BLOPE

A story of segregation, plastic surgery and religion gone wrong

by

Sean Benham

SeanBenham.biz

Lulu.com Print-to-Order Edition

ISBN 978-0-9916755-2-4

TABLE OF CONTENTS

CHAPTER 1 - EPILOGUE

TIERRA PODRIDA, M PREFECTURE, THE UNION

TUESDAY, JULY 6, 2010

Billy Lopez staggered out of Saint Basil's Cathedral and Nightclub partially seared and on the verge of death, his mouth stained with the blood of Clint Masters. He desperately wanted to head back inside and make one last attempt at dragging Clint out to safety, but it was not to be. His escape from the converted warehouse ushered in a gust of oxygen that quickly upgraded the inferno within to raging. The searing heat forced Billy to make a feeble retreat into the desert. Whatever final knowledge the grizzled pornographer could have imparted to Billy was lost in the fire.

Doctor Timothy was trapped, lying face up amongst the piles of antiquated consumer goods that surrounded Saint Basil's. Given their uncomfortable history, Billy could have been forgiven for allowing his sexual assailant to bake, writhing in the scorching desert sun, forever trapped by the very apparatus designed to allow mobility.

Billy took the moral high road for purely selfish reasons. He had lost both arms and buckets of blood along with them. Doctor

Timothy was to only person in the Prefecture with any hope of helping Billy live to see another day. Plus, in Billy's experience, leaving anyone to die at the hands of M Prefecture's harsh elements was one hell of a mistake. He had learned that one the hard way. With the last of his strength, Billy doubled over at the waist and bit down hard on Doctor Timothy's nose. He toppled over backwards; Doctor Timothy stumbled upright. Billy watched flames lick off of the top of Saint Basil's blue and white spiraled onion dome as he faded to unconsciousness.

Billy spent three days in the vault of Tierra Podrida Savings and Loan, lost in the fantastical dreams brought about by his induced coma. He awoke with a start, jolting up from his cot grimly determined. If his subconscious had imparted anything through its hazy broadcast of non-sequiturs and quarter-baked ideas it was that Billy had to start setting things right.

He would start small. He would make the trek back to the charred nightclub. He would give Clint a proper burial. He would reclaim his lost arms. But first, he would have to get out of the gleaming steel bank vault. Billy suppressed concerns of what may have happened while he was under, swallowed his pride and expressed his gratitude to Doctor Timothy for dragging him back and patching him up. It was time to get started.

At first, Billy insisted on going alone, counter to Doctor Timothy's wishes. This was Billy's mess to clean. He was less insistent following his embarrassing armless struggle to free himself from his cot and the spell of dizzy vomiting that followed. Doctor Timothy was far from the ideal escort, but Billy was in no shape to travel alone and he had no one else to turn to.

Billy's determination gave way to confusion and despair once he and Doctor Timothy set foot into the blackened brick husk of a building. Clint's body was nowhere to be found. Neither were Billy's severed arms. The remnants of the Black Pope's body still lay where he had fallen, but sticky brown pools of blood on the broken light-up dance floor served as the only evidence that either Clint or Billy had ever set foot in Saint Basil's.

Rather than conceding utter defeat, Doctor Timothy decided to rebuild Billy using the materials available. Billy was skeptical, and vocally so. Reliving the fight and the fire would surely be unpleasant and the prospect of having two reminders permanently affixed to his shoulders didn't sit well with him. But, it was preferable to the alternative of life without arms. Eventually Billy had to give in; it was the only sensible course of action. His submission to surgery came with the decision to try and ignore the poetic justice inherent in what Doctor Timothy was going to have to do to mend him.

It had been four days since the operation and Billy's rehabilitation was nearly complete. This was testament to Doctor Timothy's surgical skill, not to Billy's commitment to becoming a complete, fully functional man again. Billy wasn't happy with his new arms. But, if you asked him, he would begrudgingly admit that he was grateful to have them. He just wished they weren't so black. Black enough already from the melanin, blacker still from the fire. As far as he could tell, with his new ultra-high contrast skin, Billy would be an outcast *anywhere* in the U.S.A.

The lilting, Australian-accented assurances that it was 'far better to have four limbs and the ability to control them flawlessly' than it was to 'fit into a cracked and crumbling mess of a society' were repeated ad nauseam throughout the rehabilitation in an attempt to lift Billy's spirits. Billy couldn't argue against his surgeon's advice, or at least, by the second day of his recovery he couldn't be bothered to try any longer. Doctor Timothy's talk of Billy being 'as handsome as ever before, maybe even more so' was still wholly repugnant, no matter how many times he heard it.

Doctor Timothy's cot was in the corner of the vault closest to the operating table and the glass-front boxes that once held people's valuables, but had been converted to hold their body parts. Billy had shoved his cot from directly beside Doctor Timothy's into the opposite corner as soon as he had the energy to stand. He was further from the pails of toilet powder and wedged between an oildrum labeled UNSORTED ORGANS and the rickety bookshelf full of *LaRue's Longing* romance novels that Billy blamed for rotting part of Doctor Timothy's brain. These concessions were well worth the peace of mind.

Billy hadn't measured, but he was pretty sure his new biceps were almost as large as his thighs, or maybe just a little bit larger. They were big enough to necessitate removing the sleeves of his prized pink western shirt and adding slits through the shoulders. Billy was pleased to see that the embroidered chest panel depicting a chase on horseback made it through shirt surgery, but he kept that information to himself. Even as unfinished pieces of surgical art, Billy could tell that these new arms were incredibly powerful. His strength hadn't just returned, it had multiplied. But, to what end? Billy still had to run his way to the border if he was to leave M, and by his uneducated estimate he would have to run at top speed to make it there before the desert did him in. How badly would these bulky new arms slow him down? It was almost time to find out.

Sitting in silence in his corner, Billy played with the Halo device Doctor Timothy had nicked off what was left of Life 29, tossing it back and forth from one oversized black hand to the other. He had been doing this for days, trying to teach his new synapses to get along with the old. The pings and clangs that resonated when the device hit the tiled floor were now a memory, relegated to days past. His new fingers had yet to betray him that day and he'd been tossing the shiny golden ring back and forth for hours. As his success rate climbed, so did his self confidence. He gripped the Halo tight in triumph after one last toss. *'I'm fixed.'*

He wasn't just fixed. He was hungry, really hungry. The sustenance gel pouches stamped 'FOR DISTRIBUTION AND CONSUMPTION IN M PREFECTURE ONLY' were every bit as disgusting as he had been warned, but not in the way he had been led to assume. It wasn't the taste that turned Billy off; they weren't exactly appetizing, but they tasted no worse than B pouches. It was the strange, hot sensation in his stomach that lingered long after he ate that kept Billy from sucking back any more gel than he felt he had to. He wondered how Norm and Ry managed to catch those tasty lizards and cursed himself for failing to ask.

Billy looked the Halo over for what seemed like the hundredth time, idly poking at the inset metallic buttons. Had he cared to learn of the latent abilities held within the seemingly inoperative device, he might not have treated it as an idle plaything. Billy held no interest in the mysterious technology itself; it was the words of the homicidal Holy Man who once wore the Halo that concerned him. If what he said about his father was true... Well, there was no way to verify his story now, not with the Holy Man dead and Billy stuck within the bank vault. One thing was clear; Billy's questionable lineage left him a marked man.

If the first ambush was any indication, there would be no warning before the second. The time for action was now; even if Billy wasn't exactly sure what form that action would have to take. Plan or no plan, it was time to move. Aside from 60% of his skin, there was no reason for Billy to stay in M. Not anymore.

Doctor Timothy had been immersed in God-knows-what on the safety deposit box side of the vault, finally taking a break from doting upon Billy. This was his chance. 50 feet and a heavy steel door were all that separated Billy from freedom. There would be no farewell speech. He strode for the door, wearing everything he owned, eager to start anew. Again.

BZZZZT **BZZZZT** **BZZZZZZT** The buzz of the intercom stopped Billy in his tracks.

"Oh good. He's here." Doctor Timothy spun to face Billy, large, battered suitcase in hand. "Get the intercom, would you?"

'Christ... what now?' Billy's recent experience with strangers had been uniformly unfortunate. But, no matter who or what was waiting on the other side of the huge vault door, they couldn't do any worse than taking his life. Billy knew that in M, life wasn't worth a whole lot. "Yeah, sure." Billy walked over to the panel next to the vault door and smothered the small red button underneath his black sausage of a finger. "Hello?"

The reply came after a long pause. "Lopez? That you?" The gravelly growl was instantly familiar and, strangely enough, the most uplifting thing Billy had heard in some time. Billy smushed his finger back against the button.

"Oh my God! Yeah, yeah, it's me!" Billy chirped in his excitement, quickly shifting tones as he let up off the intercom and turned to Doctor Timothy. "Do you plan on telling me just what the hell is going on here?"

"Sweet, simple Billy. You weren't planning on leaving without me, were you? When I said I would forever be by your side, I meant it quite sincerely. After all, you cannot hope to survive in this cruel world with your feeble wits acting as your only guide. You spoke volumes while you were under, mumbling a plan you could never hope to achieve alone. You wish to kill your father and I wish nothing more than to help you do so. It will be ever so romantic."

'What? No! NO! ...Kill my father?' Billy considered the brief time he shared with Doctor Timothy to have been far too long already. He did not relish the prospect of spending another hour together, let alone forever. And his father? Billy got to wondering what his coma dreams knew that he didn't.

BZZZZZZZZZT

"Lopez? You OK in there?" The growl held what sounded like a twinge of concern.

"Yeah, sort of. Hold on." Billy didn't want anything to stand between him and the man who would be his only guaranteed ticket out of the Prefecture, even if that ticket did come attached to a living load of baggage that made his skin crawl. Billy spun the wheeled lock on the door and shoved, the pneumatic hinge started slowly cracking the door wide.

"Thanks. Told myself I'd never come back here, y'know? Man, I hate *everything* about this place. No offense, Doc." The visitor growled as the door crept open. "But, hey, I'm not dumb enough to refuse a taxi job that pays in Ashanti Orthodox gear. Dr. Timothy, how'd you even get your hands on..." The visitor cut himself short as the vault door swung wide enough to reveal its contents, his surgically altered face showing as much of a confused expression as it possibly could. "Jesus Lopez, what the hell happened to your arms? And who the hell is that?"

"C'mon in, Garbage Bag. It's a long story."

CHAPTER 2 - ETERNALLY FREE TAIWAN & THE UNITED PREFECTURES OF AMERICA

TAIPEI, ETERNALLY FREE TAIWAN

TUESDAY, JULY 4, 1933

The name 'Eternally Free Taiwan' was misleading. It wasn't eternal. Entropic forces acted upon it as they would act upon any civilization. It wasn't free, either. Dissenters were silenced, and their 'silence' was made public spectacle. Most of all, it wasn't Taiwan. That is to say, it wasn't *only* Taiwan.

Under the rule of Zhang Yao-Fong, self appointed President for Life, the small island nation had mushroomed into a pan-global network of dependent territories, each loyal to the Eternally Free Taiwanese flag. Eternally Free Taiwan had been the world's greatest colonial power for decades.

Despite his far flung influence, Zhang preferred to remain close to home. He made certain that the capital city of Taipei grew around him rapidly as his empire flourished. Modern infrastructure sprouted like weeds in amongst the ancient temples and pagodas, choking out the traditional architecture in the name of progress. Thick ribbons of asphalt criss-crossed the northern half of the isle of Taiwan, linking swaths of sleek, skyhigh steel construction. The booming growth made Taipei a magnet for immigration; the area's population having grown 500 fold since Zhang forcefully took control of the country in 1871.

No symbol of this growth was as obscenely decadent as Zhang's Presidential Palace. The dominant figure in the panoramic Taipei skyline, the Palace was a milky green colossus, completely covered in thin sheets of translucent jade. As the tallest building in the world by an incredibly wide margin, the Palace dwarfed the forest of surrounding skyscrapers and was visible from any point on the island. Zhang lovingly referred to his impossibly proportioned abode as the Erect Dragon. Mass executions following the Erect Dragon's grand unveiling quickly taught the populace that pointing and snickering would not be tolerated.

Mr. Wong, Zhang's longstanding Minister of Foreign Affairs, was slowly rolling towards the Erect Dragon. The squat, balding, 45 year old sat in silence in the backseat of his luxurious Taiwauto EX Class, a scowl etched across his pinched features. The time for shrill screaming had passed and he'd already given his driver an earful.

'Taking the Northstar Expressway? At this hour? Jesus Christ...'

The bottleneck eased somewhat and Wong's driver was able to maneuver off of the expressway. This offramp wasn't anywhere near the Presidential Palace, but at least they were making headway. It was 8:13 and Wong was a 43 minutes overdue. His ulcer had been eating away at itself for the last 45. Zhang Yao-Fong was widely regarded as the World's Most Powerful Man, and Wong was terrified of getting on his bad side.

In the southwest corner of the Erect Dragon's penthouse suite, the World's Most Powerful Man was slumped atop his lacquered mahogany toilet. Silk, floral print pajama pants bunched around his ankles. Thin tubes snaked out of his nostrils and trailed down over his sunken cheeks and wrinkled neck, disappearing into his half buttoned pajama shirt. His bald, spotted head lolled off to the left, snoring quietly. With each soft inhale, a surge of vibrant blue liquid coursed through the tubes into Zhang's nose.

KNOCK KNOCK

The distant rap on the exterior bathroom door snapped Zhang back into the world of the waking. "Come in, Mr. Wong" he intoned, his rumbling baritone still maintaining an impeccable air of command even at his advanced age of 88.

Zhang opted to hold important meetings in his bathroom, preferably as he was engaged in a scatological act. He had accidentally stumbled upon this system early in his presidency while he was racked with a bout of food poisoning. During that maelstrom of uncomfortable purging, Zhang was able to broker the purchase of every Bauxite mine in Vietnam. For a period afterwards, he had considered this method of holding conferences to be something of a lucky charm, not to mention an excellent manner of flaunting his state of the art indoor plumbing. But, that was over 40 years ago. Now, his pipework was no longer a bragging right, the Bauxite had long since been stripped from the Earth and his eccentricity had simply become habit.

This habit was all too familiar for Minister Wong; he had been acting as Zhang's Foreign Affairs Minister since the early '20s. He had made his way through the high arched, black marble corridor that led to the bathroom's gargantuan inner sanctum hundreds of times. 25 foot high, ornately inlaid, precious stone mosaics depicting a youthful Zhang decapitating mythical beasts and sexually servicing buxom concubines lined the walls of the hallway.

Wong walked past them purposefully, keeping his eyes trained on the floor.

He kneeled at Zhang's feet in silence and softly kissed his bare knees. Right, left, then right again, all without daring to make eye contact. This show of respect was uncommon for an official as high ranking as Wong, but Wong knew better than to anger the President, and he had already left him on the toilet for nearly an hour. Wong spoke in a hushed, reverent tone.

"My deepest apologies sir. My fool Arab driver is to be blamed. Though, I must be the one who to bear the brunt of your punishment, for I did not take it upon myself to train him in the appropri-"

"Arab?" Zhang interrupted, his eyes suddenly sparkling. "Most interesting. For the love of Taiwan, look at me Wong! Better. Now, tell me, is this driver of yours a dark skinned Arab, or is he fair?"

"Rather dark skinned, I suppose." Wong replied, eager to shift the conversation in any direction away from his tardiness. "Moroccan I believe."

"Moroccan? Entirely inconsequential. Trivial. That information is almost insulting, Wong! But dark skinned... Fascinating." A sly smile cracked across Zhang's staid visage. "Do you know of the Chantone Conjecture, Mr. Wong? It is quite the cutting edge theory, why, I only learned of it days ago myself."

"No. No sir, I'm afraid I do not."

"No. Of course not. My apologies Wong, at times I forget that you are not a man of science." This was a lie, and intentionally condescending. Zhang knew that Wong had a passing interest in the latest developments in the world of science. A passing interest was as much as the scientific community would ever allow him to have. The scientific symposiums Zhang frequented were restricted to the elite of the ruling class, and the topics discussed were generally limited to innovative methods of controlling those beneath them. It was not information to be disseminated amongst commoners, but from time to time, Zhang was forced to relay some of this knowledge to Wong. It was a compromise that suited them both. Zhang had no desire to dirty his hands by getting personally involved in the day to day minutiae of civilian pacification and Wong was a sniveling bootlick with lofty, entirely unattainable, goals of one day rising to power himself. Wong always made for an eager pupil when it came time for Zhang to discuss science.

"Simply put," Zhang continued, "the Chantone Conjecture, postulated by the illustrious Professor Chan, states that a man's innate, scientifically quantifiable attributes – vigor, covetousness, ineptitude, moral fiber, et cetera, et cetera – all share a direct correlation to the amount of melanin contained within his skin."

"Fascinating sir!" Wong over-enthused.

"Yes. Yes it certainly is. And, if true, this would clearly explain why your dark skinned Arab driver, likely a 'B', was unable to complete a task as simple as navigating our tranquil, modern thoroughfares in a timely manner. Moroccan or not, if his skin color fell in the 'F' range, he would most certainly have the necessary dexterity and reasoning ability to deliver you to my home without making me wait with my pants around my ankles!" With that, Zhang lifted himself off of his perch, and hovered over his toilet seat. "Abrade me, Mr. Wong."

"Of course sir!" Wong sprung to his feet and scurried over to Zhang's opulent golden medicine chest, returning with a handful of sandy granules. "F range, sir?" Wong asked as he vigorously rubbed the treatment into the nether region of Zhang's posterior.

"The *chosen* range. That's quite enough Wong. You are free to rinse off." Zhang waited for Wong to manually brush away the soiled powder before standing upright and cinching the cord of his pajama pants around his waist.

"Yes sir."

"As I was saying," Zhang continued as Wong rinsed his hands in the giant clamshell wash basin. "Human skin tones have been measured and divided into 13 Chantone ranges; from the darkest 'A' range to the lightest 'M' range. The 'F' range is the range of skin tones into which you, I and most of our fellow countrymen fall. Clearly the superior Chantone."

"Yes sir. I would have to agree sir."

Zhang walked to the western facing window. He beckoned for Wong to join him at his side. Wong dutifully sidled up and the two gazed down upon the bustling grid far below.

"With the clear superiority of the 'F' range established, it is troubling to me that I said it is the range into which *most* of our countrymen fall, and not *all* of our countrymen. Men of your driver's... 'ilk' may have provided the mindless toil that built Eternally Free Taiwan into the envy of the world, but, is it wise to allow them to continue to live among us? Can we afford to let those with less than ideal Chantones sully our National reputation?"

"Well, you, I..." stammered the Minister. He had no intention of disagreeing with the President for Life. But, he also didn't want to blindly agree with a line of thought that would result in the deportation, or worse, of his nubile, lily-white, Prussian trophy wife. "That is a difficult question sir."

"Is it? I suppose it could be, for some. But, difficult questions require difficult answers, do they not? Here is an easier question for you, Wong. What has become of the land the United States ceded to us?"

Officially speaking, the large parcel of land that straddled the Colorado River was a gift from the United States of America to Eternally Free Taiwan. The details of the seemingly unwarranted land offering were never made public record. This omission was not by chance. The truth behind how Zhang won the land from President Carnegie at a recent symposium would raise a host of questions. Zhang could not afford to allow those questions to be asked.

It had been Carnegie's first symposium and he was cocky; eager to prove he belonged amongst the cadre of the highest rollers. Zhang was more than willing to put the brash upstart in his place. The pair retreated to a quiet room during a period of inactivity between lectures.

Carnegie went first; it was his gun and his idea. Zhang was a powerful man, yes, rich in resources, but was he rich in spirit? This would be the test. A wager was set. 250,000 square miles of land were to be ceded to the winner's nation. The loser would receive a state funeral.

Carnegie loaded a single cartridge into the cylinder, spun it and clicked it back into place. Hammer cocked back, he slowly raised the muzzle to his temple. Eyes closed. Deep breath.

CLICK

Following a deep, exhilarated exhale, Carnegie smugly passed the revolver to Zhang.

Zhang calmly raised the muzzle to his temple. Eyes wide, focused on Carnegie. Breathing normally, blue liquid surging into his nostrils.

CLICK **CLICK** **CLICK** **CLICK** **BANG**

The wisps of smoke cleared. Zhang peeled the flattened metal slug from his temple and dropped it in Carnegie's lap.

With that, Zhang won himself a segment of the North American continent. More importantly, he had put a young ruler in his place. It was both the first time and the last time that the United States of America would challenge Eternally Free Taiwan in any manner.

"The trade debt repayment in the southwest of the continent, sir?" Wong asked, parroting the story behind the acquisition of the land in the Americas that Zhang spoon-fed his underlings. "Nothing much to report. Small scale mining operations, mostly. Some agriculture."

"Excellent, much as I had assumed. The land will serve as our testing ground."

"I'm sorry sir, testing ground for what?"

Zhang turned from the window and draped himself over a nearby rhinoceros-leather fainting couch with a disdainful sigh.

"I'm certainly not foolish enough to forcefully segregate our grand nation without a dry run in the colonies first, am I Mr. Wong? Listen to me carefully. No need to take notes, the plan is quite simple." Zhang paused to gather his thoughts. "First, we will divide the American land into 13 Prefectures, A through M. These prefectures are to be hexagonal in shape, following the laws set forth in Professor Ichnisanshi's Honeycomb-Form Worker-Compliance Corollary. The borders between these Prefectures must be well guarded. We will be sorting the colonists into the Prefectures by their Chantone ranges and intermingling of skin tones will only serve to sully the results of our testing. A system of automated sensors calibrated to restrict entry only to those of the correct skin tone will need to be established. Junior party members will be appointed as Chancellors to oversee the experiment. Do not concern yourself with matching the Chantones of the Chancellors to their appointed Prefectures. They will serve as experimental arbiters and will not be included in the test data. The Chancellors will administer tests on the populace, report their results back to us, and be generally be thrilled to rise so quickly through the ranks in the service of our glorious nation."

Wong was careful in phrasing his reply. "Sir, this is a very *interesting* plan! But, I must admit, I am concerned."

"Oh?"

"Yes sir. You see, the land in question is sparsely populated and not nearly as diverse as Eternally Free Taiwan. I do not believe we would be able to populate many of the Prefectures if you wish to have every Chantone range represented." Wong knew bringing this up was a mistake as soon as he said it. Not only was the grimace on Zhang's face a dead giveaway of his displeasure; Wong realized that by bringing up the notion of equal Chantone representation he was practically begging for his wife's deportation to the American colony.

"Mr. Wong, your unfounded pessimism and shortsightedness are dampening my enthusiasm. I did not bring you here today to be second guessed."

"My apologies, sir." Wong presented his most sycophantic air, desperate to weasel back into Zhang's good graces and to ensure he could keep his sexy new plaything in the country. "This is indeed a very wise plan, and a surely most noble cause. Please continue."

"If the population of test subjects is that much of a concern to you, Wong, I would like you to personally rectify this so-called problem. Spread word to our colonial embassies. 'Free land in the west! New Hope!' Dirt poor scum of every color will flock to the Prefectures. And, see to it that we establish factories in select locations before they arrive, I'd like to turn a profit on this experiment."

"Yes sir, very well sir." Wong was quite pleased with this outcome. This would require him to perform far more actual work than he was accustomed to, but it certainly seemed that he had saved his wife from deportation. "I will be in touch with the embassies right away. Unless, there is anything else you require of me?"

"There is one more thing, Wong. See to it that our new test subjects are kept forever ignorant of what is at hand. I do not wish to deal with a group of angry, self aware lab rats."

"At least the lab rats will be overseas, sir" said Wong with a cruel smirk.

"Yes, good point. Make sure we invest in a reliable rat cage all the same. Good day, Mr. Wong. Please see yourself out."

CHAPTER 3 - UNREST

TAIPEI, ETERNALLY FREE TAIWAN

FRIDAY, JULY 3, 1970

"Come in Wong!"

Minster Wong had been retired for 16 years and dead for 7. President Zhang's incredibly advanced age would have made a fine excuse as to why he could not keep his Minister's names straight. However, Zhang's mind was as sharp as ever. On top of that, he was not the type of man that made excuses.

Zhang had made a game of toying with Wong's replacement; seeing how long he would respond to a name that was not his own. The game had been underway for nearly a decade and Minister Lin had yet to correct the President for Life. Zhang had disliked his new Minister of Foreign Affairs from their first meeting. He was of the new breed of bureaucrats; born in the boardroom, not on the battlefield and far too eager to allow emotion to cloud his judgment. Lin's limp wristed decisions rooted in resolve between parties tended to be immensely profitable, far too much so to have him removed from his post. To Zhang, Lin's success was his most damnable offense.

Lin was a tall, reedy, perpetually nervous man of 40 with a shock of bone white hair. He strode down the black marble corridor with his head high and his shoulders pinned back in an attempt to mask his unease. He had news that he was sure Zhang would find displeasing and Zhang never responded well to even the best of news.

Lin had certainly planned on kneeling before Zhang and kissing his bare knees. Anything to lessen the negative impact of what he had to report. He would not be afforded the opportunity. By the time he reached the end of the corridor, Zhang was rinsing his hands in his giant clamshell.

"I hope you're happy, Wong." Zhang said with a sneer, not making any attempt at eye contact with Lin. "I have been reduced to cleansing myself. What a disgrace."

Lin tried to be subtle as he wiped his sweaty palms on his trousers. This was not going to go well. He cleared his throat and cut to the chase.

"I am sorry sir. I am also sorry to report that I have terrible news from the colonies. Can I get you a towel sir?"

"I'm not sure Wong. Can you?"

Lin rushed over and dabbed Zhang's dripping hands in reply.

"Oh, it seems that you can. Barely. That will do, Wong." Zhang retreated to a nearby pile of mink pillows and began flipping through a pile of erotic postcards, feigning interest in the nude forms. "So then, what is your excellent news?"

Lin pressed on, feeling particularly ill at ease.

"My apologies again sir. I'm afraid I do not bring excellent news. Word has come from the Americas, sir. Prefectures H through M are no longer under our control, the Chancellors have been assassinated."

Zhang stopped shuffling through the postcards. "An uprising. In the *American* colonies?" He counted on his fingers as he quietly mouthed letters. "H, I, J, K, L, M... so, the pale faces stirring are stirring up trouble? Hmph! Inconsequential."

This news was of dire consequence to Zhang.

The United Prefectures of America were troubled from their inception. This latest crisis was only going to exacerbate those troubles. The experiment in the Americas wasn't the first colony Zhang had established to act as a scientific testing ground. It was, however, the first of those colonies to have the scientific theory in question be thoroughly discredited while the experiment was still underway. Professor Chan was exposed as a swindler with dubious credentials shortly after the symposium that planted the seed of skin tone segregation in Zhang's mind. Zhang, eager to save face, was quick to rally his contemporaries to exact punishment upon the fraudulent Professor.

For years after Chan's execution, Zhang had little reason to pay any mind to the Prefectures. The factories were immensely profitable, the masses appropriately browbeaten and the whole mess was fenced off halfway around the world. The phone call Zhang had received minutes before his meeting with Minister Lin made this brewing conflict feel awfully close to home. Father Superior had called and he had a favor to ask.

The President for Life had never met Father Superior, but Father Superior needed no introduction; as the spiritual leader of the Ashanti Orthodox, he was by far the most influential Holy Man of the era. Zhang fell on the opposite end of the religious spectrum, having purposefully eschewed the practice of any and all religion within his empire. This was likely unpopular with Father Superior, but it had never been enough of an issue for him to have attempted any discourse with the Eternally Free Taiwanese. Apparently, a breaking point had been reached and Father Superior finally saw fit to reach out to Zhang. His request was as simple as it was bizarre; Father Superior wished to embed an agent in M Prefecture, preferably as Chancellor.

A request from the Ashanti Orthodox to gain a foothold in the United Prefectures of America was troubling. That Father Superior specifically asked for his agent to be put into power in M was especially troubling. Lin's news of the rebellion in the pale-skinned Prefectures and the chaos that was sure to follow were the final layers of trouble-flavored icing on the cake.

Zhang had agreed to harbor a high profile fugitive in M Prefecture back in the mid 1950s. Now, he had good reason to suspect that his fugitive's cover had been blown and worse, that his fugitive was soon to meet his end at the hands of an Ashanti Orthodox enforcer. Even on the slim chance that he was incorrect in his assumption, Zhang could not afford to incite any fanatical ill will. The Ashanti Orthodox were as powerful as they were influential. If they were so inclined, they were the only group who could challenge Zhang's dominance on the world stage.

Zhang had no choice but to agree with the Holy Man's whim and to agree readily. Now, he could only hope that he was wrong and that the Ashanti Orthodox had not picked up Satan's trail after all these years.

Satan and Zhang shared a long history. The two had met in the late 1860s during the tail end of the Taiwanese War of Independence. Satan was keeping casual tabs on the atrocities of war, as he was wont to do, when he caught wind of a particularly cruel military policeman stationed in Tainan City. He arranged for passage to the southwestern corner of the isle of Taiwan and surreptitiously observed Zhang, then in his early 20s, as Zhang tortured and killed hundreds of Chinese prisoners of war. Satan was charmed, not only with this young man's pitiless bloodlust, but with his callous disregard for the weak-willed orders of his superior officers as well. He arranged to meet with this brash, Caligula-in-the-making; the young torturer seemed to be ideal for Satan's grand scheme.

He offered to imbue Zhang with the awesome power of the Messiah's Impenetrability and to ensure that Zhang rose amongst the Taiwanese political ranks at speeds previously unheard of. Zhang readily agreed to the proposal. He knew full well that he was making a deal with the Devil and he considered it odd that there were no caveats of what he would have to pay in return for these gifts, but the offer was too good to refuse. Within four years of their initial meeting, Zhang had cemented his status as Eternally Free Taiwan's President for Life.

Satan's request to be repaid for Zhang's swift rise and perpetual reign didn't come until nearly a century after their deal was struck. In the spring of 1954, a Knight in Satan's Service, planted as a mole high within the ranks of the Ashanti Orthodox, had given Satan word. 'The Star' had been spotted over what was now known as M Prefecture.

Zhang was all too happy to oblige Satan's request for clandestine refuge in this far flung land. Practical invincibility and autonomy over a world superpower in exchange for passage into the backwaters of America was an excellent deal. Or, so it had seemed at the time. Satan had neglected to mention to Zhang that he would be hunting for the newborn Messiah while he was holed up in M.

It had been 16 years since Satan made his way to the desert and for the first time in those 16 years, President Zhang was beginning to have second thoughts about holding up his end of the illicit pact. He was torn between the only two forces more powerful than himself, neither of whom could be denied, betrayed or truly trusted.

Lin's news of an uprising in the Prefectures left Zhang downright frightened, fear was not an emotion he was comfortable with. The added volatility in the region meant that Zhang would have to be exceptionally vigilant in order to keep his Satanic alliance a secret. There was no telling what would become of him if that news was to leak and Zhang had no intention of finding out. While he could not control the outside influence of the Ashanti Orthodox, he could control the outcome of the brewing civil war. Anything that could be done to stop this situation from spiraling further out of control would have to be done. Luckily for Zhang, he was well versed in the art of smothering a rebellion.

"Yes sir. This news is entirely inconsequential. I deeply apologize for bringing the matter to your attention." Lin said before turning to leave. He turned too soon.

"Wong. Turn. Face me. *Listen* to me. The Eternally Free Taiwanese are strong, decisive." Zhang lowered his mail-ready erotica. "We will stop this uprising."

"Yes sir. Right away sir."

"No, Wong. Not right away." Zhang lifted himself from the pillows and strode towards his toilet; he needed to gather his thoughts. Zhang loosened the drawstring of his pajama bottoms and lowered himself gently, letting the expensive silk gather around his ankles. "There are elements at work here that you cannot hope to understand. This must be a delicate retaliation. I expect you to take notes, dullard."

"Of course, sir." Minister Lin produced a black, patent leather notepad from his breast pocket. "Please proceed, sir."

"Yes. This must be very delicate indeed. To begin with, we will cripple the infrastructure of the pale-faced Prefectures. Airstrikes, Wong. Accurate, precise airstrikes. Our ground troops have proven ineffective. You are to ensure casualties from this initial wave of attack are minimized. I do not wish those who oppose us to be treated to the sweet release of an immediate death. Once the fire from the sky has quelled the fight in the white man, we must put him back to work. See to it that Phase 2 Manufacturing Centers are installed in the urban areas. Unprofitable wars are not worth waging, Wong. Circle that. Very good. We must also ensure that the notion of an uprising does not spring up again. Inform the Chancellors of Prefectures A through G to institute widespread re-education programs. As of today, Prefectures H through M never existed. Any mention of these traitorous territories, in either past or present tense, is to be punishable by death. Finally, you will see to it that the dissenting Prefectures are chemically sterilized. Eradicate the bloodlines of the rebels."

Lin was taken aback. He was used to Zhang's severe autocratic rule, but as he was not yet a Cabinet Minister during the Battle for New Zealand he had never been in the position to act upon his genocidal orders. Lin took a moment to collect himself, trying his best not to stammer. "Yes sir, most wise sir. I will see to it right away."

"When will you learn Wong? You will act upon my direct command, and not a moment sooner. There is one further American wrinkle you must iron out. As luck would have it, my close personal friend, Father Superior of the Ashanti Orthodox wishes to establish a presence in M Prefecture. You will ensure he is able to institute a Chancellor of his choosing. There is no need to find replacements for the Chancellors representing Prefectures H through L."

"Yes sir, I will be happy to make arrangements for Mr. Superior's request." Lin could not fathom why the Ashanti Orthodox of all people wished to hold any influence over the palest of the Prefectures, but knew he had no business inquiring. However, in light of this odd development, there was one question that needed to be asked. "Shall we proceed with the military retaliation in M? And the... other retaliation as well?"

"We will continue as planned. With one exception, we will not establish a Phase 2 in M. Traditional production will suffice for the time being. No sense in giving the Good Father a technological leg up. At least, not for free. Oh, and Wong? See to it that the Ashanti Orthodox Chancellor is put in place *after* the bombs drop. The last thing I have time for is a repeat of the Auckland situation."

"Yes sir, of course. Is there anything else you wish of me sir?"

"No, after your disgraceful display with the hand towel, I would prefer to abrade myself. Wait! Wong, there is one more thing. Be subtle in your actions. See to it that none of this can be traced back to the Erect Dragon. I do not wish to look like a monster."

CHAPTER 4 - THE FIGHT

TIERRA PODRIDA, M PREFECTURE, THE UNION

FRIDAY, AUGUST 4, 1978

Tierra Podrida wasn't a pretty town, but it was still a town. It was the only settlement in M Prefecture that could still make that claim. The depressing color palette of dusty rock brown, cinderblock grey and oxidized tin orange had been generously coated with white and purple-blue; mimeographed flyers were posted everywhere. The flyers were posted up in the windows of the greasy spoons and small shops that lined the town square. They were tacked to the bulletin boards in the Manufacturing Center. Every lamp post and telephone pole were covered. People's modest homes were spared the paste brush, but their rock garden front yards made perfect resting spots for flyers caught in the breeze.

MASTERS vs. HUGHSON

THE MAN WITH THE IRON SKIN
vs.
THE KID WITH THE STEEL FISTS

LIVE AT SAINT BASIL'S
AUGUST 4

DOORS OPEN AT 9

$2 IN ADVANCE
$3 AT THE DOOR

ALL SING PRAISE
TO THE NAME OF THE LORD MOST HIGH

NO REFUNDS

There was no one in town to read the flyers. It was 9 PM, August 4.

As the site of the Prefecture's lone Manufacturing Center, Tierra Podrida had long been a magnet for those looking for work. Now that the smaller settlements had emptied in the wake of the civil war, Tierra Podrida was home to the vast majority of M's remaining populace. It was a decent place to live, considering the lack of viable alternatives. These days, decent was as good as it got in The Union, as Prefectures H thorough M had taken to calling themselves.

It had been eight years since the rain of bombs fell on The Union, leveling communications infrastructure and cutting any ties to the outside world. The security systems established between Prefectures made it through the war unharmed, leaving the Prefectures cut off from one another as well. This left the citizens of M Prefecture totally unaware of how lucky they were, at least in comparison to the rest of The Union. Their monotonous factory work wasn't glamorous, but in comparison to the working conditions found in the Phase 2 Manufacturing Centers that had sprung up in the rest of the rebellious Prefectures, it was downright luxurious.

The laymen had no idea their button pushing, quality checking and raw-materials-into-a-vat-emptying jobs would have no longer have existed if it wasn't for President for Life Zhang's fear of Jonathan Wright and the potential threat he represented. That was far from the breadth of what the town of Tierra Podrida didn't know about their Chancellor. They didn't know that evening's fight was the culmination of a plan Wright had set in motion eight years earlier. They certainly didn't know that the execution of his plan would mark the beginning of the end of civilized human existence in M.

Until his appointment to M to serve as the last of the Union Chancellors, Wright had been *the* rising star amongst the Ashanti Orthodox. Five-time Ghanaian fencing champion, personal bodyguard to Father Superior and a deeply devout religious scholar, Jonathan Wright was the obvious choice to undertake the very task for which his order had been founded.

Zhang had been incorrect in his assumption years earlier. Wright had not been appointed to his post to track and destroy

Satan. The Messiah had returned in the guise of Clint Masters and Jonathan Wright was tasked with shepherding him into the flock of the Ashanti Orthodox.

There was nothing the good people of Tierra Podrida enjoyed more than watching two men pound one another to the point of unconsciousness. No one in M drew the fans in quite like Clint Masters. Masters was a decent boxer, but more than that, he was an incredible sideshow attraction. Born with extraordinarily tough skin, he would not bleed, no matter what his opponents unleashed upon him. A small, slight man in a sport lacking any height or weight restrictions, he lost fights far more often than he won and his losses tended to be ugly, one sided affairs. Masters had never suffered so much as a split lip in his career. His body would bruise, his face would swell, his blood would not spill. The crowds admired Clint's underdog spirit. Like M Prefecture itself, he could take quite the beating and live to tell the tale.

Trixie, Clint's long standing girlfriend and Anna, their six year old daughter were about to head to their car parked outside of Saint Basil's Cathedral and Nightclub. "Don't get hurt." Trixie sighed, followed by a soft kiss as she passed Clint his water bottle.

"Against this chump?" said Clint with a laugh, "That's advice you should be giving him! Ha!"

"Yeah... just be careful, OK? C'mon Anna." She grabbed hold of Anna's hand and started towards the dressing room door. Anna looked just Trixie in miniature; light blond hair, big green eyes and a thin, willowy physique. Trixie hated watching Clint fight and she steadfastly refused to let Anna watch, which led to both Anna's long standing fascination and loose understanding of what her father did for a living.

Anna wriggled her hand free from Trixie's and ran back to give Clint a big hug and a kiss on the belly. Apart from her pointy nose, Anna didn't share many features in common with her Dad and his curly brown hair, eyes fixed in a permanent squint and tightly wound muscles piled on a compact frame.

"Good luck punching, Daddy."

"Aw, thanks little lady! You and your Mom have fun with your dolls at home."

"OK!" Anna ran off to join her mother and the pair made their way out into the summer night. Trixie was nervous, she hoped Clint hadn't noticed. All of her hopes were pinned on Mr. Wright's plan being a success. Something had to change; she could not keep living the life of a prizefighter's wife-for-all-intents-and-purposes any longer, especially now that she knew that Clint was wasting his incredible potential.

Back in his dressing room, Masters stood, stretched and started to jog lightly on the spot, mixing in the occasional jab. He polished off the remainder of his water bottle. It tasted sweet.

Jonathan Wright paced the length of Rex Hughson's dressing room in the eastern wing of Saint Basil's, frequently checking his oversized silver watch. If his six foot, six inch, 300 pound frame wasn't imposing enough, his form fitting white double breasted suit was a reminder that he was a man who commanded attention. His cinder black complexion was in stark contrast to the suit. He would have been nearly achromatic if not for the massive ruby encrusted silver crucifix he wore on his lapel. Thick lips pursed thin, his broad features were set in a expression of stoic determination.

"Are you ready?" asked Wright as he shifted his gaze from the hands of his watch up towards Hughson.

"Ready." Hughson snarled as he bounced back and forth on the balls of his feet and stretched his neck from side to side. At 5 feet, 10 inches and weighing in at exactly 148 pounds, he was less than half the man Jonathan Wright was.

"Alright let's get you out there." Wright draped Hughson in his kelly green robe. There was little else for him to say that he hadn't said before. This night had been a long time coming.

Eight years earlier, when Jonathan Wright arrived in M, all he had to work with was a directive and a name - Clint Masters. Father Superior was notoriously stingy with information, lest that information fall into the wrong hands. Luckily enough for Wright, Masters would soon be something of a celebrity in Tierra Podrida. That was as far as his luck would take him.

The color of Wright's skin immediately aroused misgiving amongst the locals. M Prefecture had been a bastion of pasty whiteness for nearly forty years before Wright arrived. Even those old enough to remember a time before being sequestered in M had only seen Africans in picture books. Wright's title of Chancellor did little to endear him to the people; it hadn't yet been a year since they caved in the skull of the last man who held that position. If not for his hulking physique, it was likely that Jonathan Wright would have met the same fate, or worse.

During his first year in the Prefecture, Wright's sole focus was gaining an audience with Clint Masters. No one would speak to Wright directly about Masters, or much of anything else, but word about Masters got around. Clint Masters was an up and coming street fighter back in the early '70s. All Wright had to do was find a raucous, bloodthirsty throng; chances are Masters would be in the middle of it. Initially appalled at the barbarism displayed in these matches, Wright grew to admire the primal physicality of bare-knuckle boxing. It wasn't long before he would attend matches for the sheer spectacle, regardless of whether Clint was fighting that night. By the time Wright managed to arrange a face to face meeting with Masters, he was as much of a fixture at the fights as anyone else in the Prefecture.

Their initial meeting did not go as Jonathan Wright had hoped, far from it. They met for lunch in a diner overlooking the town square. Masters was on edge from the moment he arrived, and listening to Wright did nothing to alleviate his angst. Wright had spared no time in getting to the heart of the matter. He spoke in reverent tones of Masters' incredible destiny, the greatest of destinies. He waxed poetic of the eternal era of peace and goodwill that only Clint could usher in. Clint grew increasingly uneasy as Wright declared that he must accept the divine guidance of the Ashanti Orthodox to realize his true potential. When Wright spoke of the power of God that flowed through Clint and the word of God that Clint must have heard calling out to him, the young boxer bolted to his feet, growled that Wright was the 'crazy one' and stormed out. Jonathan Wright had anticipated skepticism but not animosity from Masters. He received both; Masters had made it clear that he wanted nothing to do with Wright or Wright's agenda.

Seemingly defeated, Wright phoned Father Superior for guidance. His mentor's advice was simple. "He is young and confused, angry. Do not be discouraged. When words fail, turn to deeds. Show him the positive energy of our faith. He will lead us when he knows we are worth leading." Wright took the words to heart.

Jonathan Wright set out to improve the lives of those around him. Societal mainstays had crumbled past the point of repair after of the civil war, but he did what he could. He established a makeshift hospital for the sick and kept a vigilant eye on the quality of the town's drinking water. He re-established bi-weekly garbage collection and saw to it that children orphaned by the war were fed and clothed. It wasn't long before the people of Tierra Podrida warmed to Jonathan Wright; he had become a beacon of positivity in their dreary post-war lives. Soon he had amassed a following of volunteers to assist him in these selfless acts and Wright found himself with time on his hands, but no direct focus. He decided to make an effort to spread the gospel. The people of M were ready for the word of God.

Wright set about building a house of worship. An abandoned warehouse sat on the outskirts of town, about a fifteen minute drive from the core. It was not centrally located, nor was it attractive, but the whitewashed brick slab was the only building large enough to house all of Tierra Podrida's citizens for Sunday Service. In that regard, it was perfect.

Using resources airlifted from Africa, the warehouse was renovated into a Cathedral of the Chancellor's specifications. The warehouse building was windowless and Wright had to make do without the stained glass he had hoped for. Undaunted, he more than made up for that omission. The cavernous central space was adorned with giant, floor to ceiling religious tapestries, detailed portraits of Ashanti Orthodox saints. Life sized bronze statues of Biblical figures capped the end of each row of pews. To literally top it off, an enormous, blue and white spiraled onion dome was installed on the warehouse's roof. It had taken months, not to mention a sizable donation from Father Superior, but Saint Basil's, as Wright had christened it, was complete. It turned out to be an incredibly expensive folly.

Despite Wright's good work in the community, Tierra Podrida showed no interest in Wright's 'word of God'. Attendance was limited to the curious at first, and promptly dwindled to no one at all as the curious were alienated by archaic language and confused by tales of questionable morality. Disappointed, but not yet completely disillusioned, Wright set about to convert his Cathedral into something the people would use. Once he replaced the pews with a light-up dance floor and installed loudspeakers, Saturday night 'church' attendance began to flourish.

Jonathan Wright's years of good deeds had paid off; the people of Tierra Podrida had finally warmed to him. All except Clint Masters. On the rare occasion that the two ran into one another around town, Wright made a point of never mentioning Clint's Messianic destiny as it riled Masters so badly when they first met. Nevertheless, Wright's cheery 'hello's and 'good morning's were greeted with stony silence from Masters, often accompanied by a sneer and a quick turn in the opposite direction.

Wright had faith that Father Superior's plan would succeed eventually, but as the years passed and as Clint grew even more distant, doubt began to creep into the back of his mind. He knew that failure in his mission would not be an option. The last man who failed to awaken a Messiah paid dearly for it.

It was well known in religious circles that Pope Innocent X allowed the previous sleeping Messiah to slip away from the influence of his order. Innocent X's rash carelessness and the ensuing outcry from within his own ranks led directly to his ouster. The infighting that followed served as the catalyst for Roman

Catholicism's downfall and the subsequent uprising of the Ashanti Orthodox.

That all took place nearly a century before Wright was assigned to shepherd Clint Masters. Despite the change in eras and creeds, the similarities between the situations loomed large over Wright. He feared the damage another Messiah left sleeping could do to his own faith. Masters had to be awakened and the longer it took the more anxious Jonathan Wright grew.

He had historical religious texts sent from overseas by the crateload, eager to learn as much as he could of Innocent X's catastrophic disgrace. There was no shortage of information, the Roman Catholic collapse was impeccably documented and cast Innocent X in a terrible light. The texts were fiercely critical of the then Pope. They spoke of a pompous Innocent X ignoring his advisors claims that the Messiah had returned. They spoke of Innocent X's insistence that he was the lone voice of God on Earth and that there was no need for a physical manifestation of the Lord. They spoke of the calls from the Cardinals to forcefully remove the Pope for his blasphemy. They spoke of the eventual tragedy, the man who would be Messiah found dead, face down in the shallows of the Tiber River.

The broad strokes of this story were not new to Wright; the collapse of Roman Catholicism had been one of the first lessons taught at divinity school. However, he did come across one piece of information that had been glossed over during his studies. Handwritten pages tucked inside an obscure text spoke of a lone Cardinal vociferously demanding that the Pope test the would-be Messiah by causing him to bleed. The Cardinal had theorized that the Messiah's full power would not be revealed without the spilling of the Holy Blood. His suggestion was quickly dismissed by Innocent X and stricken from the official record.

Innocent X's dismissal and attempted cover-up of this odd, but seemingly benign suggestion piqued Wright's interest. If the story was true, it painted Innocent X as a frightened man desperate to cling to power. He was the only person with something to lose if the Messiah was to awaken. Could he have rejected the simple blood test solely so he could retain his status as 'voice of God'? Why would he remove mention of spilling the Holy Blood from record unless he was afraid of the notion coming to light a second time?

Eventually, Wright's interest boiled over into obsession. He *would* spill the Holy Blood to awaken Clint Masters and he would convert a Prefecture of non-believers in the process.

Wracked with guilt, Trixie told herself over and over again that helping Mr. Wright was in Clint's best interest, Anna's best interest, her own best interest. The tears in her eyes blurred her view of the road. Luckily, Trixie's car was the only one heading north, back towards the residential section. If the rest of the town wasn't already at the fight, they were stuck in southbound traffic trying to get there. Everyone wanted to be able to say they were there when Clint Masters was finally split open. Word had spread that they had a good chance. This Hughson kid had only fought in three matches, but his opponents in all three ended up bloody messes. Fans couldn't recall a man who could throw a punch half as powerful.

Trixie and Anna made it home safely that night. Anna fell asleep on Trixie's lap as Trixie watched the door, aching for Clint's safe return.

Masters and Hughson made their way towards the middle of Saint Basil's impromptu ring, nothing more than a clearing in the crowd. The cheering fans pushed and climbed to get the best possible view of the fight to come. Much to the chagrin of the people standing behind him, no one had a better view than Jonathan Wright. The light grid on the floor was activated. Different colors, their squares scattered seemingly at random, lit up in turn and reflected off of the bronze statues surrounding the crowd. White, yellow, pink, blue. White, yellow, pink, blue. The cheering grew louder and louder as both fighters were introduced, each spinning with arms raised to acknowledge the cheers.

They tapped fists. The bell rang.

The men circled, throwing jabs to keep the other fighter honest. Masters leaned out of the way of an arcing haymaker. Hughson was fast and strong, but he was sloppy; his left hand was drooping. Masters didn't waste his opportunity, connecting with a right hook to the jaw. Hughson was stunned, but only momentarily. He countered with a vicious body blow, landing it in front of Masters' right kidney.

The roaring crowd fell silent, then erupted. Clint Masters was bleeding, badly. His body had split open like an overripe piece of fruit. Blood was gushing down his side, running down onto his trunks. The crowd was chanting Hughson's name. He had delivered. He made Masters bleed.

As the blood began to pool at his feet, a faint, white, ethereal aura began to emanate from the body of Clint Masters. Hughson stopped to stare at what he had accomplished, his ego swollen from the adulation of the crowd, his curiosity overriding his desire to win. That was his undoing.

The crowd fell silent once again; the white aura had grown in intensity. White flames were flickering off of Masters' body as he hunched over, badly weakened from the blood loss. Hughson's mouth was agape. Masters sprung back to life and crushed it with his fist. Hughson's jaw bone was destroyed. The bell rang. And rang. And rang. Clint Masters was pulverizing Rex Hughson with a series of ferocious, un-countered blows.

The bell kept ringing. By the time Masters stopped throwing punches it was too late. Rex Hughson was dead. That much was clear. What wasn't clear is what became of his head. Masters had shredded him, only leaving behind arms, legs and a horribly mangled torso.

Clint dropped to his knees; blood still pouring from his wound. His ethereal flames had receded, he was barely glowing. The crowd was shocked, no one more so than Jonathan Wright. He had hoped to unleash the power of the Messiah, but he never could have guessed that this was how the power would manifest itself. He rushed towards Masters, but was blocked by a stout, young medical woman on hand for the fight. Hers was a new face in a sea of familiar ones. Gretl was her name, or so said the embroidered patch on her coveralls. Wright surmised she must have recently straggled in from the outlying areas of M. The panic amongst the crowd drowned out any second thoughts.

"Pardon me, this man needs treatment immediately." Gretl said as she hoisted the limp, badly bleeding body of Clint Masters onto a foldable gurney.

"But, I must..."

"Please," she interrupted. "He is in grave condition. You can check on him in the hospital tomorrow."

"Yes. Of course. Thank you."

Gretl wheeled Clint past what was left of Rex Hughson. Stoicism was meant to have been integral to her mission. Try as she might, she was unable to hold back from breaking into a malevolent grin as she plugged Clint's nose with clear plastic tubes and made her way out into the night.

CHAPTER 5 - PRELUDE TO AN EXECUTION

TIERRA PODRIDA, M PREFECTURE, THE UNION

SATURDAY, AUGUST 5, 1978

The last of the crowd had filtered out of Saint Basil's shortly after Clint Masters was carted away, leaving Jonathan Wright alone with his self-congratulatory thoughts. His plan had gone far better than he had hoped, but the giddy anticipation of meeting with the newly awakened Clint Masters was keeping him up. It was early in the morning when Wright finally decided to forego sleep and head into town.

Wright had never felt any affinity for the drab brown vistas that fringed Tierra Podrida. Waking every morning to the stark rocky formations on the horizon made him long for his gulfview suite back home in Accra. He began to view the landscape differently as he made his way towards the town core that morning, the sun peeking over an eastern mesa. To Wright, this was no longer just a shell of a desert town; this was the birthplace of the Messiah. Soon, the devout would be making pilgrimages to these hallowed grounds, the site of the newest chapter in the Holy Scriptures. Wright couldn't help but wonder how the historians would retell his part of the story, or what rewards awaited him upon his triumphant return to Ghana.

Thoughts of Sainthood danced through Jonathan Wright's mind as he reached the converted bus station that served as Tierra Podrida's hospital. What had once been a snack bar now acted as a makeshift reception desk. The orderly standing behind the desk informed Wright that there was no record of Clint Masters being admitted the night before. Wright's chipper mood quickly grew somber.

"Surely he must be here. Could it be that he was checked in under a different name? Or, perhaps no name at all?"

"I don't think so, Mr. Wright. I'm sure I would've recognized Clint when I made my rounds earlier, especially after what happened to him at the fight last night. You can take a look for yourself if you like."

"I would like to. Thank you."

Wright made his way past each of the bricked-in bus bays, there was no sign of Clint. He made his way back to the old snack bar and asked to use the telephone. Trixie was hysterical. Clint never made it home. Wright made his best effort to calm her down, comforting her with insincere assurances that everything would be alright. He hung up a beaten man. He knew that medical woman had done... something with Clint Masters.

"Thank you for your help." Wright mumbled to the orderly as he headed for the door.

"Sure thing, Mr. Wright. I can let you know if Masters shows up, if you like. Say, maybe you should check with Dr. Timothy in the meantime. If I was bleeding that badly, he'd be the first guy I'd go see."

"Yes. Yes! Of course! I should have... Thank you, my good man!" With that, Wright ran from the hospital, headed towards a private clinic across town. If anyone would be able to aid with Masters' blood loss, it would be Dr. Timothy. After all, he was the man truly responsible for making Masters bleed in the first place.

Dr. Timothy's title was unofficial; he had not attended medical school. What he lacked in formal training, Dr. Timothy made up with experience on the battlefield. As the Eternally Free Taiwanese bombs began to drop, he had been first in line to volunteer his services as a field medic. His zeal and passion were evident. He would insist on operating even when all seemed lost and other medics had triaged onto the next patient.

Despite his heroic service to the Prefecture, Dr. Timothy's name was largely unknown until the citizens of M began to get sick. The sickness went undetected for a year or so after the war, but when almost all of the baby girls started to die, suspicions were raised. Suspicions turned to full blown panic once the other Prefecture wide symptom began to kick in.

The people of M were starting to mutate, quickly. Boys were being born with hideous physical deformities. Previously healthy adults started to show signs as well. Their symptoms were never as obvious as those born with the mutations, but once their bodies started to change, those changes usually weren't easy to conceal. In some especially fast acting cases, what looked to be a pimple on day 1 could be a pulsating tumor by day 30.

Dr. Timothy couldn't stem the tide of infant mortality, but he was able to offer hope to the living. His methods didn't cure his patients, but with his incredible skill as a plastic surgeon he was able to remove and rebuild affected areas. This slowed the spread of the mutation and left those he treated looking less grotesque as a welcome side-effect. Dr. Timothy became *the* folk hero of M Prefecture.

Despite the good deeds he had performed for the people of M, Dr. Timothy was not all he appeared to be. While he was a plastic surgeon and he did operate on those in need, occasionally completely free of charge, Dr. Timothy did not have an altruistic streak. It wasn't kindness or decency that made him tick, it was a deep-seated love of bizarre human experimentation. Like any doctor, Dr. Timothy was unable to 'save' all of his patients. Unlike other doctors, Dr. Timothy made a point of ensuring he 'lost' as many patients as he could without arousing suspicion. After all, he couldn't very well send them back home, not after what he had done to them. It was his macabre fascination with human modification that lent him his incredible surgical skill, and he grew better at his job as M grew sicker.

Like the rest of the Prefecture, Jonathan Wright had no knowledge of Dr. Timothy's peculiar bent. Although, he might have deduced that something was not quite right with the doctor when they had met earlier. Dr. Timothy effortlessly produced a serum that could make any man bleed; even a gentle poke would be enough to break the skin. At the time, Wright was too amazed that such a tincture could be produced to consider how Dr. Timothy came to concoct it. As far as he knew, Dr. Timothy was a skilled surgeon and nothing more. It would not be long until Jonathan Wright experienced the truth firsthand.

Dr. Timothy operated out of the building that once housed Tierra Podrida Savings and Loan, three stories of rough hewn sandstone surrounding a reinforced steel core. It hadn't served as a bank since the war. Cash was in short supply after the bombs dropped and that supply dwindled further with every accidentally torn bill. People had no interest in handing over the little they had left for supposed safe keeping. The spacious vault had been converted into an operating room. Dr. Timothy needed to be sure he could not be interrupted while he worked.

Wright marched through the room that once served as the bank's lobby, dirty maroon carpeting muffling the sounds of his heavy footfalls. He passed the wooden teller's posts, headed for the vault and gingerly pressed upon the intercom button.

BZZT

"Hello?" Came the accented reply from the other end of the intercom console. As M's lone ex-patriot of the Northern Australian colony, Dr. Timothy's voice was instantly recognizable, even when distorted through a crude speaker. Ironically, given his line of work, Dr. Timothy looked much older than his 30 years of age. His skin had wrinkled prematurely in an experiment gone awry years earlier. Given his pale complexion, thin hawkish nose and thinning hair he looked as though he had been parboiled.

"Dr. Timothy! Thank goodness you're here! Have you seen Clint Masters?"

"I did indeed, Mr. Wright! That was quite a bout! I take it you are pleased with the results of the serum?"

"No! I mean, yes. That worked very well, thank you. I meant to ask if you had seen Clint this morning."

"I'm afraid not, Mr. Wright. I haven't laid eyes on him since yesterday."

"I see. Very well. Thank you for your help."

"My pleasure. Do not hesitate to ask if you require anything further."

Wright couldn't bring himself to reply. He began his slow shuffle back to Saint Basil's, wallowing in his failure. He knew that Masters was beyond a lost cause, he was a liability. Innocent X's Messiah died before he could be awakened. For that, Innocent X's millennia old sect crumbled around him. Jonathan Wright's Messiah was now fully awake and had been carted off by a stranger under the cover of night; there was no telling what incredible damage this would do to the institutional credibility of the Ashanti Orthodox.

Father Superior picked up on the first ring. Wright spared no detail as he laid his failure bare. Theirs was not so much a conversation as it was a confession. Wright's sincerity was met with a terse "Goodbye, Jonathan" and the hum of dialtone. He slumped to the floor of his sparsely furnished office in the upper floor of Saint Basil's, knocking over a stack of Manufacturing Center Productivity Reports in the process. The dialtone turned to a string of beeps.

Halfway around the world, President for Life Zhang was unaware at how quickly and efficiently his plan to sterilize the population of the Union was working. He would have been quite pleased to learn of the effects the tainted sustenance gel pouches were having on the populace, but it would have been no match for the overwhelming pleasure he was about to receive via telephone.

"Hello, Mr. Zhang." Were the first words Father Superior spoke after hearing of the debacle in the M Prefecture desert.

"Father Superior, good day to you! To what do I owe this call?" Zhang plastered a counterfeit smile on his face as he sunk into his wingback office chair, gingerly cradling his head in his hand.

"I am afraid I have unfortunate news, I must ask you to rescind a favor."

Zhang bolted upright out of his seat, astonished, a genuine grin spreading between his ears. There was only one thing that Father Superior had ever requested of Zhang.

"Rescind a favor? Why, what do you mean?" Zhang replied causally, making an attempt to sound as old and confused as possible.

"I am afraid our order has erred in the selection of Jonathan Wright for the Chancellor's post. I know this was not in our initially discussed in our agreement, but I was hoping he could be... dealt with."

Zhang couldn't believe his luck. He had to take a moment to compose himself before replying. "Oh. Well, I suppose that could be arranged. A deportation then?"

"No, Mr. Zhang, that will not be necessary. Jonathan Wright is no longer welcome amongst the Ashanti Orthodox. Please, do with him what you will. At this time, there will be no need for a replacement from amongst our ranks. I thank you and the Ashanti Orthodox thank you. May the Lord be with you always."

"And you, Father Superior. I trust in your most wise judgment. Good day."

The wave of relief that washed over Zhang was so great he could barely stand. He fell backwards into his seat, beaming at the ceiling. The immense paranoid burden he carried for eight years was finally to be lifted. He raised the telephone receiver once more, chuckling at his good fortune.

"Get me Wong!"

Jonathan Wright spent days sprawled on the floor of his office, immobile, taking neither food nor drink, his thoughts all consuming. Amongst the swirling clouds of guilt and self pity, Wright began to wonder what form his inevitable punishment could take. His failure was too egregious of an offense for the Ashanti Orthodox to ignore, but this fell too far outside of the Four Friar's jurisdiction for Wright to fear their involvement. Father Superior preferred to keep his personal muscle close at hand; the thought of him weakening his own defenses to mete out justice overseas seemed farfetched. Even if an outside party was sent there was no chance a hired gun could find entry. Wright had clear recollection of the difficulties he faced in reaching the Americas, let alone M, and he had been appointed to lead the Prefecture. He deduced his punishment would be handled locally, and that meant it would be upon him shortly.

New questions bubbled to the surface and the idea of his being a just punishment began to fade. If the Messiah refuses to save mankind from itself, is mankind worth saving? If two 'Messiahs' had refused to embrace their righteous responsibility, could there be others? How many? He had been unable to shepherd Masters, but is it so wrong to allow a man to live as he pleases? If God has been reborn in an earthbound form, why would he need any coaxing to lead his people?

Wright questioned what he had long labeled his 'relationship' with God. Even on the surface, it appeared awfully one sided. Wright often spoke of the voice of God, but he had never actually heard it. The thoughts in his head were his own. Questions he asked of God were answered through his own reasoning, or went unanswered entirely. What of his Ashanti Orthodox Bible, the Holy Book said to contain the word of God transcribed? Wright was said to be speaking the words of God when sermonizing back in Accra, but as a religious scholar, he knew of the numerous errors in translation. That they were errors was never mentioned in his sermons, they were passed down, verbatim, to those who would not have known better. This was intentionally misleading. Whatever faith his followers had drawn from his heavenly discourse was tainted. The words he spoke may once have been God's own, but they had been twisted by men, time and error. He had devoted his life to deceiving a simple flock.

He had long stifled the immoral cries bubbling up from the recesses of his psyche in order to adhere to the chaste ideals of the Ashanti Orthodox. His selfless devotion had led him to what seemed to be the brink of ruin; he longed now to act in his own best interest and only in his own best interest. This crisis of faith granted those immoral cries a raucous new voice. Hedonistic thoughts, long suppressed under the weight of religious belief and a lifetime of sexual suppression pushed their way to the forefront. He yearned to give in to carnality, the forbidden delights of the flesh, any and all depravity he had passed upon in the name of holy devotion. If he did not have long until his punishment, perhaps this was the only chance he would have to act upon his long muffled desires. These dark thoughts and the insight that his 'holy' overlord was punishing him for another man's noncompliance pushed Jonathan Wright's faith to the brink. And then, over it.

When his epiphany rained down upon him, Wright felt reborn. If the Ashanti Orthodox were founded upon the unjust ideal of forcing the hand of the Messiah and upon serving a God who is said to speak but refuses to listen, then the rest of their doctrine must be flawed as well. He had been serving the wrong set of principles, leading mankind down the wrong path. He knew now what had to be done. He had a new gospel to spread; a gospel that ran contrary to that of the Ashanti Orthodox, one of self-gratification and the pursuit of pleasure. In order to truly save M Prefecture, Jonathan Wright would have to refuse his punishment and live on to see this new divine prophecy come to light. He knew he could not stave off his punishment alone and he knew of the best man to turn to for help. Jonathan Wright stretched to awaken his painfully stiffened muscles, rose to his feet and picked up the telephone receiver.

Dr. Timothy did not question Wright, he was elated to be asked to conduct a surgical experiment of such perverse complexity, regardless of motive. The first two stages were already complete. Jonathan Wright's face had been removed. His head had been wrapped in fine gauze; eyeholes cut so he could watch the final stages unfold.

Arthur Keys, the heftiest white man in M, had been skinned from head to toe, his face replaced with Jonathan Wright's. He was the spitting image of the Chancellor from the chin up. From the chin down, it was a different, much messier story. Keys was sitting in a bare corner of the vault, leaking crimson onto the floor as he rocked his naked, nearly skinless body back and forth. His eyes were glazed and he was moaning softly. The cocktail of drugs he was administered had worked wonders in diminishing his howls of agony. Everything had gone smoothly so far, now it was on the delivery boy from B Prefecture to hold up his end of the bargain.

BZZZZT

Dr. Timothy stirred from his perch on his cot and grabbed his blunderbuss. The delivery boy was unlikely to cause a scene, but Dr. Timothy didn't want to leave anything to chance. The 30 inches of polished brass and delicately carved black walnut he held at the ready ensured that there would be no last minute changes of heart. Dr. Timothy pushed the button on the intercom. "Gary, please come in. So glad you could finally make it." The wheeled lock was spun hard to the left and the heavy steel door slowly swung wide. The final stage was underway.

Gary Bagwell had a difficult time getting from B Prefecture to M, but little of the difficulty was due to the barriers erected between Prefectures. Gary was a Highway Star, a member of a nomadic group of thieves and hustlers who made their living transporting goods from one Prefecture to another. Bypassing the barriers was no easy feat, but it was nothing new to Gary. At 20 years old, he had spent more than half of his life driving between one Prefecture and the next. His trip out to M would have been fairly routine, if it weren't for the personal matter that had been gnawing at him.

Gary knew Dr. Timothy was the kind of man who made good on his deals; he had acted as his chief broker of medical supplies and out-of-Union sustenance gel for years. There had never been any misunderstandings between the two regarding payments, scheduled deliveries, or anything, really. If it wasn't for their solid working relationship, there was no way he would have considered Dr. Timothy's offer, let alone accepted it. It was farfetched to the point of being absurd, but if anyone could pull this scheme off, it was Dr. Timothy. If everything was to go according to plan, no Highway Star would be able to traverse the Prefectures like Gary. He would be unstoppable, the best. The price he had to pay was steep, insanely so, but Gary knew it would be worth it. Still, he felt terrible about having to leave his protégé behind. Wilhelmina was 13, plenty old to take care of herself, but she was short. Too short. Thoughts of Willy unable to see over the steering wheel and careening through God-knows-what haunted Gary as he high-tailed it into M.

Gary was hesitant to enter into the vault, up until now he and Dr. Timothy had only done business through the intercom. He knew all about the macabre line of work Dr. Timothy was in, and he braced for the worst as he stepped inside. The skinless man was gross, yes, but Gary had expected worse. The massive hand cannon made for an imposing weapon, sure, but Gary had been a Highway Star long enough to have stared down dozens of muzzles. He exhaled a quiet sigh of relief as he extended a hand.

"Thanks for having me, Doc. Do I, uh, want to be introduced to these two?"

Dr. Timothy didn't offer his hand in return, nor did he offer a reply. Gary wasn't surprised, even through the intercom, Dr. Timothy had always been cold to him. Antique gun at the ready, Dr. Timothy turned to Wright with a small shrug. Wright spoke for himself, his voice raspy and hoarse.

"No introductions will be necessary my son. Please, turn around. Slowly."

Gary did as the man with the bandaged face instructed. Standing 6'4" with a stout build, Gary was a big black man, just as advertised. Wright glanced between Arthur Keys and Gary before speaking to Dr. Timothy.

"Excellent work! This young man *is* the perfect size." Wright turned back to Gary. "Please, undress."

Gary knew this was coming; Dr. Timothy had been very forthright in what was going to be involved in the procedure. It was one hell of a weird plan, but Gary had seen what Dr. Timothy's was able to sculpt out of the clay of humanity. He was the greatest in his field, bar none. Gary kicked off his cowboy boots, peeled away his crusty yellow duster and his threadbare white t-shirt. His dirty jeans dropped around his ankles.

"Thank you. Please, step closer." Wright croaked. Gary stepped towards him, stopping as Wright placed a hand on his knee. Wright peered through the holes in the gauze, leaning in close to where his hand met the delivery boy's knee. He straightened, his smile masked by the wrappings. "Perfect! His shade is a perfect match! Let us begin; my time is growing ever shorter."

"Do not be concerned, Mr. Wright. Once I begin, the procedure will not take long. But, first there is the matter of the contract." Dr. Timothy lowered his gun slowly and deliberately in order to reach a hand into his lab coat. He produced a pen and sheet of paper and handed them to Gary, raising his blunderbuss to the ready as Gary grabbed the sheet. "Please, look this over, sign at the bottom."

Gary skimmed past the complex medical illustrations and squinted to read the fine print. His eyes widened in shock.

"Whoa. Doc, this is a lot more than we talked about over the phone." Gary said, shaking his head in disbelief. "I mean, I'm no medical expert, but I'd say it would take me at least 20 years to round up so many. I don't know if..."

Dr. Timothy was quick to interrupt. "Gary. Supplies are scarce, and growing ever more so. I am offering you the deal of a lifetime. Now, I mean that quite literally, as I could easily kill you where you stand and take your skin for free." He paused to take aim at Gary's head. "Remember, you serve me no purpose from the neck up."

It didn't take Gary long to come around. "Sorry, Doc. You're right. You're right. I don't know what I was thinkin'." He bent down, curled the page over his knee and signed on the dashed line.

"Apology accepted. You will find pills on the operating table." Dr. Timothy said, gesturing to the table in the corner by the converted safety deposit boxes. "Take three, lie down and count to fifty. We will begin immediately."

Jonathan Wright lay prone alongside Dr. Timothy atop a 2-story building overlooking the Tierra Podrida town square. With spyglass in hand, Wright watched the Eternally Free Taiwanese officer clad in rusty red military fatigues pull the rope towards him slowly, allowing it to coil at his feet. The metal cage rose higher and higher over the town square with each tug. The day of reckoning had come.

Wright opted not to partake in the final stage of the procedure. Gary's face was to be his, but Wright wanted a constant reminder of his newfound rededication. Living life without a face would be that reminder. Dr. Timothy held onto what was left of Gary's skin for safekeeping; a malleable black face was not easy to come by in M. Wright had Dr. Timothy fashion a faceplate of surplus porcelain to protect his skinless visage. The faceplate was tall, reaching skyward far past the crown of his head. It was smooth, completely featureless apart from two small eyeholes and it was gleaming white, a perfect color match to his double breasted suit.

The leisurely public assassination came without warning or explanation. A small squadron of EFT officers arrived via dirigible earlier that morning and had been able to extract a groggy and disoriented 'Jonathan Wright' from Saint Basil's with surprising ease. A call was then sent out to the Manufacturing Center; the workers were forcibly 'excused' from the day's tasks and escorted to the town square to watch the grim spectacle.

The cage reached its apex. Slow, slurred cries of "Get me out of here!" croaked out of 'Jonathan Wright' overhead. The large crowd below, penned in amongst the concrete tables and benches that circled the town's flagpole, were unable to hear him over their bewildered murmurs. The officer tied off the rope, securing the open air prison and barked a heavily accented edict through a bullhorn.

"Magnificent Day! Rule of tyrant, no more!"

This did little to placate the visibly panicky crowd. The man they had grown to respect, even admire, had been left for dead forty feet above the ground. Their murmurs grew louder, faster, more frantic. One brave man stepped forward from the throng, crying out to the mysterious assassin.

"Why have you done this? Now who is in charge?"

"Now Phase 2 Manufacturing Center is in charge. Address concerns to Shift Supervisor." was all that was offered in response. Within minutes, the Eternally Free Taiwanese officers had boarded their red and white striped aircraft and taken to the skies, leaving the crowd in baffled disarray below.

From their perch above, Jonathan Wright and Dr. Timothy were left with every indication that their plan had worked. Wright had not expected his doppelganger to have been disposed of in such a public manner, but he was thrilled to have seen it unfold that way. Not only did he manage to skirt his grisly fate; he was able to convince the whole Prefecture of his death in doing so.

"Thank you, doctor. I am forever in your debt." He rasped.

"And I yours. The knowledge I have gained through this experiment will aid my work immensely." Dr. Timothy was quite pleased. Not only had his complicated set of surgeries gone perfectly, he now had a powerful ally. Hopefully one who would allow him to push the boundaries of human physicality even further. "Dare I say, our work together is just beginning, Mr. Wright."

"Indeed it is. But, you are wrong on one count. Jonathan Wright is soon to die, as you can clearly see. From this day forth, I am reborn as the true voice of God's Will on Earth." He rose to stand, nearly seven feet tall with the addition of his faceplate. "An eternal era of peace and goodwill be damned, the glorious reign of the Black Pope has begun!"

CHAPTER 6 - LAST PAGE IN THE LEDGER

20.3 MILES SOUTHWEST OF TIERRA PODRIDA,
M PREFECTURE, THE UNION

MONDAY, APRIL 2, 1979

"You're sure about this?" The younger, taller, sandy blond man asked, shielding his eyes from the sun as he surveyed the horizon. He was heavily freckled, it was clear he spent more time outdoors than most men in M.

"Jesus, Rollo, pretty sure. I guess. Here, take another look." The older, shorter man handed Rollo a ledger of work orders. His bald head, tinged a permanent rosy pink, was testament to his days spent out in the sun.

Rollo McPherson and Ken Walker worked for M Prefecture's telephone company, a branch of the Manufacturing Center. It had been a place of employment for 21 years for Ken, 8 for Rollo. It was the only job either of them had even known, both men having started straight out of school at 17. If you had asked before today, they would have told you they'd seen it all. There's a lot of strange, off-putting stuff the average man doesn't think to conceal when the phone company drops by to repair a line. But this work order, this was a different kind of strange.

"Yeah, I seen the order. Seen it five times. Still doesn't make any Goddamn sense."

It had been ten minutes or so since they arrived at what was supposed to be their work site. A small rock outcropping, standing all of three feet above the parched desert floor looked to be the only thing around for miles.

"Well, look over here, there's a little gap between those rocks... You think?" Ken gestured towards the rocks with a doubled over phone cable. There was indeed a small gap nestled in between the two large stone slabs that accounted for most of the outcropping. No more than a foot and a half high, maybe three feet wide and covered by a slight rock overhang, the gap between the slabs looked like it would make a fine resting spot for a transient whiptail lizard. It didn't look like much of a spot to install a telephone.

"Yep, guess so." Rollo said with a shrug. "Coordinates are dead on. I just don't get it. Want to take a look down there?"

Ken walked towards the gap and got down on his hands and knees. He gave the gap a quick swing of his flashlight, nothing, at least no lizards. "I don't see why not. Let's see if this goes anywhere." Ken popped his flashlight into his mouth and wriggled into the gap up to his shoulders, only to stop and wriggle back out again. He righted himself and spat the flashlight back into his hand, letting out a defeated groan. "Oh man."

"What? What is it?" Rollo crouched down next to the gap, trying to peer into the darkness within.

"That's just it. It's nothing. A big, empty nothing. Some kind of cave, looks like."

"OK, what now?" Rollo looked up at Ken. "We actually going to do this?"

"You want to tell the New Factory no?"

Rollo didn't need to answer that. There was once a time when a factory employee could voice a concern to a foreman. That time passed with Jonathan Wright.

The installation of the Phase 2 Manufacturing Center was underway hours after 'Wright' was left to die high above the town square. Airlifted as one enormous, prefabricated compound by a fleet of zeppelins and installed overtop the original Manufacturing Center, the Phase 2's installation was complete before the sun set that evening.

Phase 2 Manufacturing Centers were technological marvels, the pinnacle of automated efficiency, designed to be entirely self-sufficient. Developments in automation meant that delivery, processing, manufacturing, packaging, shipping and even the generation of power could all be performed without pause and without the need for any human interaction. Automated flight meant that raw materials could be shipped in and processed products could be shipped back out without anyone so much as flicking a switch.

Workers from every stage of production had been re-assigned. In a Phase 2, what remained of the human workforce was used solely to power the factory. While the workers could easily be replaced with rechargeable fuel cells, those fuel cells didn't come cheap. Now, a factory worker's job consisted of nothing more than causing turbines to spin for hours on end. They were expected to toil until they no longer had the physical capacity to convert their kinetic energy into electric. It was a temporary solution, but a profitable one.

The 'Shift Supervisor', a grainy video feed of an Eternally Free Taiwanese man, was the only form of authority in the Phase 2

Manufacturing Center. It took a little over a week before it became clear that he was nothing more than a video loop spouting inspirational messages. You could lodge as many concerns or complaints to the Shift Supervisor as you liked, all you'd receive in return was a staccato lecture about the importance of peak productivity. Otherwise, work was unsupervised and attendance was far from mandatory. But, for most, the repetitive physical exertion was their only means of survival. The lion's share of the goods produced in the Phase 2 Manufacturing Centers made their way overseas; only items deemed absolutely necessary were made available to the workers and meeting a daily wattage quota of was the only way workers could hope to pay for those items.

Ken and Rollo were some of the few remaining lucky ones; for the time being they were able to continue working as they had before the arrival of the Phase 2. They didn't know it yet, but this was going to be their final work order, the last phone line laid anywhere in the Union. It wouldn't be long until they were tasked with spinning copper between magnets along with the rest of the Prefecture.

Ken secured a rope ladder outside of the cave and wriggled back through the gap between the rocks, free end in hand. He let the ladder fall the five or six feet to the floor below and climbed down with Rollo close behind. The pair dusted themselves off and gave cursory swings of their flashlights. Ken was right. This was a big cave, probably three or four hundred feet across at its widest point. They had landed in a large, chalky brown clearance flanked by stalagmite pillars. Several craggy passageways branched out from the center. The ground beneath them was fairly smooth and level, having been filed down by an underground river eons ago. Time had reduced the river to a slow steady trickle, no more than two inches across.

"So, where are we going to do the install?" Rollo asked with a sigh.

"Let's just hang it on the wall." Ken chuckled. "And, to think, I usually brag about how I get to spend my days out in the sun."

"Yeah, very funny. Now you can brag about how much solid rock you get to drill through." Rollo grimaced as he scanned the ledger with his flashlight. "Then, maybe you can let this Mr. 'C.M.' know how much we appreciate him asking us to run a phone wire for miles underground out to the Goddamn middle of nowhere."

"Christ, Rollo, calm down. I'm just trying to lighten things up a little. If being underground pisses you off so bad, why don't you go get the drill from the truck? Otherwise, I'd say you'd better get used to this uh... natural beauty, down here." Ken rapped his knuckles against the solid rock wall. "Looks like we'll be drilling for a while."

CHAPTER 7 - ROOSTER LIQUOR

TIERRA PODRIDA, M PREFECTURE, THE UNION

SUNDAY, JUNE 3, 1979

Livestock was rare in the Union, rare to the point of being treated as mythological. Rooster Liquor was not a poultry product; there was nothing chicken about it. It just happened to be the brainchild of an unbalanced man with a penchant for sly wordplay. Dr. Timothy dreamt up the process of distilling medical waste into an inebriating sludge before the civil war broke out. But, without an ample supply of the leftovers of humanity, he had been unable to brew much more than a test batch. The scores of dead countrymen that came along with the war were repurposed as Dr. Timothy tinkered with his Rooster Liquor recipe. By the time the rain of bombs ended, he had perfected the science behind the cloudy, pink drug.

Dr. Timothy took great pleasure in concocting his swill, but none in consuming it. He was a man who made certain that his senses were never dulled. He had long wished to share his invention, especially with those whose ancestors were instrumental in Rooster Liquor's development. Now that he had aligned himself with a man of guile and resources, his wish was finally to be fulfilled. The Black Pope flooded the market with Dr. Timothy's brand of liquid immorality.

The time was right for a habit forming inebriant to grip the Prefecture by the throat; Rooster Liquor proved to be immediately popular. Production ramped up as the people of Tierra Podrida grew ever sicker and sought surgical treatment, unwittingly delivering themselves as walking lumps of raw product. With the healthier segment of M's populace reduced to human batteries used to power the factory, people had nothing to lose and little to live for. Busy, hole-in-the-wall bars sprung up in the abandoned storefronts that ringed the town square as the depressed masses embraced the drug's temporary relief from reality.

As the only product not dispensed from the Phase 2, Rooster Liquor was all that was still available for cash purchase in Tierra Podrida. The Black Pope was sole purveyor. In time, he was able to amass all of the hard currency that once changed hands within the Prefecture. M's economy to mutated alongside its citizens, sustenance gel pouches became the currency of choice. Morale dropped as the cumulative time spent spinning turbines in the factory climbed. Demand for Rooster Liquor grew as morale dropped. Within the first month of the inception of this new cashless system, the price of a bottle of Rooster Liquor had jumped from one pouch to four.

Swigging the addictive, cannibalistic brew snuffed out the human decency that once resided within the people of M. They had been reduced to savagery, eager to please only themselves regardless of the harm to others. Getting wasted had become M's most popular pastime, just ahead of getting laid.

Rooster Liquor's unexpected encephalitic side effects played a large role in the Prefecture's swift moral decline. With brains swollen and inflamed, obscene self-gratification had replaced civility. Crude free enterprise began to flourish. By the time a ten-pouch box was the going rate for a bottle of Rooster Liquor, the local women had abandoned factory work. It took around 200 hours toiling in the Phase 2 to earn ten pouches. An enterprising gal could spend 15 minutes on her back in exchange for a bottle of Rooster Liquor. Word spread quickly. It wasn't long before all the gals in town were enterprising.

The Black Pope's depraved vision of the Lord's true will was taking hold. With his subjects trapped under the spell of Rooster Liquor's revolting charms, unable or unwilling to dissent, his power was ultimate in Tierra Podrida. This was not cause for celebration, it was cause for concern. The Black Pope's self-imposed isolation gave him time to think, he thought of unseen enemies from parts unknown. Paranoia defined the Black Pope during the early stages of his sovereignty over M. Before long someone would come to lay claim to his Prefecture. But, who?

The Eternally Free Taiwanese didn't appear to be a threat. The red and white striped delivery dirigibles from overseas maintained their beelines to and from the Phase 2 Manufacturing Center, never once veering towards Saint Basil's. From what the Black Pope knew of the EFT, factory profitability would be enough to keep them at bay from any interference. At least, that was the hope. He knew he wouldn't be able to muster any defense against an aerial assault.

The roads could be defended. Fevered suspicions of an outside force storming into town and impinging upon his rule changed the Black Pope's opinion. The roads *must* be defended. The Inter-

Prefecture Highway, or what remained of it, was the only route through town. It was a vein of vulnerability, a hole in the dike seemingly too large to plug. Tierra Podrida needed to be fortified, no matter how. The solution to the problem was as drastic as it was violent and shortsighted. With one emphatic plunge of the detonator, the buildings overlooking the highway at both ends of town burst apart; lighting the night sky, showering the streets with flaming debris and choking the air with rolling grey clouds. Huge piles of smoldering rubble blocked all easy wheeled entrance into Tierra Podrida. In sober, level headed times, the people of M would have been horrified. As it stood, they barely registered their explosive entrapment.

The satisfaction of barricading his domain against the fantasy of foreign invaders did not last. The Black Pope's paranoia directed itself inward, towards his unwitting flock. They were weak, docile, but that was only due to the effects of the Rooster Liquor. If the illicit booze-well ran dry, the simpleminded morality of times past would surely return. He knew his subjects could wrest control away from him, if they were so inclined. That inclination had to be snuffed, but that was not a task the Black Pope was willing to undertake personally. Face to face interaction with his subjects was out of the question; he was to be a figure of legend, not a mere man of the people. He needed representatives, a force to ensure that he could maintain control over his domain should circumstances change. Once again, he turned to the only man he felt he could trust.

Dr. Timothy was given a simple instruction to begin, return with a woman. He left the bank vault and set off into the heart of town, sack in hand, blunderbuss over his shoulder. He would never dare fire the gun; it was merely for show. He knew full well that a firearm of its age was more likely to blow up in his hands than it was to fire properly. It wasn't much for shooting, but it made for a great intimidation accessory. Dr. Timothy returned dragging the sack behind, heavy with victim.

She was young, 16 or so, rather pretty. Her nose was a mess, but that would be an easy fix. She must have been a patient of his at an earlier date, though Dr. Timothy couldn't recall operating on her; she was one of thousands. It looked as though the sickness had been concentrated in her neck. He was quite pleased with the results from his earlier surgery. The skin tone of her graft was nearly a perfect match and the flesh underneath showed no signs of rot. Dr. Timothy was also pleased she hadn't opted for any of the extreme procedures that had come into vogue amongst the town's working girls, work of this scope and scale would be best upon a relatively blank canvas.

The Black Pope drew his surgical specifications by hand; he was many things, a talented artist was not one of them. Dr. Timothy pressed on without question. He had been told to turn in his work as quickly as possible and the simple line drawings made the intent of most of the cosmetic procedures obvious. Her nose and chin were reshaped, ears pinned back. Breast and buttock implants, ribs removed. Liposuction, brows-down perma-hairmelt. 'Invisible' heel implants, vaginal tautening. Hand and foot reduction, enhanced pheromone release implant. Powerblonde Eterni-Coif. Muscle and bone toughening, improved night vision. That much the diagram had made clear. There was one final element that seemed particularly bizarre, even by M Prefecture's standards. Dr. Timothy pressed forward with a shrug, suturing a thick, bushy mustache above his patient's obscenely plumped lips.

With the physical modifications complete, Dr. Timothy turned to the invasive work. It was the first aggro-tranq lobotomy he had performed in years. Judging by the results of her reflex and sensitivity analysis, he hadn't lost a step. Within the day, she was ready for testing at the hands of the Black Pope.

She was a sight to behold, standing well over six feet tall, proportions reflective of the Black Pope's virginal misinterpretation of female anatomy. Her unnaturally flawless face marred by a pushbroom mustache, her extreme hourglass figure straining her bloodstained medical gown well past the point of modesty. If her looks were his only concern, Dr. Timothy would have been overjoyed with his work. Her intricate transformation was his second most complex piece to date, trailing only Gary's rebuild. But, looks were only the beginning. She had to be obedient, ferocious, worthy of the Black Pope.

Dr. Timothy crouched at her feet, gently poking at her nearly spherical calf muscle. "How do you feel? Any lingering tightness?"

"No, Dr. I feel fine." Her reply was cold and emotionally dead but beautifully melodious. Her vocal cord adjustment was a resounding success.

"Excellent. Lift me."

She did as she was instructed, effortlessly scooping Dr. Timothy up and cradling him in her toned, svelte, superhumanly strong arms.

"Now, run!"

She gracefully sprang forward and bolted out of Tierra Podrida Savings and Loan. Dr. Timothy issued directions as she sped towards what was to be her new home.

The Saintly tapestries had been defaced and re-hung upside down. Aside from that, little had changed at Saint Basil's since the naissance of the Black Pope. The bronze statuary proved too difficult to remove and the Black Pope still had a soft spot for his illuminated dance floor. He had turned it on for the first time in months in anticipation of his lady caller. White, yellow, pink, blue. White, yellow, pink, blue.

The glowing squares seemed to agitate the test subject, or it could have been the initial stages of Rooster Liquor withdrawal. An ugly, dark haired man with a reputation for being boorish and argumentative, Calvin Clarke had been handpicked for the trial. He was exactly the breed of malcontent that could rile the common people against the Black Pope (or so the Black Pope led himself to believe). He had also been easy to dupe. Calvin's mood grew worse as he waited, audibly grumbling as he staggered his weight from one foot to the other, his hands loosely tied behind his back. He was beginning to suspect the bottle of Rooster Liquor Dr. Timothy had promised in exchange for making the long walk out to Saint Basil's wasn't forthcoming. He was right. It wasn't.

The heavy double doors burst open. She set Dr. Timothy down on the dance floor and stood at attention awaiting instruction. The Black Pope was immediately impressed by the physique Dr. Timothy had created at his request, but that was literally for show. If she couldn't perform, he would have to rethink his plan.

"Take him down." he rasped.

She ducked low and quickly swept the ground beneath the test subject with her long, lean leg. Calvin collapsed with a moan as she popped back upright.

"Very nice. Kick him while he is prone."

She reared back and delivered a swift, bone crunching boot to the test subject's spine. He howled and began to twitch.

"Yes. Again."

Another kick. Another howl. His twitching grew more spastic.

"Sickening. Step on his throat."

Calvin Clarke's gasp turned to a long thin wheeze as her bare foot, now permanently arched into a tiptoe, came down hard upon his neck. The wheeze faded as she applied more pressure, forcing the life from his body. The Black Pope turned to Dr. Timothy, his faceplate masking his grin.

"Incredible work! Tell me, what is her name?"

"Candi was the name she gave."

"Candi... A heavily refined treat. Delightful! Come Candi. Allow me to inspect you." he leered.

Her obedience ingrained, she swayed over to the Black Pope. He relished his inspection, eying her slowly from head to toe and back again, finally running a hand across her cheek, stopping short of her mustache.

"Excellent. Simply excellent. But, tell me, Dr. Timothy. Why on Earth did you give her... this?" He asked, bemused, twisting a corner her facial hair between finger and thumb. Dr. Timothy had anticipated this question. He produced the Black Pope's surgical schematics from his lab coat.

"It is as you drew in the diagram. Here." He passed the crisply folded sheet of paper to the Black Pope. A gurgling roar of a laugh came from behind the gleaming porcelain mask.

"That was meant to be a menacing smile, Dr. Timothy! But this, this is... appropriately disturbing. Savagely erotic. A splash of machismo dripping from the petals of my deadly, delicate flower.

You have done well, very well. Better than I could have imagined. Is there any possibility she could turn on me?"

"No. Docility towards her master is ensured."

"Her master... I do like the sound of that. Now, we will need more of them. We must be vigilant in our defense. Make me as many as you can, mustache and all. I want each one to be more similar than the last." The Black Pope reached out and gingerly pulled on the collar of Candi's ill-fitting gown, letting it fall to the floor. "A man of my stature must not be limited to a single bride."

CHAPTER 8 - AFTERBIRTH

63.8 MILES NORTH OF TIERRA PODRIDA,
M PREFECTURE, THE UNION

SATURDAY, OCTOBER 23, 1993

Anna Masters wasn't feeling well. Her soft, hazy sense of discomfort was the first thing Anna could remember feeling in months, maybe years. The physical pain wasn't pleasant, but Anna had felt pain before. The emotional pain she was beginning to feel was something entirely new. Other feelings, bad feelings, came back to her as her brain struggled to break free from its drugged stupor. Anna knew she had done something... She was pretty sure it was something terrible.

She had served Satan little purpose over the last nine months, other than acting as a vessel to gestate his seed. Impregnating Anna had been quite the coup, considering her lineage. Now, with the child born and the child's sacrifice having gone awry, she didn't serve him any purpose.

Anna was stumbling through the parched flats of M Prefecture, completely nude. Her feet hurt. It would be a while before she was able to register that the elements were assaulting the rest of her body as well. Her feet were easy to pay attention to. They kept plodding on, one after another, headed anywhere, just so long as it was forward.

She didn't notice the congealing blood that was slowly caking onto her thighs; she was too concerned with trying to straighten the horizon in her field of vision. Evil people. She had been dealing with evil people. Evil people who wanted to hurt her. But why? Left. Right. Left. Right. Keep going. Find somewhere comfortable.

Anna never found somewhere comfortable, but she did find a bare patch of ground. She made her way down. It was a coordinated effort until she was bested by gravity. She didn't really feel it when she hit the ground, she was too disappointed in the diagonal horizon. Nothing felt better, but everything felt smaller, colder. Then, nothing was felt at all. The circles the vultures were tracing in the sky overhead grew smaller and smaller as they descended upon Anna.

Wilhelmina Hung was careening south towards Anna's last known whereabouts, slung low on the back of her Taiwauto 600cc racing motorcycle. Wilhelmina and Anna had never met and never would, but their lives were about to be directly linked. All thanks to the four pillars of light in the distance – stretching down from the heavens to the cloud of thick black smoke hovering low over the horizon. Wilhelmina needed a change, it was long overdue. She would have given the pillars a curious glance followed by a wide berth if she had known of the change to come. But, Wilhelmina was a thief, not a clairvoyant and those pillars were beautiful, hypnotically so.

Things hadn't been the same since Gary left. They made a great team during their time. With Gary's brute strength and his long list of connections and Wilhelmina's sly charm, they were adept at turning trouble into profitable adventure. When they rode together, stealing whatever wasn't nailed down and selling their spoils to the highest bidder, Wilhelmina felt life was worth living, life was good. Now, life was only the best option because death was too frightening to face.

Gary had been the only person Wilhelmina ever grew to be close with. She never knew her mother and had decided to run away from her father's house in F by the time she was four. She didn't have the nerve to do so until she was six. Her bravery didn't last long once she stormed through the front door for the last time. Gary found her only hours after she left, chancing to drive past a little girl bawling by the side of the road. They spent the next seven years traversing the Inter-Prefecture Highways together.

A bright kid immersed in a violent, lawless underworld, Wilhelmina quickly took on her share of unsavory traits. She gravitated to thievery, out of necessity at first and for the thrill of it before long. She was good, too. Small enough to squeeze into places she shouldn't, cute enough to get out of most jams, and backed by a burly enforcer to get out of jams where her cuteness couldn't cut it. Wilhelmina grew to be a shrewd broker as well. She had a natural advantage when she was younger, the black marketeers she and Gary dealt with were immediately thrown off by having to negotiate with a foul mouthed, 75 pounder. Her favorite bargaining trick involved crocodile tears streaming down her cheeks and a lit stick of dynamite. It didn't matter that the dynamite was fake; she always got her way long before the fuse had the chance to burn down.

When Gary was given the offer, he told Wilhelmina he couldn't pass it up. Then, he told her that she didn't want anything to do with it. He said this was the one score they couldn't split and that he could never forgive himself if she had anything to do with paying for his end of the bargain. Wilhelmina wanted nothing more than to follow in Gary's shadow, even if she didn't grasp the consequences of doing so. He didn't give her the option to tag along. When she awoke the morning after their argument, Gary was nowhere to be found. He left at a bad time; Wilhelmina's Highway Star apprenticeship was far from complete.

She had picked up enough skill with a makeup brush to get past the Chantone sensors that separated the Prefectures, but without Gary's connections, she now found herself two steps behind his exhilarating trail of larceny. Even worse than being cut off from his old associates was the psychological toll Gary's absence took upon her. Wilhelmina grew meek, knowing that she didn't have anyone to back her up in times of need. Threats of violence became frightening, rather than laughably insulting. Fight was no longer an option; flight became her way of life.

Wilhelmina always held out hope that she would see Gary again. She grew to regret that hope once her wish was fulfilled, nearly two years after he left. As emotionally painful as Gary's absence had been, his return was torturous. To say that Gary came back a changed man was an understatement. Physically, he was hard to classify as a man. He adopted a name that wasn't suitable for a man, and in Wilhelmina's mind, he adopted an outlook that certainly wasn't befitting of a man. He told her he had to do bad things, things far worse then what she had been exposed to. She knew exactly what that meant. That meant murder. Gary taught her at an early age that no matter what, no one was to die because of their actions. A man can always get back what he has lost, but he only has one lifetime to do so. Nothing else was off limits. Wilhelmina took that ideal to heart, adopting it as a code.

Apparently, Gary didn't feel as strongly as he had let on years earlier. He never said outright that he was in the business of taking lives, he never had the chance. Their final face-to-face meeting ended in a cloud of dust; an enraged Wilhelmina cut Gary off mid-sentence, gunning the engine of her freshly pilfered bike and speeding away into the distance.

Wilhelmina was still miles from the four pillars of light. Her excitement grew as she raced closer and closer. Whatever they were, Wilhelmina had a strong feeling that these pillars would be the key to finally shrugging off the weight of Gary's absence. Their awesome glow offered her assurance that her days of small time burglary and a life on the lam were coming to a close. But, what the hell were they? Wilhelmina had seen her fair share in her travels, but never anything like this.

There was good reason she had never seen anything like the pillars; no one ever had. The pillars of light were a by-product. Beautiful, certainly, but nowhere near as interesting as the devices that created them, or the legion of men who wore the devices. The Four Friars, elite strike force of the Ashanti Orthodox, were headed back to Earth.

Father Superior was forced to deviate from the Ashanti Orthodox's stated intent of awakening the Messiah, opting instead to increase focus on battling the ancient force of evil. Only Father Superior and Jonathan Wright knew of Clint Masters slipping through their grasp. The attention of an entire faith was turned to eradicating Satan; Wright's failure was successfully swept under the rug. With no Messiah left to awaken, Satan's death would have to make do as the crowning achievement of Father Superior's holy career.

The Four Friars had been fitted with Halos, the net result of longstanding technological one-upmanship between Ghana and the Eternally Free Taiwanese. The Halos cast a golden sphere of light around the heads of each of the Friars, but life imitating art was the least of the Halos' functions. Each Halo acted as a self contained stratospheric flight device. In theory, the ability to quickly travel anywhere in the world was to give them a decided speed advantage over Satan and the Knights in his Service. For the Four Friars, simple to use, incredibly accurate, intercontinental travel was an incredible boon. With the Halos, their quest to destroy Satan became more than just a hopeful mission statement.

Formed in the late 19th Century, the Four Friars were the Ashanti Orthodox vanguard in the fight against Satan and his forces. Theirs had been a legacy of failure. As an order, they had yet to confront Satan in the flesh. They were best known for repeatedly dying at the hands of the Knights in Satan's Service. The Four Friars did not relish their sullied reputation; they preferred to be recognized for their piety and strict adherence to tradition. Since their inception, the revolving cast of battle tested Holy Men who comprised the Four Friars have been granted one of four titles – Prosperity, Peace, Abundance and Life. These titles were not assigned at random, as each title carried with it a specific set of responsibilities. Prosperity acquired and disseminated information, and acted as chief negotiator. Peace planned battle tactics. Life served as tracker and it was up to Abundance to kick in doors and knock heads together. As the members of the order fell in battle with the Dark Lord's forces, new recruits were anointed with the names of the fallen as they joined rank.

Prosperity 3 was the elder statesman of the group and acted as their unquestioned leader, having served as one of the Four Friars for over half a century. At 67, his physical abilities had deteriorated but his first hand knowledge gained from surviving dozens of skirmishes with various Knights was said to be invaluable.

Peace 9, 40, was second in command. While he would never dare say it outright, he viewed Prosperity 3's 'experience' as a career of incompetence. Not only had he been unable to come close to killing Satan, but Prosperity 3 had also spent decades avoiding a glorious death in battle. It was not a written rule, but as Peace 9 saw it, if you did not come home with news of your victory, it was best to not come home. The internalized lack of respect Peace 9 felt for his leader was nothing compared to his own self loathing. Peace 9 had been obeying Prosperity 3's cowardly orders of 'Retreat!' for nearly 20 years.

The newest recruits, Abundance 12 and Life 29, rounded out the group. At 24 years old, Abundance 12 was in the physical prime of his life, and it showed, he was the tallest and broadest of the bunch. Life 29 stood on the other end of the spectrum. Only 13, he was naturally the smallest of the Four Friars, not at all physically intimidating but preternaturally gifted at following a trail. He wasn't only a hyper-adept tracker, Life 29 was perpetually worried. It wasn't that he was thrust into a mission better suited to someone twice his age that concerned Life 29, it was his title. As the 29th 'Life', he knew that 28 men had died manning his position before him. His was the unlucky title. Life 29 wanted nothing to do with Satan, at least not yet. For now, all he wanted was to make sure he wouldn't be replaced by Life 30.

The inaugural mission of the latest incarnation of the Four Friars did not get off to a promising start. The devout had gathered en masse in Accra to watch the launch of the heroic men who were to forcefully rid the world of evil. The Four Friars patiently stood at attention, each tall, muscular member decked out in a loose, beige combat robe, Halo activator rings hovering an inch above their heads.

Father Superior issued quiet blessings to his Friars before addressing the crowd. His speech to his followers was brief; time was of the essence. He should have prepared a backup speech. The Halos' first launch was an exercise in anti-climax. The Four Friars gazed towards the heavens as the golden spheres engulfed their heads. In theory, once the spheres were engaged, they were to soar into the sky. In practice, they stood looking skyward until the murmurs from the crowd grew loud enough to warrant drawing a curtain over the embarrassing display. The error had been one of simple oversight; Prosperity 3 had input the destination telemetry, but overlooked inputting the current location. He mumbled something about being old and the buttons being too small as an excuse. By the time the engineers had the problem pinned down, the opportunity for pomp had long passed. The Four Friars winglessly took to the skies with only Father Superior and a handful of technicians looking on.

Wilhelmina reached the smoldering church before the Four Friars had the chance to land. She stood in silent admiration at the base of the light pillars, trying to determine what they could possibly be. A cry pierced the air, snapping Wilhelmina's attention towards the church's scorched remains. The sound was unmistakable; there was a baby amongst the wreckage. The time for wonder was over, instinct and adrenaline took hold.

She revved the engine and roared between two blackened, sagging beams that looked as though they could snap in two at any moment. The fire had died down inside, but it was still incredibly hot. Wilhelmina's neck to toe, white leather motorcycle suit and matching helmet only made things hotter, but they did provide protection from the embers that rained down from the creaking, moaning roof.

The bone-white baby, still coated in the goo of afterbirth, lay wailing on a stone slab, encircled in pools of black wax. His tiny, wrinkled arms were clasped like a vice over his heart, grasping the tip of a dagger nearly as long as the child himself. Wilhelmina reached for the handle, the infant loosened his grip and allowed her to toss the dagger aside. His cries ceased as she cradled him in her left arm and sped outside, eager to avoid being crushed by the fire-decayed wood overhead. She stopped short, no more than 50 feet from the church. The pillars of light had faded, replaced by four men in tan robes, their faces obscured by glowing golden orbs.

The Halo devices allowed the Four Friars to talk to one another while remaining practically silent. Their words were clear as crystal amongst themselves, but registered only as a barely audible hum to Wilhelmina.

"We are too late. It is clear we have failed." Prosperity 3 announced to his brethren. "Worse yet, it appears the initial reports were correct. Satan has fathered a child."

"We have *not* failed." Peace 9 countered. He was furious, but tried his best to hide it. If it weren't for the old man's technological incompetence, they could have finally had Satan in their grasp! "We have been given an opportunity to strike a fierce blow against Satan's forces. The child must be destroyed! Abundance, seize him!"

Abundance 12 strode towards Wilhelmina, now clutching the infant to her breast. Prosperity 3 grabbed hold of Abundance's arm before he could get too far. Wilhelmina, still astride her motorcycle, trembled visibly even as Abundance was held back from her.

"We shall do no such thing." Abundance stepped back in line as Prosperity overruled Peace 9's command. "Our orders were to destroy Satan and the Knights in his Service. Those are the only orders we shall follow. Despite his lineage, the child has done no wrong. The Four Friars will not be responsible for his death. Nor shall we be responsible for the child's life. This young woman will watch over the child in our stead; she is to become a Sister of Joseph. Come now, lower your Halos. We must begin."

The Four Friars tapped a combination of buttons on their activator rings, some Friars more resentfully than others. Their golden orbs faded from view. Wilhelmina was relieved to see that these odd figures were in fact men and not some otherworldly sphere-headed creatures, but she was not relieved to the point of complacency.

"Who are you? What is going on here?" she blurted, her terrified sobs muffled by her helmet.

Their response was just as bizarre as their arrival. They were chanting. Wilhelmina's frustration and confusion quickly lifted as they droned as a group, replaced by a feeling of serenity beyond anything she had ever experienced. She could not make clear the words that were being chanted, but their intonations went beyond comprehension. The effect was one of compulsion.

Suddenly, Wilhelmina wanted nothing more than to protect this mysterious child. She had a burning desire to take him home and provide him with an inert, sheltered lifestyle, one devoid of conflict. She knew that she was to contact these men, these Four Friars, if anything was to stand in the way of her new wishes. Before she could ask any more of the Four Friars, their heads were once again covered by golden orbs and they were ascending towards the heavens, swathed in pillars of light. Wilhelmina Hung kicked her bike awake and began the long ride back to F Prefecture, where she belonged and where the child in her arms most certainly did not.

CHAPTER 9 - WELCOME TO CASTILLO

THE CASTILLO ACADEMY, F PREFECTURE, U.S.A.

MONDAY, JUNE 21, 2010

"At The Castillo Academy, the opportunities to thrive are limitless. Offering a wide range of academic programs to encourage the emerging talents of our students, Castillo strives to create the leaders of tomorrow."

That's the paragraph printed below the four smiling brown faces on the cover of the Castillo Academy recruitment brochure. The fresh faced teenagers in the photo weren't actual Castillo students, they were models. Outfitted in the Castillo school uniforms - dark grey blazers, shorts and caps, white dress shirts, red ties and shiny black dress shoes - they had been bused in for the day to stand in for Castillo's best and brightest. Photographs had been taken all over campus. They sat smiling and pointing at textbooks in the glass and stainless steel beam library. They sat smiling on the freshly trimmed grass in front of one of Castillo's ivy covered brick walls. They stood smiling and looking sporty around the groomed gravel racetrack. They forced laughs in front of the 20 foot tall, ornately carved double doors that acted as the Academy's main entrance. Then they were bussed back to their modeling agency, far down the highway, in a much poorer area of F Prefecture.

The model students conveyed the look the Castillo Academy wished to portray. Wholesomely pretty girls, ruggedly handsome boys, all decidedly clean cut, all eager to learn. Indeed, the model students could have made fine Castillo students, if their parents could afford the staggering cost of a Castillo education.

The Castillo Academy was the most prestigious private preparatory school in F Prefecture. Every one of the students was a 'somebody'. Juan and Inez Montenegro were the son and daughter of a bank president. Samida Al-Farouq was the daughter of the Prefecture's most popular singer. Fabricio Martuzzi was the son of a real estate mogul *and* an award winning actress. On and on it went. Everyone was set to live the good life on account of their lineage. Everyone, that was, with the exception of Billy Lopez.

Billy Lopez was an orphan and a Ward of the Prefecture. He had grown up in a middle class group home and was admitted to Castillo in a move the Academy would later describe as an act of 'giving back to the community'. He was the only student ever admitted under such circumstances in the 70 year history of the school. Perhaps in other schools being different from the rest of the students may have made Billy an interesting figure, someone worth getting to know, someone with a different perspective. Not at Castillo. At Castillo, without proper social standing you were a pariah, meant to be ignored, mocked for your failures and grumbled about when assigned as a lab partner.

At least his high school days would soon be behind him. He had been granted a scholarship at the Alpha Center, F Prefecture's most prestigious *public* institution of higher learning. He would have a fresh start, surrounded by thousands of new people. Billy couldn't wait, but he had to. It was fifteen minutes past noon, second last Monday in June. Only four and a half more days to go.

Having no record of his parents, there was no telling Billy's actual ancestry. His last name was a pretty good clue, except, that was assigned at random when he was granted Ward of the Prefecture status. Based on his angular facial features, a Latin American background (heavy on the conquistador blood) would be a good guess. All in all, he was fairly handsome, tall and lanky with medium brown hair and eyes. Based on looks alone, Billy should have had little trouble fitting in. If his father owned a chain of auto repair shops he would have been a big hit with the girls at school.

The Castillo student body was an amalgam of Chinese, Greek, Arab, Guatemalan, Taiwanese, Italian, Turkish, Colombian, Persian, Mexican, Peruvian, Korean and Japanese ancestry, all of whom had been born and raised in F Prefecture. They made for a sea of brown faces in dorky grey suits. As different as their backgrounds may have been, the students had all been conditioned to think and act as a group; individuality was frowned upon. Today the group was in a good mood - the afternoon's classes had been cancelled for the annual track meet. With no further classes to attend, most students who had the earlier lunch period stuck around the cafeteria into the later lunch period. There were kids everywhere. Like the library, study hall, all three gymnasiums, auditorium, and most any other room at the Academy, the cafeteria was covered with a steel ribbed glass dome. The powerful air conditioning units were humming furiously, keeping the crush of students from melting in the greenhouse.

Billy stood alone in the lunch line, the other kids made a point of giving him an extra wide berth. Over the course of his time at the Academy, he had stopped noticing these things and began to accept the extra personal space he was afforded.

"Here you go, Billy." said Imelda with a smile, as she passed him his lunch tray. The cafeteria staff knew Billy better than anyone else in the cafeteria. He worked there as a janitor after hours and they would exchange pleasantries as their shifts ended and his began.

"Thanks Imelda." Billy checked out the contents of his tray. It looked like today was fried krill patties and a side of mealworm paste. One thing Billy could say for the Academy was that the food was great. He had never eaten half this well in the group home.

Lunch tray in hand, Billy scanned the rows of tables for a seat. With the cafeteria pushed well past capacity it was even harder than usual for him to find a spot where he could keep enough of a distance from the other kids to avoid offending anyone with his presence. He strolled up and down the aisles, temporarily quieting the conversations around him as he passed. Nothing. Billy had long since accepted being alone at lunch, but he wasn't about to accept having to stand to eat.

Heading down the final row of tables, he finally spotted his best option and his best option was far, *far* better than he had hoped. Gina Theoulis, daughter of the Prefecture's wealthiest River Kelp magnate, was sitting alone. Gina Theoulis! Alone! Gina Theoulis was easily the most popular girl in school, at least as far as the boys were concerned. Amongst the girls, she was easily the most reviled. To drastically understate, Gina was good looking. And she knew it. With a flawless olive complexion, bouncy chestnut hair, big, almond shaped eyes and an inviting smile, she would have made an excellent candidate to act as one of the models for the Castillo Academy brochure. However, that wasn't likely. Gina wasn't the sort of woman who would ever have to work for a living.

She already had it down to a science. She rolled her skirt up at the waistband, raising it three or four inches above the approved knee length and she never wore her tie, opting instead to unbutton the top half of her dress shirt to display her ample cleavage. Loathe as Gina's male instructors may have been to admit it, her blatant disregard of dress code violations routinely skewed her grades much higher than they deserved to be. Not that the grades meant anything to Gina. It was only matter of time before she was married. To a man at least 30 years her senior, if she had her way. Atomic weights and past participles don't matter much when you're sleeping your way to an inheritance settlement.

Most days, she would have been flanked by Paula Chow and Mary Ramirez, both nearly as beautiful as Gina, both equally as adept at milking the desire of the male faculty for good grades. Today, they were nowhere to be seen. Had they been seated with Gina, Billy would have given up hope and accepted a standing room only lunch. But here she was, alone, just like Billy. Maybe he had a chance.

As an outcast, Billy had even less luck attracting the girls at school than he did fitting in with the guys. It wasn't for lack of trying, at least at first. After being roundly rejected by every member of the fairer sex he struck up a conversation with in his freshman year, he quickly learned that not trying was the easiest way to avoid having his ego stomped upon. Taking the path of least resistance was nothing new to Billy. He was raised to not make waves.

Today was different though. Gina sitting by herself had filled him with a confidence he had never felt before. After all, he would only be at the Academy for a few more days and then he likely wouldn't see any of these people ever again. Even if he crashed and burned, he'd only be taunted for a little while and his social standing couldn't dip any lower. Plus, Gina sure was dressed like she would let him feel her up behind the shrubs that separated the school from the parking lot – what did he have to lose?

"Is this seat taken?" he asked, sitting down before she had a chance to answer.

"Ugh, I guess it is now." she replied, making no attempt to disguise her disdain.

That didn't go quite as smoothly as Billy had hoped. As Gina began to pay rapt attention to her krill patty, Billy's mind was racing, trying to come up with something, anything, he could say to make himself seem interesting, appealing, or at least, not poor. As thoughts blurred together in his head, he caught himself staring. He knew leering at Gina's breasts wasn't going to win him any points with her, but she wasn't paying him any attention, and look at them, I mean... no, no, he had to stop staring.

Billy's eyes drifted upwards. They had only made it up about an inch when inspiration struck. Gina's diamond encrusted crucifix necklace. That was it. That was his in! Sure, he would have to lie to get her attention, but his horny intentions were far from noble to begin with. Also, if he wasn't going to tell his lie now, when would he? He had made up his mind. Billy was going to tell Gina the Satanic sacrifice lie.

CHAPTER 10 - THE SATANIC SACRIFICE LIE

THE CASTILLO ACADEMY, F PREFECTURE, U.S.A.

MONDAY, JUNE 21, 2010

Billy knew it wasn't a good idea to open with the lie, he figured he had to take things slow. "I thought" is all Billy managed to croak out before having to clear his throat and start over. His nerves were not helping his confidence. "I thought you usually sat with Paula and Mary?"

Gina didn't look up. "Yeah, yeah I do." is all she offered Billy in response, never shifting her attention away from her krill patty.

"Oh, so um, where are they today?"

"I *wish* I knew." she said brusquely.

Billy's plans to strike up an actual conversation were falling apart. Gina swallowed the last mouthful of her tinned water. Her tray was empty, she would be leaving Billy and his line of questioning behind as soon as she was finished wiping her mouth. Billy had to go for it.

"I like your necklace, is your family religious?" he asked. There was an excellent chance that they weren't. Citizens of the U.S.A. (this stood for the United prefectureS of America, a lasting consolation to violently opinionated loudmouths from past generations) had long been dissuaded from practicing any religion.

"Not really, why?" Gina was still speaking to Billy with an icy tone and she had ignored his compliment, but at least she made eye contact as she answered. Billy's hopes were officially up. He could feel the lump in his throat melt a little.

"I find religious families interesting." This was the beginning of Billy's lie, but not the crux of it. He had no interest in religious families, or religion in general, but his lie was far more complicated than that. He wasn't prone to lying; in fact, he was usually truthful to a fault. The story he was about to tell Gina was a huge lie and Billy recognized how out of character it was for him to have concocted such a tall tale. It had been churning in his brain for what seemed like years, growing in scope and scale each time he retold it to himself. He wasn't sure where this lie had come from, or why he was so compelled to tell it to someone. He was sure he would end up looking pretty good after he told it, though. This was going to knock Gina's socks off. Even better, maybe it would knock her shirt off and hike her skirt up even further.

"Did you know I was born in a church?" Billy continued.

"No, that's weird." said Gina before applying a fresh coat of lipstick. Gina said weird to mean gross, rather than interestingly out of the ordinary.

"Yeah, really weird." Billy was operating under the assumption that she meant interestingly out of the ordinary. "It's also really weird because I can remember the whole thing." Billy paused for dramatic effect. Gina seemed interested. Sort of. At least she was still looking his way. And sneering a little less.

"I was born onto some kind of stone altar, a big rock slab in the middle of the church. This place must've been really old, paint was peeling and windows were smashed and stuff. There were these black drippy candles all over the place and me and my mother, we were surrounded by a bunch of guys wearing black robes. They were all chanting about 'Satan's power' or something and sort of swaying back and forth."

Another pause for dramatic effect. Maybe it was working. Gina's crimson lips had parted slightly. Billy couldn't say for certain, but he thought her eyes might be getting wider too. Time to get to the good stuff.

"My mother was shuddering and whimpering the whole time, but then, when she saw the knife she got up and ran. Not me though, I was brave, even as a baby. I can still remember the knife. It was long and kinda wavy. I remember it 'cause one of the guys in the robes thrust it at me, like he was trying to stab me through the heart. Crazy right? Trying to stab a baby! I was only like 5 minutes old!"

"That *is* crazy!" said Gina, with a slight gasp and a tone of genuine interest.

"It's not even the craziest part!" Billy continued; he couldn't believe how well this seemed to be working. "I caught the knife."

"No!" said Gina, with a full-on gasp and legitimately wide eyes.

"Yeah, caught it right between my tiny baby hands." Billy wished he hadn't said tiny baby hands, but he couldn't take that back now. "I must have been really strong, or something, 'cause the guy in the cloak couldn't get the knife back. He pulled and pulled on it but I wouldn't let go. The knife got really hot too, like glowing white hot, so hot he had to give up and drop it. Then everyone started to run, leaving me all alone. After that my memory gets kinda fuzzy. I think the heat from the knife must've started a fire; the last thing I can remember is lying there on the altar while the church burnt down around me."

Billy didn't have anything to follow his lie with, but that didn't seem to matter. Gina looked positively stunned and Billy felt great. The lie was finally out of his head and it sure looked like he had made an impression on Gina. It turned out to be the wrong kind of impression.

Gina dropped her 'tell me more' act in a flash. Her eyes narrowed and her lips curled up in a sneer. She laughed, scoffing and dismissive, as she picked up her lunch tray.

"So, your mom didn't want you, your dad didn't have the balls to kill you and they had to burn down a church to get rid of you? I don't blame them! You're a freak, Bobby. A freak and a loser." she said as she sashayed away from the table. Her swaying hips seemed to be laughing at him as she walked away.

'What? What? No! It's Billy! Who said he was my dad?' Billy Lopez was crushed.

Billy Lopez was also the captain of the track and field team. If he knew a bit more about impressing girls, he might have tried playing that angle.

CHAPTER 11 - FINISH LINE

THE CASTILLO ACADEMY, F PREFECTURE, U.S.A.

MONDAY, JUNE 21, 2010

Billy was the fastest kid at the Castillo Academy by a wide margin. There were rumors that he may have been the fastest kid in all of F Prefecture, but that was hard to tell. The Castillo Academy had a longstanding policy of not sharing test scores or athletics results with their rival, Xixi Prep and Xixi Prep acted in kind.

His foot speed was the one and only reason he received his Alpha Center scholarship. His grades ranged from just below average to failure. Billy ended up taking remedial courses at the Academy over the last three summer holidays.

Knowing that he would be spending his summers in his dorm room, regardless of his test scores, likely contributed to his poor showing in school. Ms. Hung had always been careful not to let Billy stray far from her eye. She had to work at Castillo during the summer, so Billy had to live in Castillo during the summer. There was no room for discussion.

This summer was going to be different. His recruiters had set him up with an apartment a few blocks away from the Alpha Center for the upcoming summer and following school year. Ms. Hung was hesitant to agree to this arrangement, but gave her half-hearted consent after she heard of the apartment complex's high security and strict policies on weapons, visitors, unarmed violence, loud noises, drug use, non-pastel colors, sharp corners and spending too long in the bathroom. Billy's test scores spiked after he heard this news. He wouldn't be taking any remedial classes this summer.

It had been almost an hour since Billy lied. He couldn't help but replay the embarrassing scene over and over again in his mind. Of all the days she had to be sitting alone... of all the people to be sitting alone... *'Concentrate'* he told himself. He had a 400 meter race to run.

Billy was in the fourth lane. Julio, Kenneth and Charles were getting into position to his left. Gus, Will, Kenji and Mike were on his right. Those seven guys made up the rest of the Castillo track team. They had raced against one another hundreds of times and by this point they all knew that Billy was going to win. None of them liked Billy; that was ingrained in the code of the school. They all respected his speed though.

"Runners to your marks!" hollered Mr. Estevez, the track coach.

It was a formality, all eight of them had been idling around their starting blocks for some time now. They stretched one last stretch and began coiling themselves into human springs. In this bent over position you couldn't tell one from the next – eight identical sets of dark brown hair, light brown skin, red shorts and ash gray t-shirts.

The bleachers ringing the gravel oval were packed. Classes may have been cancelled for the afternoon, but the Castillo Academy was the kind of school where attendance at *all* functions was mandatory.

"Get ready!" Mr. Estevez offered another unnecessary formality.

The students weren't the only ones in the stands that afternoon. With classes cancelled and the campus situated miles and miles away from anything, the faculty members were there to take in the bizarre spectacle about to unfold. So were Mr. Chen and Mr. Chen, the two men who had scouted Billy for admission to the Alpha Center. Not that they needed to be there; Billy's paperwork had already been submitted and processed, but they wanted one last look at the boy who would soon be the face of their athletics program. They were about to get an eyeful.

BANG

The white smoke from Mr. Estevez' pistol didn't have time to form into a puff before the sixteen feet were kicking up gravel. Within seconds, before the race was one third of the way finished, it was clear that Billy was going to win, and win by a good margin. The crowd cheered him on. The status taboo kept them from cheering Billy on by name, but it was pretty clear that they weren't cheering for Gus, now a distant second. Normally Billy loved the cheers, today he didn't pay them any thought. The Gina situation still weighed heavily upon him. *'Why I have to go and do something like that? Why'd I have to make myself look even weirder? Faster. Go faster.'*

By the time the race was two thirds finished, Billy could have walked to a victory. Still, he kept on, giving it his best effort. Billy's best effort appeared lax in comparison to everyone else's. Running came naturally to Billy. He took part in the twice weekly training sessions with the rest of the team, but he never felt the need to spend his early mornings with the other seven members during their informal practices. He had no specific training regimen to speak of, no specialized diet either. He was just fast, the fastest. He had been ever since he was a little kid in the group home. It was the afternoon heat that caused him to break a sweat, not the exertion.

He broke through the tape. Gus wouldn't meet him at the finish line for another four seconds. He took a look at the scoreboard. '43.85... *Whoa!*' In what would be his last race at Castillo, Billy had smashed his old record, beating it by nearly a half second. He broke into a broad smile. Finally, Gina was the furthest thing from his mind.

The second furthest thing from his mind was his meticulous post race routine. Billy may not have trained or eaten in a specific manner, but he *always* finished a race the same way. Grab a tin of water and a towel. Drink the water, pat dry with the towel. Grab another tin of water. Repeat step two. *Always.*

Looking back, Billy wouldn't be able to tell exactly why he did what he did that afternoon. Maybe it was his new record time, or maybe his freshly hurt pride, or maybe a combination of the two. Regardless of the cause, there's no questioning the outcome. On his way to the water station, he wiped the beads of sweat from his forehead with the back of his forearm. His smile disappeared, replaced with a look of pure dread.

He had blown it, blown the whole thing. The crowd's cheers turned to silence. The silence turned to derisive comments and cruel laughter.

Billy had wiped the brown makeup off of his forehead, revealing a streak of pasty white skin underneath.

CHAPTER 12 - AND STAY OUT

THE CASTILLO ACADEMY, F PREFECTURE, U.S.A.

MONDAY, JUNE 21, 2010

The chant of the Four Friars had a profound, lasting effect on Wilhelmina Hung. Their hypnotic intonations had been the guiding force behind every facet of her life, and by extension, the life of Billy Lopez. Ms. Hung oversaw every aspect of Billy's life, surreptitiously aided by the incredible influence wielded by the Ashanti Orthodox. Shortly after the encounter at the burnt church, they ensured Ms. Hung was installed as the matron of the group home in which Billy was to be raised. When it became clear that F Prefecture's public school system was too risky of an environment, they ensured Billy was granted access to a Castillo Academy education. They were even able to establish Ms. Hung as Principal of Castillo. The Ashanti Orthodox did anything and everything to aid Ms. Hung in her duty as a Sister of Joseph. No corners were cut, no expenses were spared.

As a Sister of Joseph, Ms. Hung was tasked with making certain a Billy lived a quiet, inconsequential life. Those orders led to a cold, emotionless rearing, one that resulted in a child ill adjusted to life as a social individual. He didn't lash out, quite the opposite, he withdrew. When he was in the group home he was the good, quiet kid amongst eleven other not so good, not so quiet kids. At Castillo, it was more of the same, only on a larger scale.

The color of Billy's skin was a constant concern. In the Prefectures, the punishments for 'Improper Chantone Within Established Perimeters' varied. The level of punishment meted out depended on previous transgressions and whether or not the crime was committed in adjunct with another, less severe infraction. Permanent expulsion was the softest of the penalties, minors were granted no leniency. It was up to Ms. Hung to make certain that Billy's secret was never discovered.

Until he was old enough to do it himself, she would wake Billy up and cake on a fresh coat of brown makeup long before the rest of the kids in the group home woke up. It wasn't long before Billy realized that it wasn't normal for Ms. Hung to use her bizarre suitcase full of paint to slather him in a foreign skin tone every morning. He used to ask why he had to be a different color, but he never received a straight answer. Even as a four year old, Billy grew tired of her standard responses of "It's just a skin condition" and "Because you are very special". Billy sure never felt special, just confused.

Billy had reapplied his makeup, changed back into his school uniform and snuck his way up to Ms. Hung's office on the school's top floor. It hadn't made for a fun trip; he spent most of his time on the way there hiding in classroom doorways, waiting for other students to pass. Once he was safely inside her office, he made every effort to look as though nothing had happened. He didn't realize it, but his 'every effort' consisted of sitting up straighter than usual and nothing more. Sitting up straight did very little to appease Ms.

Hung. Short and sharply dressed, her black hair pinned to her head in a tight bun, the entranced Wilhelmina Hung usually gave off an air of superior, monotonous calm. That air had begun to fade, ever so slightly. This was the first time that there had been any kind of incident involving Billy and the stress involved had weakened the power of the chant. Wilhelmina Hung was feeling nervous for the first time in nearly two decades.

They sat in silence across from one another. Ms. Hung shuffled papers on her desk, muttered to herself under her breath and made three attempts to address Billy that ended with a head shake and a sigh.

"I *always* told you to pat dry, *not* rub dry!" she managed to blurt out on her fourth attempt. Choked with emotion, she cleared her throat before speaking to him using a subdued tone, tinged with anger and fear. Billy was unnerved. He had never heard anything like this from Ms. Hung before.

"You will not be receiving your scholarship to the Alpha Center, Mr. Chen and Mr. Chen both made that abundantly clear. But that should be the least of your concerns. You are very, *very* lucky not to have been arrested today, Billy, and it is only a matter of time before that luck runs out. This is where things get difficult. Thanks to your... *indiscretion* earlier today I have had to erase any record that you were ever a student here, or anywhere else for that matter. I contacted your elementary school and pulled some strings. As of today, you were never enrolled there either. This means, as far as the official records are concerned, you haven't done anything of note since being admitted into the group home. If and when I am questioned, I will have to say you ran away from the home years ago, and that you are most likely dead. Do you understand?"

Billy didn't understand at all. *'Now I'm dead? Dead enough not to be arrested I guess. And no scholarship? What am I supposed to do now? All of this because of my skin condition? How is that fair?'* All he knew was that he had a lump in his throat and wanted to get out of Ms. Hung's office as quickly as possible. This was too much.

"Yeah, I understand." He managed to croak, trying to end the conversation. It didn't end.

"Good." Ms. Hung said, seemingly satisfied with his meager response. "Billy, have you ever wondered what life is like outside of F?"

"Uh..." She handed him an envelope before Billy had a chance to stammer out any kind of answer.

"People are going to be suspicious. I'm going to have to answer a lot of questions. More than that, I'm going to have to instruct a lot of people on how to properly answer a lot of questions. You've put yourself in quite a spot, Billy. This is *not* how things were meant to be. I've arranged somewhere safe for you to stay. Part of me wishes I could come with you. But..." Wilhelmina trailed off, never to complete that thought. Memories of the man she had been forced to rely upon cracked through her chant-induced fog ever so briefly, flooding her mind with regret. "Goodbye Billy. I hope we will meet again under better circumstances."

"OK. Yeah, OK. Goodbye." Baffled, Billy lurched to his feet and staggered out into the hall, without so much as a glance back to Ms. Hung. Aside from his brief farewell, Billy was dumbfounded. Not that it mattered. Apart from the cafeteria staff he didn't have anyone left to talk to. Ms. Hung had never really been warm with Billy, but the way she ended their conversation was downright cold. As far as Billy knew, that was it; that was the end of their relationship. No hug, no nothing. She seemed kind of sad, but...

only kind of. That was it, it was over. Unless the letter she had given him said differently.

At least Billy thought it was a letter – he decided not to open the envelope until he got back to his dorm room. If he didn't like what was written inside, he sure didn't want to make any kind of emotional outburst if front of everyone. He'd had enough attention today.

Envelope in hand, he quickly made his way through the halls, headed towards the dorms. The whispers and snickers behind his back were nothing new and the unwritten 'do not speak with Billy' rule was still in effect. He stared straight ahead as he walked, making sure not to make eye contact. If anyone decided to break the rule, he was sure he didn't want to hear what they had to say. He nearly made it to the dormitory wing without incident. Then he saw Gina.

She was leaning against the wall admiring her fingernails, Paula and Mary stood nearby. They were both wearing casts on their arms; Paula's was on her left, Mary's on her right. Billy had forgotten his 'looking straight ahead' plan and was fixated on Gina. She was looking bored and beautiful, oblivious to Paula and Mary acting out whatever it was that left them with broken limbs. *'Why did I have to tell her the lie? What the hell was I thinking?'* And, oh no! *God no, she saw me!'* Gina shushed her henchwomen and gestured at Billy. Making sure she caught his eye (and making extra sure Paula and Mary were watching) she flashed him a devil's horn hand sign and delivered a mocking "Oooooo!" This sent her friends into faux-hysterics.

"Don't stab me, I'm a baby!"

"Please mama, don't burn the church! Waaa!"

That was it. Of course she would've told her friends about his lie. *'What was I thinking? Now everybody will know I'm a freak and a liar!'* Billy could no longer maintain his brave façade, he sprinted to his dorm room.

He slammed the metal door behind him. And locked it. Finally alone, Billy burst out sobbing. His internalized anger gave way to a feeling of complete confusion as he sat on his bed. Thoughts turned from *'Why?'* to *'What now?'* Ms. Hung didn't actually tell him he wouldn't be finishing his year at Castillo, but that seemed pretty obvious. But, that didn't tell him what was coming next, only what wasn't. Sniffling, he opened the envelope.

As suspected, it was a letter and nothing more. Billy unfolded it and wiped the tears from his eyes.

Billy,

I've arranged transit to M Prefecture and a place for you to lay low. The bus will pick you up at 5 tomorrow morning in the parking lot. Do not be late.

I will be in touch when the time is right.

Ms. Hung

Billy couldn't put it together. He didn't have much to work with and what he did have didn't add up.

'M Prefecture? Everybody knows that the Prefectures only run A through G in the U.S.A. It's pretty clear on the flag – 7 red stripes, 6 white. 7 white hexagons on a blue square in the corner. And why do I have to lay low? What the hell is going on?'

It didn't really matter – Billy's mind was made up. He had no future in F Prefecture. He had no other options. He was headed to M. Whatever or wherever that was.

Billy rolled over and switched off his alarm clock before it had a chance to ring. Having slept away most of the previous afternoon and all of the evening, he was wide awake long before sunrise. This would be his last morning at the Castillo Academy, four days ahead of schedule.

He was still disappointed he wasn't going to start fresh at the Alpha Center, but the prospect of cutting all ties with the last four years of his life was enough to fill Billy with a little optimism. He did his best to hold tight to that shred of optimism as he prepared to leave. He wouldn't have admitted it if anyone asked, but the prospect of deserting everything he had ever known was terrifying. Clinging to his familiar routine, Billy reapplied his fake brown skin and dressed in his Castillo uniform. He tucked the makeup canister into the breast pocket of his blazer. It was starting to feel light. Lighter, anyway. *'I'll have to ask Ms. Hung to get... oh, right. Oh man.'* In hindsight, Billy would realize that his janitor coveralls or even his track outfit would have been a much better choice than his dress grays. But, at the time he figured he should aim to make a good first impression, even if he had no clue who he was trying to impress.

Without a suitcase, packing wasn't an option. Billy wasn't thrilled with the prospect of only being able to bring one change of clothes. He stuffed his pants pockets with socks and underwear. Better than nothing.

Leaving the dormitories after 10pm and before 7am was against the rules. Billy was fine with breaking that rule. Having been expelled from the whole Prefecture, Billy knew he had larger concerns than punishment at Castillo. Opening the door leading to the field triggered a silent alarm. Silence aside, it was pretty easy to tell that something was up. The flashing red light was a dead giveaway. *'Aw crap. I should've known. I'd better... No, that's stupid.'* Feeling defiant for the first time he could recall, Billy decided not to run. His pace was still brisk, just short of a jog, but that was only to make sure he wasn't late. At least that's what he kept telling himself. He reached the path leading down into the parking lot with 20 minutes to spare.

Billy's eyes adjusted to the faint orange glow beneath as he walked downhill towards the lot. There weren't more than ten cars in a lot that could accommodate dozens; no surprise at that early an hour. What was a surprise is what had happened to the car closest to the road leading away from the school. Was it even a car? *'Huh... I wonder what, oh no...'* As he got closer Billy could see he wasn't the only one who got to the parking lot early. The car closest to the road wasn't just a car; it was a bus, 'parked' on top of a car. The car's hood had been crushed under the weight of the bus' driver side front wheel, leaving the bus angled slightly skyward. Shattered glass twinkled on the ground, reflecting the orange light. *'I'll be riding in that?'* Billy couldn't see inside the sky blue bus. Its small porthole windows were streaked an opaque, dingy brown.

Billy's stomach was in knots. He cautiously approached the bus, absentmindedly folding and unfolding the letter from Ms. Hung. *'If I knew the bus was going to be like this I would've...'* Billy couldn't complete that thought. He knew this was his only option, and he had brought it upon himself, with a little 'help' from Ms. Hung. *'I do not want to get on this bus. I do not want to get on this bus.'* He stopped, too apprehensive to continue. *'I'll just turn and run. Easy.*

Head up into the foothills. And... wait until I starve to death. I guess.' Billy wouldn't have been able to get far on his own and he knew it. A lifetime of institutionalized instruction had left Billy with very few skills aside from showing up on time and doing as he was told. If he was going to make it he would need help. Equal parts emboldened and defeated he started towards the bus once more.

He had only taken two steps before the hinged door creaked open. He caught the wave of stench first. It was powerful. If he had any appetite the night before, Billy's dry heaves would have been a lot messier. The smell was worse than his first day cleaning the cafeteria's walk-in fridges after they had been left unattended during the summer. Far worse. But, not all that different. *'Who would let mealworms rot in a bus? Oh God! Oh God that stinks!'* The painful dry heaves had subsided to a point where Billy was able to shift focus to the swarm of tiny flies that had erupted from within the bus. The flies didn't hold his attention for long.

"Lopez!?"

The bus driver thrust his dull green head out of the door. It was hairless and featureless apart from the ragged holes encircling deep black voids where a man's eyes and mouth should normally be found. Billy stopped gagging and swatting. He was unable to do either in the state of pulse racing panic he found himself in.

"You Lopez!?"

Billy was normally fairly articulate. He wasn't going to dazzle anyone with his eloquent banter, but he got by just fine. At that moment, his diction failed him.

"Y-yes. Billy. Billy L-Lopez" followed by another dry heave. This time he was rewarded with the sour tang of bile. Billy gagged a little as he swallowed in fear.

The bus driver cackled and wheezed, his laughter sounded like a rusty lawnmower engine firing up. "Well c'mon in; I've got a tight schedule!" He went on laughing like this was the *funniest* thing he'd ever heard. Billy didn't really hear him; he was still fully freaked out by the driver's green head. Trying not to stare, he caught a glimpse of the driver's hands – melted paw shapes, the same green color.

'Run! Just run!' Billy's natural instinct was to dash off really fast, that was always his instinct. As badly as he wanted to run, he was drawn towards the door, as if his feet were now completely independent from his brain. Billy shuffled forwards, covering his mouth and nose with one hand, fanning flies away with the other.

"Well, get on already!" growled the driver. "Willy's not payin' me to watch you stand around a parking lot."

Billy did as he was told. Even if he did run, he couldn't outrun a bus. And he didn't want to try and outrun a bus driven by a man who was comfortable parking on top of a car. *'Can I even call him a man?'*

"Welcome aboard, Lopez. Next stop – M!" The door creaked shut behind Billy. His heart skipped a beat – the other passengers were all gleaming white, just like he was. That was a shock. They were all dead and chopped into pieces. That was even more of a shock.

CHAPTER 13 - BLUEBELL

258 MILES EAST OF THE CASTILLO ACADEMY,
F PREFECTURE, U.S.A.

TUESDAY, JUNE 22, 2010

When the Castillo Academy was founded, promotional materials boasted of its "two hundred acres of lush green lawn". It wasn't true. The school grounds sat on a total of 191 acres, and at least a quarter of the land was either paved over or had been built upon. It didn't matter that the numbers were padded. The mere mention of a 'lush green lawn' in F Prefecture was enough to grab people's attention. If you were able to grow a lawn in F, it meant only one thing – you had more money than you knew what do with. That resonated with the Prefecture's wealthy elite. Having a child enrolled at Castillo was still the kind of thing mothers made a point of 'casually' bringing up at social events.

The bus had navigated the tight knots of freeway onramps outside of The Academy and had been roaring down the highway for hours. Castillo's expensive, geographically incongruous greenery had given way to an expanse of brown, rocky terrain. Water was hard to come by in F; the region's plant life was a testament to that.

Knee high, spindly black bushes were the only flora of notice along the ribbon of road.

The sun setting behind the bus let Billy know they were heading east, even if that didn't register consciously. He had never been through this section of F Prefecture, but his group home had been situated in nearly identical surroundings. It had been years since he had been anywhere that wasn't green and groomed. Now, back amongst the dusty rocks of his childhood, Billy was more ill at ease than he had been at any point during his four years at Castillo. He would have gladly spent another forty years at Castillo in exchange for not riding with the Green Man and his corpse pile for another minute.

The mound of flesh took up the back half of the bus; the benches in the rear had been removed. It wobbled and slid as they rolled down the road, shifting as one partially gelled mass. Billy had the misfortune of making eye contact with the blob. He couldn't tell if he was looking into the eyes of one person or two.

By the time it had grown dark, Billy's cowering and quivering had dropped off and he was beginning to grow used to the fetid reek of death. While his initial terror may have had subsided, things had grown disconcertingly quiet. Half of this was Billy's doing. He hadn't dared speak since the doors shut behind him. The Green Man hadn't said a word to Billy since they left the parking lot hours and hours ago, but until recently he'd been grunting and mumbling to himself. Now, all that was left to listen to was the rumble of the road. Without his all encompassing panic, a series of unsettling questions crept into Billy's head. Most of them centered around the corpses, but the man with the green skin responsible for the corpses was a mystery himself.

'Who is this guy? He called Ms. Hung 'Willy', so they must know each other somehow. But how? Why would she know a bus driving monster man? And seriously – a monster man? A monster man with a truck full of dead white people? What the hell is going on? Maybe I don't have a skin condition. I mean, look at them all, just as white as me. What are the odds?'

Billy did look at the pile of parts. That was a mistake. The pile had shifted, the pair of eyes he had looked into before had become a trio. Another wave of nausea started to churn in his stomach.

'OK, OK, keep it together. Don't give him a reason to get angry. Does Ms. Hung want me dead? Is that it? I'm as good as dead back in F, she would get away with it... At least I'm still alive – that's a strange thing to think. He would've killed me by now if was going to kill me at all, right? Or maybe he only does that when it's light out. Probably harder to do in the dark. But he had all day, today... No, no, need to keep focused. The bus has to stop for gas at some point, and when it does, I'll just...'

SKREEEEEEEEEEEEEEEEEEEEEEEEEEEE

Billy's attention snapped forward to the front of the bus. The bumper was scraping against the guard rail; metal on metal sent sparks flying. The Green Man didn't seem to be dealing with whatever caused the bus to smash into the divider; he didn't seem to be doing anything. The bus was still racing ahead, grinding its front end. The screeching got louder, the rumbling grew more and more intense. Billy had to do something. He sprung from his seat in the second row of benches shoved the Green Man aside. He stomped on the brake, grabbing the wheel and turning it away from the divider as he did so. The bus fishtailed and lifted up onto two wheels, nearly rolling over in the process. It righted itself with a bone jarring thud.

SHNICK

The business end of a switchblade was pressed against Billy's neck, shattering the post-impact calm.

"First rule of the road – never wake a sleeping Highway Star!"

Billy bolted backwards, landing awkwardly in the stairwell and curling up into a whimpering ball. The Green Man's lawnmower laugh started up again. Slowly shaking his head, the Green Man folded the blade back into the handle.

"Jesus, sorry about that kid – old habit. You hungry?"

He pulled a pair of sustenance gel pouches from the pocket of his yellow duster jacket and offered one to Billy. It had been years since Billy had eaten from a pouch. They were the lowest form of food available for consumption, but Billy was hungry.

"Yeah, thanks" Billy said between sniffles. The Green Man tossed Billy a pouch as he fired up the engine, sending the freshly scarred bus back down the highway.

"Good manners, I like that!" the Green Man guffawed. "Thanks to *you* for steering Old Bluebell outta trouble! And you can thank Willy and her 5 AM pickup time for makin' me fall asleep there!"

"Bluebell?" Billy had torn the pouch open with his teeth and was slurping on the goo inside. He had no shortage of other questions he wanted answered, but opted to stick with the line of conversation that was offered.

"My rig. Highway Star needs a bitchin' rig, yeah?"

"Uh, yeah, yeah..." Billy righted himself out of the stairwell and took a seat on the first bench. He didn't know what the Green Man was talking about, but at least he was talking. It gave Billy something, anything else to pay attention to. Allowing his focus to shift away from the situation he had been forced into helped Billy fake his way into feeling a bit more at ease. Now, having eaten, he was less jittery and he was doing his very best to pretend he wasn't surrounded by a heap of rotting body parts.

"How do you like the B pouch? Salty right?"

"Ha, yeah it's good." Billy said, looking to appear as agreeable as he could. An unfortunate revelation sprang to mind as the words left his mouth. *'Poison. That's how he does it, poison. He's poisoned me.'* Billy thought he could feel the gel swishing around in his stomach, eating away at him from the inside. "How do you mean salty?" he added, trying not to show his fear.

"Y'know, tastes like salt does. I figured you'd be able to tell the difference, figured you'd be used to the taste of F pouches."

"Oh!" Billy paused before continuing. "Sorry, I don't get it." Billy really was sorry, the last thing he wanted to do was get on this guy's bad side.

"Christ, they really *don't* teach you U.S.A. kids anything do they?" The Green Man said, making no effort to hide the impatience in his voice. "Look at the back."

Billy flipped the deflated pouch over in his hands. It looked like the back of any other pouch he had ever seen. *'OK, now what? Oh!'* There was one small difference from the pouches he had fuzzy recollections of from his time in the group home. The fine print stamped on the bottom of the pouch read 'FOR DISTRIBUTION AND CONSUMPTION IN B PREFECTURE ONLY'.

"B Prefecture? How'd you get this?"

This seemed to perk the Green Man up. "I told you, Lopez, I'm a Highway Star! Name's Garbage Bag, last of the *true* Highway Stars" he said in a cheery growl.

"Oh! Oh yeah!" *'Huh?'* Billy hated to ask, "So, uh, what's a Highway Star?"

Silence, awkward angry silence, cracked by a guttural cackle.

"I tell ya kid, I *love* the way you don't know anything!' Garbage Bag let loose with an ever louder cackle. "Gives us something to talk about. This is one hell of a boring ride otherwise!"

He was right, it was a boring ride. Bluebell's lone working headlight lit the ever-approaching stretch of asphalt. Aside from the cracked black strip, there was nothing to see but murky darkness on the horizon. Billy wasn't feeling comfortable, not by a long shot, but he did feel less tense now that this Garbage Bag guy seemed to be in a decent mood. His immediate fear of death had withered; he wasn't dead yet after all.

"Yeah, beautiful scenery out this way" said Billy with a half forced laugh.

"You said it! It's kinda funny, I guess I had you pegged for someone who was on the up, someone who knew a thing or two, with you headed out to M and all..." Garbage Bag trailed off as he stood up from the driver's seat and shuffled over to the bench next to Billy's, slumping himself into a comfortable position.

Billy's panic was back in full force. "Uh, whoa, whoa! Shouldn't you be driving?" Bluebell was headed downhill. Even without a foot on the gas they were picking up speed.

SHNICK

The blade was back out, glinting faintly in the dim glow of the bus' emergency lights. "Good question" Garbage Bag deadpanned. "Although, I'd say the question is - shouldn't *you* be driving?" He fired up the lawnmower once more as he slouched back into a full recline.

Since leaving Castillo, the cracks in the asphalt had been growing wider and wider. That was one reason Bluebell was swerving erratically as it barreled down the road. The other reason was that Billy didn't know how to drive. His fear had mutated. A fiery bus crash had supplanted the possibility of a violent outburst from Garbage Bag at the forefront of his mind. A road sign up ahead said that it was another 133 miles to G Prefecture.

"Gettin' the hang of it yet?" asked Garbage Bag as he reached into his duster and pulled out another sustenance gel pouch.

"No!" yelped Billy.

"That's good," countered an unfazed Garbage Bag in between slurps of gel, "It'll be more exciting this way." He slumped sideways on the bus bench. "Hasn't been another soul on the road for miles and miles anyhow. What's the worst that could happen?"

"Uh, well..." Billy stammered distractedly before Garbage Bag interrupted.

"I'll tell you what the worst that could happen is, we could go even slower. You know that gas pedal shaped thing you've been nancying with? Step on it. And keep your foot on it. And take your foot off of it when we get there. Simple right?"

Billy followed Garbage Bag's 'advice'. As Bluebell heaved forward, a precariously stacked portion of the corpse pile tumbled apart, unleashing a new wave of stench and flies.

"Now that's more like it!" Garbage Bag bellowed.

'Is this how he does it? He tricks people into driving? Driving and crashing? Wouldn't he die too? He's pretty big, maybe he's padded... Straight ahead, keep the wheel straight. No one else to hit. I'll be the only one to die on the road. Straight. Keep straight. 135. That's fast. I think. Was he going this fast?'

"I appreciate the ride and all. But, where are you taking me?" Billy mustered the courage to ask, emboldened by the immediacy of his likely demise.

"I'm not takin' you anywhere. You're the one driving." Garbage Bag paused then broke his silence with a chuckle. "Nah, I'm just screwin' with you kid. You're a proud American, right?"

Billy didn't know how to respond. Garbage Bag didn't seem to be the patriotic type. Then again, what 'type' did he seem like? "Proud enough" followed by a small, involuntary yawn seemed to be a reasonably inoffensive response. He hoped.

"Stop the bus." The slightly playful tone in Garbage Bag's voice had disappeared.

'He's mad. Really mad... Oh God...'

Billy did as he was told, stepping down hard on the brake. Too hard. The bus veered to the right and skidded to a halt, angled across two lanes. Garbage Bag tumbled onto the ground with a thud as the pile of parts shifted and slid further towards the front of the bus. Billy was still upright in the driver's seat, hands gripping the wheel tightly. It felt like his shoulder blades had torn through his back.

Garbage Bag rose to his feet with an angry groan, followed by a slight chuckle. "OK, not bad for your first time braking. Not bad at all. Now get up already, you've had your fun. If you are a proud American, that means you don't actually know thing one. And I'm not about to launch into my history lesson if you're just gonna sleep through it. Grab a bench."

'Thank God.' Billy's knuckles finally relaxed, he no longer had to grip the wheel for dear life. He stretched as he stood and then slumped onto the closest bench seat, letting gravity do most of the work.

The sun was dawning as Garbage Bag took the driver's seat. Billy had been awake for over 24 hours and his body was aching for sleep. *'Alert. Focused and alert. He's unbalanced. Happy one minute, angry the next. Dangerous. Of course he's dangerous. Bus full of dead people...'* His alert focus didn't last long. The rigors of the day had taken their toll and Billy couldn't force himself to stay awake any longer. He didn't realize it at the time, but that morning would mark Billy's first time sleeping without dreaming of his attempted sacrifice. His subconscious had a fresh set of terrors to agonize over.

CHAPTER 14 - SKIN SWATCHES AT THE BORDER

CHECKPOINT TO G PREFECTURE,
F PREFECTURE, U.S.A.

WEDNESDAY, JUNE 23, 2010

"Just let me talk to Ms. Hung!" Billy yelled. His plea went ignored. "She has the *UGH*" The incredible weight of Garbage Bag's bulky body slammed Billy against the bus' metal wall. Then released. Then slammed into Billy again, an angry honk spilling out of what passed for Garbage Bag's mouth with each shove. At least, that's what Billy's brain was telling him before he had the chance to wake up.

The sun was high in the sky by the time Billy cut his dream short. It wasn't the sun that woke him; it was the blaring siren, screaming loud enough to rattle Bluebell's porthole windows. The force of the sirens was so immense that the waves of sound were pinning Billy to the wall. His organs compressed painfully with each squawk of the klaxon. It was getting louder. And faster. And even louder. Billy could no longer hear the windows rattle, now he could only see them vibrate in time with the mechanized honks. Through the streaky windshield, he could see that Bluebell was stopped at a chain link fence, the kind with a wheeled gate that slides away to one side.

Billy couldn't make out what was going on outside, but he figured it must be important if it was making a noise that could cause him so much pain. He pushed against the waves of sound towards the front to get a better look. Garbage Bag was hanging out of the driver's window, shifting his weight around in the window frame. Whatever he was doing, he was doing it fast. Steadying himself against a bench seat and peering over Garbage Bag's hunched body, Billy could see that he was reaching around to the backside of a metal box. The box was affixed to the blaring loudspeaker posted atop a metal pole driven into the dirt. Small blinking lights spelled out 'ERRO'. Billy figured it must have read ERROR in its entirety, but couldn't see the rest past Garbage Bag.

With an emphatic grunt that could be heard over the din, Garbage Bag yanked a panel off of the box; sparking live wires sprung from the back. He struggled back through the window frame and threw himself into his seat with a smile, or at least it looked like a smile, hard to tell with his ragged mouth. Billy was sure he had been caught sneaking up behind Garbage Bag. He had gotten too close, now only a few feet away. But, if he was caught, it didn't seem to matter. Not at the moment anyhow.

Garbage Bag reached into an interior jacket pocket and produced what looked to be a large metal pill, about the size of a tin of water. He turned it over in his hands and studied one of the sides intently. With a flick of his wrist, a beige rectangle framed in metal slid out of a slot on the side he had been eying. He cocked his head, shook it and stuffed the rectangle back into the pill. Another flick of the wrist. Another beige rectangle. This one looked a little less beige than the last. It must've been what Garbage Bag was looking for. He bolted out of his seat and shoved himself back through the window frame, all without so much as a glance in Billy's direction.

Peering over Garbage Bag's shoulder once again, Billy could see that the message on the box had changed. Now instead of ERRO it read 'VEHICUL IMMOBILIZ COUNTDO' with an 'I' underneath. When the 'I' turned to a '0' it left no doubt in Billy's mind that it was counting down to something, and VEHICUL IMMOBILIZ really made it seem like it was counting down to immobilize Bluebell. That was the last thing Billy wanted. Being trapped in a corpse filled bus that was headed somewhere was one thing. Being trapped in a corpse filled bus that was left to bake in the desert was another.

Billy was getting panicky. *'Should I ask if I can help? I should try and do something to get out of this, right? What is this?'* The siren was still getting louder and louder. Even if he could yell loud enough for Garbage Bag to 'speak' with him, Garbage Bag was hanging out of the bus... and he was pretty quick with that switchblade, too. Prodding him to get his attention seemed like a bad idea. *'Don't do anything'* was as far as Billy's thought process led him before the silence.

Whatever Garbage Bag had been doing out there seemed to have worked. The siren fell quiet and the motorized gate began to slowly roll to the left.

Billy's ears were ringing like never before. He opened his mouth, closed his eyes and tilted his head forward in an attempt to force the residual noise out of his head. It didn't work. He opened his eyes to see Garbage Bag's ragged hole of a mouth grinning back at him.

"What was that?" Billy hollered, frantically rubbing a finger in one ear, then the other.

"Checkpoint." was Garbage Bag's reply, accompanied by a gesture towards the rolling gate.

"I don't get it? Checkpoint for what?" Billy asked. He was able to speak at a normal decibel level again, even if the ringing persisted.

"For what? For G! G Prefecture! Or should I say, 'Welcome to G Prefecture'" said Garbage Bag, trying his best to affect an upper crust accent through his gravelly growl. "They've got those sensors around all the Prefectures in the U.S.A. Persistent little buggers. I betcha by the time I make my way back, they'll have it fixed up again like nothing ever happened. Doesn't matter much now, though, we're in. There's one more to go before we get where we're going, and that one's not going to be half as much fun. My 'manual override' technique isn't going to get us anywhere with that one." Garbage Bag mimed ripping the back off of the metal box in case Billy didn't pick up on what he meant by 'manual override'.

Billy's curiosity was piqued. Why would they have gated checkpoints between Prefectures? And what was with those rectangles?

"Will you have to use another one of those square things?"

"Square... things?" Garbage Bag turned and gave Billy a skeptical look.

"Um, yeah, y'know, you flicked them out of that can thing?" Billy immediately regretted asking this question. Why give him a chance to get mad?

"Oh! You mean my skin swatches!"

Billy's question seemed to have made Garbage Bag happy. Very happy. Now, he really regretted asking. *'Shut up, Billy! Just shut up! All that skin probably belonged to somebody once!'*

"Nah, they're not going to do much good from here on. I have my ways of getting by, though" Garbage Bag continued. "So, you ready to roll?"

Billy nodded, anxious to do anything that would shift conversation away from Garbage Bag's collection of ex-people. Bluebell's engine rumbled to life and they began to drive down the road into G. As far as Billy knew, this was his first time outside of F Prefecture. It wouldn't be long before he pined for F's cold comforts.

They had driven away most of the day. Breakfast and lunch, both B Sustenance Gel Pouches, had come and gone. Billy was beginning to feel the effects of the extra salt. It had been a long time since he had anything to drink. Nearly too long. It was getting harder for Billy to think. Thoughts would half form, only to be torn apart by the throbbing pain in his temples.

"Do you have any water? I'm really thirsty."

"No."

He must have water. Even monsters have to drink sometime. Or maybe they don't...' "OK, uh, do you think we could stop somewhere and get something to drink? Maybe?"

"Yeah, once we get through G. I've got another stop to make on the way, you can get some water there. You ever wonder what's past G?"

As far as Billy knew, the U.S.A. was engulfed in Canada - a warm, dusty, oasis-of-sorts within a vast frozen desert. "No, it's just Canada" was Billy's blithe reply. Past G? What did he care about that? The important thing was he would get something to drink. Finally!

"CANADA? Jesus, not even Canada would want what we're headed towards." Garbage Bag didn't share Billy's oblivious disinterest in geography. "Canada... no, we're headed for The Union, or whatever's left of it" Garbage Bag continued. "God only knows how they'll react to a skinny brown kid down there."

'Brown? Oh no! Oh no!' Billy had completely forgotten about his last makeup application. Hopefully it was still in good shape – the body parts on the floor sure made it seem like Garbage Bag and white people didn't get along. Billy's head cleared, his thoughts were lucid once again. Those thoughts were of escape – now that Billy realized he was one smear away from being dismembered. His first thought was to kick out the hinged door and fling himself to the side of the road, but, what good would that do? He had to play it cool, had to wait for his chance to escape. He wasn't sure what was up ahead, he wasn't even sure if he'd live long enough to find out. *'Water first. When we stop for water I'll make my move.'* He didn't know what that move would be. A futile dash towards an icy Canadian death was the best Billy could come up with.

"...by their Chantones. Hey! You listening?" Billy wasn't. Dread was rushing through his head like a burst dam, drowning out everything aside from thoughts of his demise.

"Y-Yeah. Yeah I'm listening." He had missed a lot of whatever it was Garbage Bag was talking about. *'Chantones?'*

"OK good, didn't think you'd be one for politics, but I didn't think I'd be putting you to sleep either!" The sound of Garbage Bag's lawnmower laughter turned Billy's stomach. Or, maybe it was the stench or the nonstop buzz of the flies, neither of which did much to allay Billy's fears.

The sign at the side of the road read 85 miles to Canada.

"So they drew up a buncha new borders, A through M. Some kinda Zodiac thing I think. Treated everybody like they were animals in a zoo, all divvy'd up by the color of their skin. Don't know why, really. It's not like anybody was payin' to see 'em." Billy started to focus. As a walking dead man, he didn't care much about what Garbage Bag was saying, but it did give him something to focus on that wasn't his nervous nausea.

"Things went pretty good at first. People had jobs, crankin' Eternally Free Taiwanese crap outta the new factories." Billy looked down at the ubiquitous sunburst flag logo on the crumpled sustenance gel pouch he had dropped to the floor.

"Problem was the EFT are a bunch of brain retards. They didn't count on people getting pissed off at being caged up. And they sure didn't count on the white folks in The Union wanting to split off on their own. The EFT, they might be dumb, but you don't want to get on their bad side. They caught wind of the white man rising up and the next thing you know H through M are blown to Hell's doorstep!" Garbage Bag was giddy as he told this part of the story, but he quickly snapped into being gravely serious. "Now listen, when the time comes, you play it cool – don't go bringing up any of my 'brain retard' talk. Wait, never mind, never mind." Garbage Bag gestured over his shoulder to his pile of body parts. "I forgot about my big plan for you."

Billy's desire to run was stronger than ever.

CHAPTER 15 - THE ERROR OF THEIR WAYS

THE CASTILLO ACADEMY, F PREFECTURE, U.S.A.

WEDNESDAY, JUNE 23, 2010

Four pillars of light radiated over the Castillo Academy. Classes were traditionally light on educational content during the final week of classes and this year was no exception. Teachers openly encouraged their students to ignore their meager lesson plans and swarm the windows to take in the mysterious splendor from the heavens. It wasn't long before almost everyone at Castillo was watching the four figures with spherical golden heads fall gracefully to Earth, their tan robes fluttering in the slight updraft.

This brazen display went against the tenets of the Friars; they were to carry out their actions as subtly as possible. Their new method of transportation rendered subtlety a near impossibility. There was little time for discretion, word had come from Wilhelmina Hung after 17 years of silence and that word was frantic. The instructions embedded in the hypnotic chant of the Four Friars had been clear, the Sister of Joseph was only to be in contact if there were any overt signs that the child was acting out in a dangerous manner. Given the ancestry of the child, the representatives of the Ashanti Orthodox could not afford to balk at any warning from his guardian.

This was not the same incarnation of the Four Friars as the group that initially landed upon Wilhelmina Hung outside the burnt church. Prosperity 3 was dead, having succumbed to a heart attack back home in Accra. This left Peace 9 as the head Friar. Having finally stepped out of the Prosperity 3's shadow, he was determined to mold the squad as he saw fit.

Prosperity 3 was weak, or so Peace 9 had thought. That he didn't die in the line of duty was more than enough to cement this in Peace 9's mind. He was quick to point out what he believed to be Prosperity 3's shortcomings to the younger, more impressionable members. They took his words to heart. Their tiresome inactivity made a shift in ideology an easy sell; the old methods weren't working. Despite the technological advances available to them, the Four Friars had been unable to pinpoint Satan's location. They hadn't been able to make any form of contact with his forces either. The bloody skirmish with the Knights in Satan's Service that brought the latest embodiments of Abundance and Life into the fold took place in the winter of 1992. As an order, they were closing in on 20 years of futility, and their tempers had been pushed past even-keeled.

The phone call they received from Wilhelmina Hung was inevitable as far as Peace 9 was concerned, the culmination of another ugly mess left behind by his predecessor. Had his advice been followed years earlier, the devil spawn would have been destroyed and they would have no reason to trek to the backwaters of Eternally Free Taiwan's American colonies. Now that he was in command, he had to atone for Prosperity 3's shortcomings, like it or not. He would not be making his way back to Ghana until this situation was resolved.

There was no word as to the exact nature of the incident in Wilhelmina's frantic phone call, but Peace 9 knew that whatever had happened, the news couldn't be good. He had long considered granting Sister of Joseph status upon Ms. Hung to be a mistake, especially once it was revealed that she and the child should, by law, be cordoned within separate areas of the colony. Peace 9 did not view habitual law-breaking as conducive to an ideal upbringing and an ideal upbringing was the only hope for staving off the rise of a new Satanic threat.

There was no telling of the child's power. If the legends of Satan's destructive force were true and if his innately evil abilities transferred through his bloodline, the child could be able to wreak whatever form of havoc he wished. Even if the child was half as strong as his father, he would still pose an incredible threat. God forbid the child grew to be more powerful than his father. Peace 9's mind was made up; the child had to be destroyed, no matter the severity of his wrongdoing.

Their golden orbs had faded and the pillars of light were dissipating as the Four Friars strode purposefully towards Castillo's towering double doors. The black men from the sky would become legend within the halls of Castillo after their visit that day, although it wouldn't be for their bizarre entrance or foreign skin tones. They would be remembered for their actions within the Principal's office.

They made their way to the top floor and into Wilhelmina Hung's office without the courtesy of a knock. Wilhelmina was not caught off guard. She had been expecting them for days and the fervent excitement throughout the school made their presence obvious.

"Glad to see you could finally make it." she sneered.

The chant's power had waned dramatically since the 'incident' at the race track. No longer was the sway of the Four Friars all powerful. Thoughts of *'What the hell am I doing here?'* *'Principal?'* and *'I've wasted 18 years of my life.'* had been swirling feverishly through Ms. Hung's head. The chant had yet to lose all of its power, however. She was still compelled to tie up this final loose end. She knew she had no future at Castillo, and now with Billy gone, furtive plans of hitting the road once again were incubating. She was curt. She wanted to be through with this ordeal.

"Let me get to the point. Billy blew his cover, in front of everyone. It was no longer safe for him here. I've sent him to M Prefecture, where he belongs. He's with an old acquaintance of mine." Wilhelmina grimaced as she mentioned her 'acquaintance'. Even in her chant-addled state, she was loathe to rely on Gary's new alter ego. But, she had no choice. Billy would only be safe in M, and only Gary was the only person she knew who could get him there.

"I see." Peace 9 replied. His calm demeanor belied his impatience. News that he would have to travel further to erase his order's previous mistake did not sit well. He did an excellent job of hiding his annoyance. "Where in M has he been taken?" he asked with a slight smile.

"I don't know. I don't want to know." Now that the bond that had been forced upon Wilhelmina and Billy was broken, she no longer had any desire to care for her foundling. She had quickly grown to resent Billy. She viewed him as the catalyst for her humdrum, button down life. Even though their sloppy work years earlier was to blame, the chant's effect was still powerful enough to deflect any thoughts of condemnation from the Four Friars.

"Very well." Peace 9 was finding it increasingly difficult to stifle his disdain for the woman sitting across from him. "Do you have a recent photo of the child?"

"Tomorrow is yearbook day." Ms. Hung bent down below her desk, emerging with a cheaply bound tome. "You can find his picture in here. Billy Lopez." She said as she passed the yearbook to Peace 9.

"Thank you. If you will excuse us." The Four Friars tapped buttons on their hovering activator rings and their golden orbs faded on to opacity, obscuring their voices.

Abundance 12 was first to speak. "What are we to do now?"

"We head for M, and destroy the child!" Replied Life 29. He was eager to please Peace 9. More than that, he had a yearning for glory. He was no longer the boy who was afraid to pass to his title to the next Life; he was now the young man who wished to reap the accolades that came with fighting Satan's forces. This mere child, this Billy Lopez, seemed like an easy target. A quick and dirty way to finally be lauded back home.

Peace 9 was pleased with Life 29's fervor. But, he knew that there was more to being a Friar than doing battle with the forces of evil. He had to make due for every element of Prosperity 3's gaffe in the desert. "Yes Life 29, you are correct, but first we must reward this poor woman, this Sister of Joseph. She has been thrust into a set of regrettable circumstances beyond her control and has performed her duties to a degree that bested our most optimistic projections. Prosperity 4, as your first act as a Friar, I shall leave this reward in your hands."

"Yes Peace 9, it will be my pleasure. Please join me, my brothers."

The chant of the Four Friars grew louder as their golden orbs faded away. Ms. Hung's confusion, anger and self doubt vanished as she heard their heavenly intonations once again. She was decidedly enraptured. The Friars circled Wilhelmina at her desk and chanted their most powerful blessings; she was to be rewarded with an eternity of God's love and protection.

Prosperity 4 drew a thin dagger from within the left sleeve of his robe and gracefully plunged it into the base of Wilhelmina Hung's neck. She slumped headfirst onto her desk, unable to sully the prayers of the Four Friars with further sin, eternally blissful.

CHAPTER 16 - INTO THE PILE

CHECKPOINT TO 'CANADA', G PREFECTURE, U.S.A.

WEDNESDAY, JUNE 23, 2010

Garbage Bag slowed Bluebell to a crawl. The bus was veering closer and closer the shoulder of the highway, finally coming to an angled stop. The lone working headlight cut through the dark of night and cast a sheen on a large metal road sign. The sign had once read 'Now Entering Canada'. With the clever application of spray paint it now read 'NoT Entering Canada'. Garbage Bag pointed it out to Billy. "You see that?"

"Funny..."

"Stupid is more like it. The border guards don't mess around; whoever sprayed that is probably back in my pile" Garbage Bag chortled. "Now you've gotta go join 'em!"

Billy's brave façade, not particularly convincing to begin with, was showing serious cracks. His eyes had grown wide with fear, his breathing had become short. He sat stock still as they resumed their slow roll towards to the border. Billy knew he didn't have much longer; his prospects were looking grim.

Six foot high chain link fence, the same kind that separated F and G, stretched to the horizon in either direction. It seemed to be the main defense keeping anyone out of The Union (or Canada as the signs preferred it to be known). A small redbrick outpost with a roadblock arm sat in a gap in the fence, facing the highway lane leading out of the U.S.A. It looked like once you were past that arm you were in The Union. Billy couldn't see well in the dim light, but from what he could make out the Union was more of the same, nothing other than a dirty brown landscape interrupted by a cracked black stripe. It didn't look like there was much of a reason to continue.

It looked to be far more complicated, and dangerous, to drive the other direction and enter G Prefecture from The Union. Billy couldn't tell for certain, but it seemed as though tripod mounted machine guns greeted visitors from the other side of the fence. At least he figured that's what they were; they sure looked like the pictures he remembered from the 'Bavarian Menace' chapter in his *Potential Enemies of the U.S.A.* textbook. The rusty red uniforms and automatic rifles made it clear the guards milling around the outpost were military. If Billy's education hadn't been specifically designed to stunt his knowledge of his homeland's colonial overlords, he would have recognized them as Eternally Free Taiwanese.

Bluebell rolled to a gentle stop. Billy had never been stabbed to death before, but he was pretty sure he wouldn't like it. He closed his eyes tight and awaited the worst. *'The neck. It'll be over quicker if he cuts your neck.'* Billy tilted his chin towards the roof of the bus, swallowing hard to stifle a whimper. He kept waiting.

"Hey! Lopez! I'm not kidding; you've gotta go hide yourself under there." Garbage Bag hissed, finally breaking the silence.

"These guys aren't going to ask many questions before they leave us both full of holes."

A wave of relief washed over Billy. *'Hide in there! Oh, thank God!'* It was unwarranted and it didn't last long. *'Wait...'* Sure, Garbage Bag wasn't going to chop him up (at least, not yet) but he did have to hide himself in a pile of body parts to keep from being shot. Not having much of a choice in the matter, Billy took a deep breath and wriggled towards the bottom of the mound.

The deep breath ended up doing more harm than good. Billy hadn't counted on the weight of the parts squashing the breath from his lungs as he made his way deeper into the pile. Working against gravity, Billy had to inhale deeply to avoid suffocating. Now, the pervasive stink had become a taste as well. Everything around him was far mushier than he had anticipated. Billy tried not to focus on the individual parts, tried to treat it all as a mound of flesh, but he couldn't do it. He knew full well that he was hidden underneath legs, arms, torsos cleaved in two at the sternum, scalps, penises – lots and lots of scalps and penises.

'At least I'm safe here. For now. I'm safe. Hell, after all this, I'd better be safe! How long am I going to be down here?'

Billy heard the creak of the hinged door followed by heavy booted footsteps. Having never considered the possibility of anyone *not* speaking English, Billy was startled by the string of barked vowel sounds that ended with whiny twangs. The Eternally Free Taiwanese adopted English as their official language for business purposes years ago. However, it wasn't out of the ordinary for EFT commoners, even those assigned to posts overseas, to have stuck with their native Taiwanese tongue. It was clear from their tone; these particular commoners stationed overseas weren't pleased to see a bus full of dismembered parts. They started walking very slowly towards the pile, taking small tentative steps, as if they were waiting for something.

Once Garbage Bag started twang barking the mood shifted. Whatever he said, he said forcefully. If he wasn't actually in control of the situation, he was putting on a good show. The footsteps stopped and then turned back towards the front of the bus. There was a long pause followed by some shuffling noises. One of the guards asked a twangy question and then broke into peals of laughter along with Garbage Bag and the other guard.

The door creaked to a close and the bus roared off through the checkpoint. Billy didn't want to take any chances, but he didn't want to spend any more time under the pile. He didn't need to wait long.

"C'mon out, c'mon out, you're in the clear – unless you're startin' to get comfortable down there!" Garbage Bag bellowed.

Billy scrambled out from underneath the pile, covered in viscous blood, dripping maggoty flesh, unleashing a cloud of flies that trailed behind him. "What was that all about?" he asked in between gasps, trying hard to inhale as much corpse-free air as he could.

"Oh that? Nothing special, just worked a little Highway Star magic. I know those two EFT guys well enough. Well enough to know how much they enjoy a good deck of bikini girl playing cards, at least. Damn near impossible to find 'em down this way. So I pick up a couple packs from over in C, drive 'em down here and next you know, we're in... Huh? C'mere Billy." The beaming grin vanished from Garbage Bag's face, replaced with a look of total confusion. Billy tried to wipe more of the goo off as he tentatively made his way to the front of the bus.

"Uh, sure, how come?" Billy didn't get an answer. Instead, Garbage Bag pulled the metal pill out of his coat pocket and produced one of his 'skin swatches'. The grin began to reappear as he held it up towards Billy.

"So *that's* why I'm takin' you to M! Oh man, you had me goin'!" Garbage Bag roared. He reached out towards Billy's face, rubbing his fist of a paw roughly against Billy's cheek, then pulling it back to show Billy the brown streaks left on his knuckles.

"How did you know? Oh God... I didn't..." Billy's flight instinct was kicking again. He shrunk back towards the benches.

"Relax, kid, relax. Hard not to notice, see?" Garbage Bag tilted the rearview mirror to face Billy. His face was streaked red, white and brown.

There was no hiding it now. Billy's cover was blown, again. But Garbage Bag didn't seem upset. But just in case... "So, are you going to kill me now?" Billy managed to squeak.

Garbage Bag let loose his loudest roar of laughter yet. "Kill you? How the hell would I get paid that way? Honestly, you U.S.A. kids... classic! Kill you..." He began to mutter to himself. "Oh wait, did I miss... yeah, Goddamn it. OK, hold on." With that, Garbage Bag jerked the wheel to the right and sent Bluebell careening across the desert. Billy didn't have the chance to hold on. He tripped over himself and fell, landing squarely on the corpse pile.

"Smooth Lopez, real smooth! Now sit tight, would ya? We're nearly there."

"Ugh. Mind if I take a bench?"

"Go for it, kid. I'd say you earned it."

CHAPTER 17 - SANDWICH

15.2 MILES WEST OF GRETL'S GARAGE,
J PREFECTURE, THE UNION

THURSDAY, JUNE 24, 2010

Bluebell's shocks were not designed for rocky terrain. The constant erratic vibration made sitting comfortably an impossibility. Billy held onto the pole leading up from the stairwell as he craned forward to see where they were headed. Dawn was breaking, and from what he could see out in the orange-tinged darkness, they weren't headed anywhere. *'I thought we were nearly there?'*

"Where are we going? Is this the way to M?" Billy asked.

"No, not really. With Bluebell dinged up and you looking like a painted idiot we need to make a pit stop. Get us somethin' to drink too."

"A pit stop? Alright!" Billy only really understood the 'stop' part. And he knew he would be getting something to drink. Finally! With the idea of hydration Billy's brain started to uncloud. "I really did think you were going to kill me, you know." he said, matter of factly.

"Yeah, I picked up on that. But, why?" Garbage Bag sounded genuinely confused and maybe even a little hurt.

"Why? Really?" Billy was confused and a little angry. *Why? Isn't it obvious?'* "Well, let's see. You've got a pile of white people parts in your bus, and I'm white. So I figured I'd be next to be chopped up." Billy's pitch was rising and he was talking faster, his emotions were taking hold. "You've pulled your knife on me twice now. You crashed the bus. Then you made me drive and I'm amazed I didn't crash the bus! And now we're headed off to God knows where! Oh, and you made me climb underneath a mountain of corpses!" Billy was yelling now, and only some of his volume could be attributed to trying to out-decibel the rattling bus chugging through the desert.

"Did you major in whining at that school of yours? Jesus." If Garbage Bag felt any sympathy for Billy's plight, he did a great job of concealing it. "If you don't like the service I provide, feel free to get the hell off of my bus at any time. I'm just doing the job Willy paid me to do, and by the way, I still haven't been paid yet – I don't get paid until you're dropped off nice and safe. So, remember that before the next time you get all teary eyed thinkin' I'm about to off you."

"Oh..." Billy had little to say to counter Garbage Bag's gruff rebuttal. "Sorry?"

"Yeah you should be. Actually no, Willy should be sorry for getting you into my bus in the first place. No need for you to apologize. You're just a stupid F kid. You always live there?"

"Yeah."

"So, I guess you've always had to keep your face painted, huh?"

"Yeah."

"Willy always was damn good with disguises. Don't know why she'd be hiding you out in F though."

"Me neither. How do you know Ms. Hung anyway?"

"Ms. Hung…" Garbage Bag shook his head in disbelief. The Willy he used to know was no Ms. "See… alright look, me and Willy go way back, like 35, 40 years back. Used to work together, kinda like partners, kinda like I was training her. She was a sneaky little one. Cocky too, maybe too cocky. Definitely the best thief I ever worked with. Then I… I uh, I got a little greedy I suppose, had to cut her outta my business."

'A thief? A cocky thief? Hey, wait a minute! 40 years? Just how old is this guy anyhow? How old is Ms. Hung? 50? This can't be right.'

"I don't mean to say you're wrong… But Ms. Hung doesn't seem like she'd be interested in doing, um, anything like that. Are you sure we're talking about the same person?"

"Ms. Hung, she Chinese or something?"

"Well, yeah…"

"Then it's her, trust me. And don't interrupt." Garbage Bag took a while to get back on track. "Look, we used to be tight, me and Willy, OK? Real tight. I did some underhanded things to get where I am today and I've got some regrets. Leaving Willy on her own the way I did is the biggest regret of 'em all. Never thought she'd forgive me for that, and I can't blame her if she never does. Something must've changed her mind though, 'cause, well, here we are. I get this call patched through to me outta the blue. Willy says she's got a kid named Lopez that she takes care of and she needs me to get him out to M, needs to stash him somewhere safe. So, I say yes. That's all I know about the situation. So, tell me kid, what's got Willy so worked up? Why's she shippin' you off out into this?" Garbage Bag gestured out into the dimly illuminated landscape. Off in the distance, Billy could see a low, wide, grey box, the unmistakable glow of fluorescent bulbs emanating from within.

"I accidentally wiped some of my makeup off. In front of the whole school. I had to leave after that." Billy said sheepishly.

"Nice move. Still doesn't explain what the hell she was doing with a white kid painted brown in F Prefecture. What's the deal?"

"Not sure, all she would ever tell me is that I was 'very special'."

"Special? Yeah, maybe back in F. Around here, you're just another pasty sucker." He said with a lawnmower laugh.

Billy no longer feared Garbage Bag. He was still very wary of him, as he should have been, but now that Billy was no longer faced with the immediate threat of death, Garbage Bag had lost his menacing edge. Garbage Bag didn't seem to have all of the answers either. Billy found that oddly appealing; at least he wasn't the only one in the dark. Even with the threat of violence reduced to practically nil and some semblance of humanity beginning to crack through the bus driver's monstrous exterior, Billy still thought Garbage Bag was a jerk. It had been a long, awful couple of days for Billy and that sucker crack was uncalled for.

Bluebell rolled to a stop in front of the grey box. It looked to be some kind of garage; Billy could see the undercarriage of a car up on a big hydraulic lift through a glass roll up door. There must have been a back door to the garage, too. Before Billy and Garbage Bag had a chance to step outside, an older woman in grimy blue coveralls had run out from the back to greet them with a beaming smile.

She was the first living white person Billy had ever seen.

Garbage Bag bolted from the bus without a word. He ran up and grabbed the squat, wrinkled woman in his arms and spun her around, kissing her deeply as he did so. It was gross, but not gross enough to keep Billy on the bus. He stepped out and made an effort not to stare. Thankfully, the woman broke the embrace before things got too steamy and made her way towards Billy.

"Who's your filthy little travel buddy, Baggy?"

Billy tried hard not to smirk, but he had to crack a little grin at the corny nickname the lady had for Garbage Bag.

"Gretl, meet Billy Lopez. Lopez, meet Gretl, mechanic extraordinaire, finest phone-patch gal in The Union and most importantly, my main squeeze. Lopez here is on the run from the law, aren't you Lopez?"

"Uh yep, sure am." Billy was taken aback by the tonal shift in Garbage Bag's voice. Had he been putting on the growl earlier, or was he trying to hide it now? "Nice to meet you Gretl."

"Nice to meet you too, Billy. Say, how does a bath a nap and a sandwich sound?"

Exhausted, Billy had slept away the morning and a good portion of the afternoon. He awoke with a start, expecting to find himself lying on one of Bluebell's benches and not on a pile of floor mats. The shock continued as he caught a whiff of himself. On the bus, his ripe, deathly odor was just an extension of the stink produced by the corpse pile. In the garage, he was the only one to blame for the olfactory assault. Now, he was crouched naked in an industrial wash basin, the last of the timer-rationed water pooling at his feet. After a lifetime of hurried predawn makeup applications, Billy was whiter than he could remember.

Finally full of food and drink, fresh and clean at last; Billy patted himself dry with rough paper towels and got back into his disgustingly crusty school uniform. He was quite pleased to have brought a change of underwear and socks – at least they weren't corpsey. Billy still stank, but the only alternative was nudity.

"Bluebell's looking shiny and new." Gretl's voice carried through the impeccably kept garage with a faint echo. Billy stepped out from around the corner to see Gretl kneading Garbage Bag's shoulders as he lounged on a stack of tires.

"Mmm, thanks Sugar."

"You've got to take better care of her."

"What? And miss out on payin' a visit to my best gal? I'm gonna try and smash her up real good next time!" They laughed. Garbage Bag's ratchety growl was almost non-existent. Gretl doubled over and pressed her withered lips against his ragged hole of a mouth with an audible moan.

Billy liked Gretl immediately. The sandwich she made for him was amazing. It marked Billy's first time eating meat that wasn't grown in a fetid pond or a writhing hive and the first time he had eaten bread of any kind. The meal and the bath were easily the nicest things anyone had ever afforded him. What Billy didn't like was watching Gretl make out with his monster of a bus driver. He made a feeble throat clearing sound, which was met by Gretl's soft laughter.

"Oh, hi Billy! Don't mind the old folks!" She said with a wave of her hand.

"Nice timing Lopez..." Garbage Bag muttered. There was no disguising his gravelly grumble this time. He rolled his shoulders as if to test them out and shifted his head from side to side, releasing mighty cracking noises.

"Now Baggy, you two had better get back out there; it'll be dark soon enough and you're supposed to meet with Dr. Timothy tomorrow."

"Yeah, yeah, I guess. Not like he's going to fire me now. But, listen, I'll drop by on my way back, should be a day or two." He snuck in a quick kiss before straightening up off of his tire perch.

They made their way out of the garage. True to her word, Gretl had Bluebell looking better than it ought to look. On the outside anyway. The windows were still caked brown with blood and God knows what else.

"Good luck Billy. I hope you have fun being an outlaw!" Said Gretl as she tousled Billy's hair and kissed him on the cheek.

"Thanks! And thanks for the bath. And the sandwich! How do you get such tasty food all the way out here?"

"It's all about who you know, Billy. I'm just lucky to have a good friend who knows how to give a woman what she wants. And I'm not talking about Baggy here, in case you're wondering!"

Billy and Gretl had a good laugh. Garbage Bag made a poor show of pretending not to hear that last part.

"Thanks for coming by, it's always such a pleasure to see new faces!" Gretl said with a smile as Billy and Garbage Bag walked towards the bus. "Hail Satan!" she added with a cheery wave.

Billy waited until he and Garbage Bag were both inside the bus, with the doors closed behind them before asking. "Hail Satan?"

Garbage Bag climbed into the driver's seat. "Pal of Gretl's. Steer clear of him, that guy's an asshole." The throaty growl was back in full force as he grunted his reply. "A lowdown, sneaky, generous asshole. Some folks out this way treat him like he's some kind of hero, not me though. I've been around long enough; I know not to trust a man who gives you somethin' for nothin'. He's the type who'll come callin' for what he thinks he's owed when you can least afford it."

"So... he gives people things?"

"So they say. Never actually met the asshole myself, but trust me. Asshole. Alright let's move – these chunks aren't getting any fresher." The key spun in the ignition and Bluebell roared back towards the highway.

'Huh...'

This was Billy's first view of 'Canada' in the light of day. It looked nothing like the vast frozen steppes his Castillo education had taught him to anticipate. "So this is what's left of... what'd you call it, The Union?"

"Yup. Gorgeous country they've got down here isn't it?" Garbage Bag coughed up a gravelly chuckle.

It sure seemed like Garbage Bag was telling the truth. He wasn't in Canada, or at least not the part of Canada he was told to expect. The drab, brown terrain continued unabated. If Billy didn't know better he would have sworn he was still in the outskirts of F. If this place had been bombed, Billy wasn't sure how much damage the bombs possibly could have done. There was nothing of note out this way aside from Gretl's, and her garage disappeared in the rearview fifteen minutes earlier. The garage looked great though, must've been lucky when the bombs fell Billy figured.

Gretl didn't just keep a neat and tidy establishment, she was indeed a skilled mechanic, having gone far beyond performing a mere cosmetic patchup on Bluebell. The ride was smoother, quieter, even as they drove along the unpaved desert terrain. It still stank powerfully, but with the pile of body parts no longer bouncing around, the stink no longer assaulted Billy in waves.

They made it back to the remains of Inter-Prefecture Highway just before night fell. Both headlights were back up and running again, the powerful cones lighting the upcoming patchy stretch of asphalt.

"Radiation?" Garbage Bag paused to take a leisurely slurp from his sustenance gel pouch. "No, that's not it, not even close. My hot and sexy look is all fake. Not fake like a mask though. You know much about plastic surgery?"

"Yeah sure. Jamilla, this one girl in my grade, she came back to school with a new nose last year."

"OK, yeah, good. So it's like that, only for me it's not a nose, it's a new shiny new wrapper."

"But why? Why green?"

"It ain't white, it ain't black, and it ain't brown. There's a reason I'm the last true Highway Star. Know why? I outsmarted most of them and then I dealt with the rest. Billy felt uneasy about the 'dealt with' part. But he was no Highway Star; at least he didn't think so. Garbage Bag went on. "You think the EFT would've let a fat black guy pass through from G to J? Hell no! Either they would've shot me on sight or carted me back to B. A fat green guy with a melt face though? Most people don't even want anything to do with me." He unleashed another lawnmower laugh, followed by an abrupt pause. "Here, you take the wheel. You got a nap and a sandwich, so now I get a nap. Plus, you owe me a sandwich. Fair's fair, and I don't want to be rusty tomorrow. Keep going down this road. When you get to the ugliest place you've ever seen you'll be there."

Garbage Bag left Bluebell in drive as he walked down the aisle, stopping to lie on a free bench near the front. Billy scrambled to take the wheel again and was forced to steer hard right, away from the craterous pothole dead ahead. The pile could be heard sliding to the side of the bus. So much for stemming the tide of stench waves.

Billy gagged a little as he glanced back over his shoulder. "Are you ever going to tell me who these people were? Or what you did to them?"

"I'm tryin' to sleep, Lopez. But, I dunno who they were and I didn't do anything other than buy 'em that way, OK?"

'Jesus! Why didn't you tell me that two days ago?' "Yeah, OK. Do I want to know what the parts are for?"

"Nope. You'll piece it together soon enough though!" The lawnmower laughter quickly turned to lawnmower snores.

Billy piloted the bus through the gaping hole in the fence that once separated J from M. He was home, whether he liked it or not.

CHAPTER 18 - MAKING DEPOSITS

TIERRA PODRIDA, M PREFECTURE, THE UNION

FRIDAY, JUNE 25, 2010

What the rising sun revealed wasn't pretty. A heaping mound of crumbled concrete marked the end of the Inter-Prefecture Highway. Rusted rebar spines jutted out in every angle, staining the broken slabs with crusty brown trails. Billy had yet to learn the finer points of braking, but he managed to lurch Bluebell to a stop long before the ramshackle barricade.

"I think we're here!" he called out over his shoulder.

Garbage Bag rolled over and slumped forward. "Ugh. Thank God this is the last time I'll ever have to be back in this crap hole."

"Yeah..." Billy wasn't particularly interested in Garbage Bag's upcoming itinerary. His focus was on the concrete mound. "What happened to this place?"

"Christ Lopez, I'm no engineer. If you're lookin' for somethin' better than 'a building fell over' you're askin' the wrong guy."

Billy took a closer look. It was a building, or maybe buildings, at least they used to be. Although rubble had filled most of them in, Billy could make out window and door frames here and there.

"C'mon, no time to stare at broken crap." Garbage Bag hoisted himself off of the bench and made his way towards Billy. "Go take a seat, I want to get this over with." He fired up Bluebell's engine and they veered left, completely off the road. They drove alongside the collapsed remains of the buildings, passing the ruins of a large, still mostly upright main floor.

The bus sped up an escarpment and the 'city' spread out beneath them. Rows upon rows of cinderblock and tin shacks stretched out into the distance, leading towards an enormous, gleaming white compound. The smooth, gently curved features of the massive building were lit bright orange by the rhythmic jets of fire it belched into the air. A swarm of red and white striped dirigibles made their way in and out of the complex, clouding the sky over the factory.

Garbage Bag spun the wheel hard right once they reached the pinnacle of the precipice. Bluebell careened down the steep face of the escarpment, headed towards a narrow gap between two midrise buildings in dire need of repair. 'Uh...' Billy had some faith that Garbage Bag knew what he was doing; his plans seemed to have worked out to this point. But this, this seemed particularly stupid. The gap grew closer and closer.

Billy closed his eyes tight and hid his face in his hands, praying that Garbage Bag was playing the angles right, going limp in case he wasn't. Even with his limited automotive experience, Billy knew a head on crash at however crazy-fast they were going wouldn't end well. 'Sounds OK so far...' Billy peered through his intertwined fingers. Things seemed a lot darker than they should be, but only briefly, sunlight quickly peeked through the hand slats. Billy uncovered his eyes to find that they had squeezed through, somehow. 'We made it!' Billy thought as he looked out a porthole window. *'Goddamn it!'* Billy's glance towards the front of the bus cut short his fleeting relief. They were headed straight for another building and Garbage Bag showed no signs of slowing down.

'Oh God! Asleep?' Billy shifted in his seat to get a proper look in the rearview. Garbage Bag seemed to be awake, though it was hard to tell. His ragged eye holes weren't closed, so he was either awake or dead. That was hard to tell too, Garbage Bag's expression was one of the utmost serenity. His glazed expression took on a smirking air as he yelled "Hold on!"

"Hold on to wha-aaaaaaaaaaaah!" Garbage Bag had braked. Hard. Bluebell spun a full 180 degrees and came to a jarring halt. Massive G force flung Billy around as the bus rotated from front to back, crushing him against his bench seat first, then against the wall, finally dumping him off the bench and onto the floor.

BEEP **BEEP** **BEEP** **BEEP**

Bluebell backed up slowly and deliberately, in stark contrast to the rest of the downhill trip. It afforded Garbage Bag a chance to guffaw loudly and yell something to Billy about 'The Lost Art of Braking'. The beeps subsided. The wheels were finally at rest. Billy picked himself up off the grimy floor and peered over the corpse mound, through the back window.

The building they were going to smash into before Garbage Bag's braking bravado was ornate but decrepit, hewn from sandstone. Sheet metal had replaced glass in the windows and there was no door to speak of, just an empty doorframe that was now parallel with Bluebell's rear emergency exit.

"I can't believe I'm finally through with this!" Garbage Bag sounded elated. "Guess that means I won't get to drive that obstacle course any more though. It's kinda fun, right?"

"Sure. Yeah. Lots of fun." Billy wheezed as he steadied himself on a bench, he could feel his heartbeat in his teeth.

Garbage Bag sprung from the driver's seat and busied himself underneath the bench behind him, popping up with pitchfork in hand. "C'mon kid, time to earn your fare!" he yelled, tossing the fork to Billy.

"What? I thought Ms. Hung paid my fare!"

"Yeah, well... shut up and start spearin'. I don't want to hang around any longer than I have to."

It took a second for Billy to grasp exactly what Garbage Bag was talking about.

"Ugh. Really? What do I once I have them... speared?"

"Yeah, really. Just dump 'em on the floor, your majesty. I'll get the door." Garbage Bag stepped outside and unlatched the emergency exit. Billy gave a slight shudder and climbed to the top of the pile. He had lost his initial revulsion to the stacked body parts several days and hundreds of miles ago, but Billy wasn't looking forward to this. His first stab at the pile was more successful than he had imagined, he was able to skewer a good 30 pounds of rotten man flesh. He gingerly stepped off of the pile, out of the rear exit and into the sandstone building. A ratty maroon carpet spread out ahead of him, interrupted by a waist high wooden counter that spread along the rear wall. Metal poles strung with velveteen ropes separated the room into a series of straight lines that led towards the long wooden counter.

'Why is Garbage Bag leaving body parts in a bank? Oh, who cares? Nothing this guy does makes any sense.' Billy jabbed the man-laden pitchfork into the ground and stepped on the speared meat, guiding it off the tines as he fully extended his leg. *'Nasty.'* By Billy's estimation, that would be the first of at least fifty forkfuls.

As Billy made his way in and out of Bluebell, unceremoniously plopping rank pile after rank pile onto the carpet, Garbage Bag lumbered towards the large reinforced door behind the counter at the rear of the building. He slammed his paw against an intercom button.

BZZZZT

"Dr. Timothy?"

BZZZZT **BZZZZT** **BZZZZZZZZZZZT**

"Dr. Timothy!"

"Mr. Bag, is that you?" The voice on the other end had an Australian lilt, dry and snide.

"C'mon, who else?" Garbage Bag sneered as he stared down the intercom speaker. "This is the last of it. We're finally square."

"I'll have to weigh it all to be certain, but yes, we should be. I cannot say it has been a pleasure, but it has been..."

"Don't worry, the pleasure's all mine. No offense Doc, but I hope I never see you again!"

"That would be delightful, Mr. Bag. Goodbye."

Billy didn't get it. *'A bank doctor?'* At least he wouldn't be riding with body parts any longer. At least not these body parts... His pile transfer was nearly complete. The big pieces had been speared and dumped. Now he was trying in vain to scrape the little sludgy pieces from the bottom of the bus with the pitchfork, hoping they would trickle on top of the pile. It wasn't working; his efforts were producing little more than piercing metallic squeals.

Garbage Bag grabbed him by the shoulder. "Lopez. I swear to God, if you don't stop it with that noise I'm gonna leave you on the pointy end of that thing."

Billy knew by now that the cheery tone behind Garbage's Bag's violent threat meant he wasn't in any actual danger. He eagerly tossed the pitchfork through the emergency exit.

"What was that all about? Are we done here?"

"Just wrapping up some old, old business. A Highway Star makes good on his debts."

'Wrapping up? Does that mean no more parts? Please, let it mean no more parts!'

"Congratulations. Right?"

"Damn straight, congratulations! And thanks. This day's been a long time coming."

'What the hell is he talking about?'

"C'mon kid. Let's move. Still have one last delivery left on this run."

Garbage Bag followed Billy into the bus. Bluebell snaked in between the same two buildings they had narrowly navigated earlier and motored its way back up onto the escarpment.

Now that he was no longer sharing his ride with a pile of corpse hunks, Billy was feeling fairly optimistic about things. He was under the hopeful assumption that he would be the final delivery. Maybe there was a school nearby. One like the Alpha Center. Maybe that's where he was headed. That's probably it. A new school. It didn't seem like the kind of thing Garbage Bag would have anything to do with, but it sure seemed like something Ms. Hung would have arranged. "Where are we going now?" Billy asked hopefully.

"Now? Now, you're gonna disappear."

'Goddamn it!'

Billy had long grown tired of not being able to understand what the hell was going on. Never knowing his parents. A lifetime of daily makeup applications. Being run out of school, and then run out of the country. Being lied to about some war, or maybe being lied to about being lied to. Dealing with a monster man 'Highway Star' and his piles of body parts. And now he was going to 'disappear' whatever that involved.

"OK." Billy replied, his hopes utterly deflated.

Bluebell rolled through the desert terrain. Headed towards nothing, or at least nothing that Billy could see. The bus stopped next to a small rock outcropping, maybe three feet tall.

"Welcome home, kid. Hoo boy, you are going to *love* it here!"

"Home? We're in the middle of nowhere!"

"You're sharp. Clint'll fill you in."

'Clint? Who? Jesus, more nonsense.'

"Say Lopez, before you go, I forgot to ask, you got a girlfriend?"

"No, not really, I mean uh..."

"Wait! What am I saying, she'd never get into M anyhow. Good thing too, she'd be *pissed* if she knew what you were about to get into!" Garbage Bag clearly wasn't listening. "Now, get outta here, climb into that hole and have yourself a good time!"

Billy couldn't fathom what Garbage Bag was talking about, but he didn't have the heart to argue. The bus door slid open and Billy stepped outside. "OK. See you around."

"You've got a lot to learn. Like what 'disappear' means! Hurry up and climb on in, Lopez! And try to keep your hands to yourself!" With a guffaw, Garbage Bag pulled hard on the lever next to his seat, sealing Bluebell's door behind Billy. The bus roared off into the distance, swerving back and forth and kicking up a huge dust cloud.

Billy had no idea what Garbage Bag meant by anything he said, or what he was about to get himself into. If he did, he would've been wise to bolt after Bluebell, grab onto the rear bumper and let himself be dragged back onto the highway. But, it was too late for that. Billy inspected the man-sized gap in the rock outcropping, took a deep breath and wriggled his way inside.

CHAPTER 19 - PSYCH

GRETL`S GARAGE, J PREFECTURE, THE UNION

FRIDAY, JUNE 25, 2010

Four pillars of light radiated over J Prefecture. Initially, the Four Friars had little difficulty following the path of oil stains and assorted vehicular debris leading away from the Castillo Academy. But the child's trail had grown cold, stopping abruptly at a secluded garage. According to Prosperity 4, J Prefecture was on the official Eternally Free Taiwanese record as being completely bereft of human life; its final Phase 2 worker having died in the mid-1980s. Something was wrong. The lights in the garage were still burning bright. Someone, or something, was still stirring in J.

Peace 9 gave a sharp rap on the glass door. He wasn't expecting a reply. It was a mere formality, an antiquated nicety serving as a precursor to the Four Friars storming the garage and destroying the child hiding within.

A short, older, heavyset woman wearing dark blue coveralls came bounding out to meet Peace 9 before he could issue his orders to move in. With a press of a button the door rolled up into the ceiling. Peace 9 would have to come up with a Plan B.

"Well, hi there! Don't get too many customers these days! The name's Gretl. What can I help you with?"

Prosperity tapped Peace on the shoulder before he had a chance to reply. He leant in and whispered into his squad leader's ear. Peace 9 nodded and turned back to Gretl.

"My apologies for this, Madam. Would you excuse us?"

"Well sure, I suppose. Kind of an odd way to greet a lady, but I guess you, uh, fellows must have all sorts of strange customs, huh? Coming from, well, coming from someplace else. I'll just be straightening things up inside." Gretl turned her back on the robed black men and headed back into the garage.

The Four Friars were silently enshrouded within their golden orbs before they spoke again. Peace 9 turned to Prosperity 4.

"Prosperity are you certain?"

"No, I cannot be certain. But, is it not worth taking precaution?"

"Most wise. Please, enlighten our brothers."

"Very well." Prosperity 4 turned to face Abundance 12 and Life 29. "I have read of a Knight in Satan's Service operating in the Americas who roughly matches this woman's description."

Peace 9 interjected. "Thank you, Prosperity. I feel it would be best to avoid taking any chances. From the intelligence we have gathered, this woman appears our only hope in tracking the child any further. We must ensure her absolute compliance, regardless of her potential affiliation."

The subordinate Friars nodded as their golden orbs began to fade. The Four Friars followed Gretl into the garage in full chant. A tray of socket wrenches spilled to the floor with a clatter as Gretl turned to face the mysterious men, wide eyed and awestruck.

"We have been looking for a young man." Said Peace 9, holding up Billy's photo, torn from the Castillo yearbook. "Like this, only white. Have you seen him?"

Gretl's reply was slow and relaxed. "Sure I have. He came through here not long ago at all. Told me he was headed to the old Coxwell Motel, just west of Tierra Podrida. That's over in M. Can I get you boys something to drink?"

"No. But, thank you, Madam. Life?" Peace 9 gestured to his underling. Life 29 tapped the two buttons on his activator ring, bringing his golden orb to full opacity. He made a quick study of the map that was projected within the confines of the golden sphere. He tapped the buttons once more, fading the orb. "There is a motel that once operated under that name. 28.4 miles due west of Tierra Podrida's town square."

"Very well. Thank you, Life. And thanks to you, Madam."

"You're most welcome. Is there anything else I can do for you? I'd be happy to take a look at whatever you rode in on, give it a quick tune up. Free of charge, of course." Gretl replied in a dreamy near whisper.

"Again, no thank you, Madam. You have been most helpful."

Gretl beamed, mouth wide. She watched as the four men took to the skies, enveloped in dazzling light that seemed to stretch to heaven, tan robes fluttering in their wake. Within minutes they had disappeared from view completely. She dropped the act as soon as the pillars began to fade. Grin replaced with a determined scowl, she ran back inside the garage and rapidly spun her phone's rotary dial.

Markus Sarpong was best known as Prosperity 3, longtime leader of the Four Friars of the Ashanti Orthodox. To a very, very select few, Markus was known in a different capacity. Markus Sarpong was a Knight in Satan's Service. For a time, he was second in command to Satan himself. It was certainly no mere coincidence that the Four Friars had been hesitant and toothless under his watch.

That morning marked the first time Gretl was able to put Markus' lessons in trance nullification to the test. His deceitful tips worked far better than she had expected; her unwelcome visitors didn't just bite, they appeared to have swallowed her story whole.

She had no idea why the Four Friars were after Billy, it hardly mattered to Gretl. She hadn't bothered to try putting a finger on who Billy reminded her of. Had she been able to pinpoint why she found him familiar, she would have been concerned for his safety, panicked perhaps. As it stood, Billy only mattered because he was riding with Garbage Bag. If they were on Billy's trail, they were on Baggy's. *That* mattered to Gretl. She would never let any harm come to her big, green sweetheart if she could prevent it. The Four Friars dealt only in harm.

Now, she had to act quickly. Disclosing Satan's location could prove to be a costly error, unless she could ensure he had the drop on those who wished him dead. Satan picked up on the first ring.

"Hello? Yes, this is Gretl. I have word on the Four Friars. They're headed your way. Yes. To the Coxwell. Just a minute ago. I'm not certain, flying, somehow. No. They have no idea, they're expecting a teenage boy. Yes. Yes. Markus did teach me well. Very well, I guess." She paused for further instruction. Her face brightened and she cracked into a legitimate grin. "A reward? Oh, that's so sweet of you! Let's see... How does a side of beef and a ham or two sound? Ooh! And pickles! Can you get pickles? Please? You can! Of course you can, how silly of me! Well, I won't keep you any longer. Stain the ground red with the blood of these insolent, holy fools! Bye now!"

CHAPTER 20 - BILLY LOPEZ, WORKING MAN

20.3 MILES SOUTHWEST OF TIERRA PODRIDA,
M PREFECTURE, THE UNION

FRIDAY, JUNE 25, 2010

When Billy hit the floor of the cave, he hit it hard. Not hard enough to break anything, but hard enough to regret not looking for a better way down first. He noticed the metal ladder bolted just below the cave's entrance as he rose from his awkward landing, gingerly rubbing the shoulder that absorbed the worst of the blow.

He thought the muffled ring he heard upon impact was all in his head, a product of his inner ear being jostled out of whack. The goldenrod colored rotary phone lying on the cave floor dispelled that notion. The handset had been knocked off of the cradle. Billy set the phone back in place without giving thought to why anyone would want to get in touch with a rock formation. There seemed to be a lot more to this cave than Billy had expected, the phone wasn't the only thing that seemed out of place down in the hole.

He shouldn't have been able to see much at all, but to his surprise, the expansive cave he'd stumbled into headfirst was bright as day. Thin, illuminated plastic strips, radiating out from a nexus not far from where Billy landed, lined the surprisingly smooth 'floor'. *What is this place?'* Billy gave the lighting grid's hub a quick once over. It looked to be sturdily built and it was adorned with the same sunburst logo found on the back of sustenance gel pouches. Seven strips of light branched out from the center. They snaked overtop the small stream that bisected the cave floor as they wound along the ground, eventually disappearing from view around the cave's stalagmite pillars.

Billy knew he wasn't going to be alone down here, at least not for long. As poor as his Natural Science marks had been throughout his scholastic career, Billy knew lighting setups and telephones didn't grow from rock floors. And there was the matter of Clint, the man who was to 'fill him in'. Or maybe the woman? *'A woman named Clint? Nah... Well... Makes as much sense as anything else around here.'* One way or the other, somebody named Clint was supposed to explain to Billy to that this cave was his new 'home' and probably why he'd 'love' it down there too.

So far there wasn't anything to love. Underground lights were kind of cool, sure. But, any affection Billy may have felt for the mysterious cavern he had wriggled down into was washed away by his brooding negativity. He'd had enough of living the life of a fugitive. The extra-thin coat of exciting polish had worn off of his adventure right around the time he was forced into Bluebell. Fleeing from unnamed assailants into a land that by most accounts shouldn't exist left Billy feeling lousy.

He made a makeshift seat of his death-encrusted Castillo blazer and parked himself on the floor, trying to come up with any semblance of a plan. He failed. Thoughts of what he could do didn't come, only thoughts of what could be done to him. It dawned on Billy that his days of eluding authority were likely far from over. He had spent enough time away from Castillo to know that the new world he found himself in was deeply rooted in deceit. This cave seemed to be perfectly suited to dirty secrets. Lighting up a hole in the ground out in the middle of nowhere was no small undertaking. If someone went through the trouble of setting this up all the way out here, they probably didn't want the outside world to know anything about it. True, Garbage Bag knew about it, but he hardly seemed like an upstanding citizen.

Billy was nervous, but his curiosity began to get the better of his nerves around the time the dull ache shifted from his recently bruised shoulder to his barely cushioned butt. *'Hell, if I'm going to disappear, I'd better find out where I've disappeared to.'* He decided to cautiously follow the illuminated strip on the floor that led down the path with the widest opening. *'If things go bad, just turn and run. It'll be OK. There's a ladder to get out and then it isn't too far back to that crappy town. Plus, you can outrun anybody that would want to chase you out of here. Right? Right. Oh God, I hope I'm right.'* He moved slowly, quietly, not looking to attract attention if he did stumble across 'Clint'. Anyone who went to lengths like this to stay hidden probably didn't care for surprises, especially not ignorant young surprises who stank of rotten flesh. As Billy crept further and further into the winding depths of the cave he heard... something. *'Some kind of motor? Must be powering the lights I guess... No, that's no motor... What the... Oh my God...Is THAT Clint?'*

He stopped short at a beaded curtain hung between two large stalactites. There was one hell of a spectacle taking place beyond the beads. A spectacle set in front of a roll-down 'Underwater Palace' backdrop, exactly the same as the one Billy had posed in front of for his fifth grade class photo.

They were having sex. And the sex was *not* like how it was pictured in *Sex for Americans*.

The black and white line drawing of the expressionless horizontal man had been replaced with a sweaty, jiggling, fat bodied, spindly legged, Lollipop of a Man. Each thrust of his hips was paired with an aggressive grunt and sent a new bead of sweat trailing down his pockmarked, possibly scorched back.

The black and white line drawing of the expressionless horizontal woman had been replaced with a vision of erotic beauty, albeit, one doubled over at the waist, her ankles seized in the grip of the sweaty blob. She was as sexy as he was hideous. No, she was even sexier than that. She made it possible to completely ignore the grotesque display of humanity that was pounding himself into her.

Garbage Bag was absolutely right, Billy was loving this. So much so that he didn't even register that they were both bone white, just like he was. But, maybe he was loving it a little too much. Billy was hit with the realization that he had been standing out in the open, and he had no idea how long he had been there. *'Hide, you should hide. You can introduce yourself after. He's really gross, you probably have a shot.'* Billy's hormonally charged thoughts were violently interrupted. In a flash, The Lollipop of a Man's hands were around her throat. Her grunts, coos and purrs turned to grunts, shrieks and gags. The frantic shouts from the periphery clued Billy in; he wasn't the only audience to these acts.

With an enraged howl, a bushy haired short guy leapt into the fray feet first, aiming a clumsy dropkick at the Lollipop of a Man. It may not have looked like much, but the kick did what it was intended to. The Lollipop of a Man forcefully slid out of Billy's newfound object of lusty desire, engorged and enraged. He couldn't right himself; his spindly legs were bent backwards and pinned under the weight of his rotund torso.

The short guy looked to be about 60, and pretty spry for his age. Lengths of surgical tubing snaked out of his nose and into the collar of his orange, western-style, button down shirt. He stood over the Lollipop of a Man in triumph; each deep inhale sent a surge of vivid blue liquid coursing through the tubes and into his nostrils.

He delivered another kick, this one swift and straight to the Lollipop of a Man's distended, skyward belly producing a guttural groan. "Lopez!" The short guy called out over the snarling wails as his vicious kicking continued, blows alternating between belly and balls. "Billy Lopez, right?"

"Uh... right!" Billy's cover was blown. Under normal circumstances, he would have panicked. Right now, the best he could muster was an affirmation. The violence on display went far beyond anything he had been exposed to during his sheltered existence back in F. Between the physical savagery and the beautiful naked woman who was awkwardly clambering away from the attack, Billy had an awful lot to process.

"Figured." The bushy haired guy grunted as he stomped on the prone man's chest. "Your cologne's a dead giveaway! My name's Clint. The pleasure's mine and all that. Now that we got that squared away, pick your jaw up off the floor and get your dick out of your hand! Don't go acting like you haven't seen a naked woman before!" Billy hadn't. "Give me some help getting this low life up the ladder! Norm, Ry, you two make sure Mona's OK!"

"Would someone please tell me what the hell is going on?" a voice croaked out from the cave's recesses.

"Jesus Christ, you blind bastard!" came the squeaky, high pitched reply from another unseen cave dweller. "The fat son of a

160

bitch nearly killed Mona and then some smelly guy showed up! C'mon! Get over here!"

Billy didn't have time to check to see who was calling out; Clint thrust one of the Lollipop of a Man's long, brittle legs into his arms. "Let's go! Help me drag!" Billy did as he was told. Together, they pulled the Lollipop of a Man across the riverbed-smooth rock floor to the base of the ladder. Clint stepped on the Lollipop of a Man's throat, pinning him with a gaspy gurgle.

"Now you climb up, pull his legs up along with you!"

'How the hell am I going to get out of this?'

"OK..." Any love Billy felt for the situation had faded quickly. Even without knowing the circumstances, he felt no remorse for what was being done to the sex-attacker; he just wished he wasn't a part of it. His upbringing had ingrained abhorrence towards conflict, and his surging adrenaline did little to quell his nauseating unease. He struggled the climb the ladder, deformed goon in tow, with Clint pushing up from below. It was an awkward affair, but the two eventually managed to squeeze the thrashing Lollipop of a Man through the mouth of the cave and out onto the desert floor.

Clint resumed where he left off in the cave, more or less. He swapped kicks for punches, sitting astride the man's near sphere of a chest, raining blows down upon his grimacing face. Billy shirked away as the blood began to divert from the pool beneath the Lollipop of a Man's head into the cracks in the sun baked ground. Clint's enthusiasm seemed to wane around the same time. He stopped punching and rose to his feet, speaking to Billy once more.

"Keep an eye on him, will you?"

"Uh... yeah..." Billy wanted nothing more than to run, but shock kept him rooted in place. As horrifying as Billy had found the first day or so of his bus ride out here, this, this was worse. The chopped corpses held the threat of violence over Billy's head, these last few minutes had thrust violence down his throat. The battered, twitching man stared at the sun in silence, eyelids wide. He belched up a bloody bubble and Billy brought up the biley remnants of the only sandwich he had ever eaten.

"Done barfing?" Clint grunted through gritted teeth. "Hope so, you need to make sure he doesn't move!" He was struggling under the weight of the large red rock he was carrying towards the man lying prone on the ground.

"What? No! Clint! No! What are you doing?" Billy blurted. He knew perfectly well what Clint was doing, and Billy wanted no part in abetting a murder – no matter what the intended victim may have done. He had to think quickly. "You don't have to kill him! Just leave him out here in the desert, there's no way he'll survive out in this heat!"

What Billy said was likely true. The sun was beating down particularly hard that afternoon and it was a pretty long drive back into town. There was no telling how long it would take to shuffle over the harsh terrain in a badly beaten state. Billy's pleading must have struck a chord with Clint. He dropped the rock harmlessly to the ground and broke out in a grin, shaking his head in disbelief.

"I knew some fresh blood was just what we needed around here! I like the way you think, Billy! You know what else I like about you?" Clint didn't give Billy a chance to answer. "Two working eyes AND two working legs! Ha! Man, oh man! Doesn't get much better than that! C'mon, let's head in, get you situated. I tell ya Billy, you sure can pick a moment to make an entrance!" he said with one final kick at the Lollipop of a Man.

Billy felt awful as they descended back into the cave, leaving the man to crawl to his death. The weight of his guilt crushed the confusing thoughts imparted by Clint's speech about having two eyes and two legs. *'Maybe he'll survive the trip back into town. Probably. It'll be dark before too long, being out of the sun should help buy him some time.'* Optimistic half lies like that one helped temper Billy's self-condemnation, but only to a point. The cold finality of the way the man was left to writher and bake resonated throughout Billy, leaving him feeling hopelessly hollow.

Clint was beaming as Billy stepped down off the ladder and turned to face the cave, his eyes were hidden in the crinkles of his squint. "It is *so* good to see the new slave finally made it! Ha ha! Just kidding, but only sort of! Seriously though, that wasn't much of an introduction I gave you earlier. The full name's Masters, Clint Masters. Wait, no, you look confused. The full name's just Clint Masters. Call me Clint. Looking forward to working with you, Billy." He thrust out a sinewy arm and Billy shook his hand as a conditioned response. His fate was sealed. Billy didn't have enough of his wits about him to worry about the 'slave' talk, let alone the talk of working together. He kept mechanically pumping Clint Masters' arm, unable to shake the awful, soul-gnawing thoughts of what he had just done and hypnotically entranced by the odd visual of the blue juice flowing into the old man's nose.

Billy was close to tears by the time he was finally able to blurt anything out. "What the hell was that? What the hell is this?"

"They sure do go for good long handshakes over in M, don't they?" Clint managed to pry himself free of Billy's thoughtless grip and stretched his freed fingers. "Ha! I'm just joking with you Billy, trying to lighten the mood a little. You sure look like you could use a little mood lightening. Not to mention mood lighting, but the cave's got that covered already." Clint paused as he gestured to the expanse of well-lit cave behind him, expecting a laugh. He didn't get one and pressed on. "Listen, try not to get too bent out of shape over all this, OK? This has a bad turn for everyone here, so you're not alone if you're not feeling great. Hell, we haven't had a day quite this bad since, well, we've never had one quite like this at all! I bet this has been a lot to deal with after the long trip out here, huh?"

"Yeah." Billy repeated himself, hoping to silence the quiver in his voice the second time. "Yeah." There was something about the way Clint spoke that had a calming effect on Billy. He wasn't feeling good, not by a long shot, but with the way Clint barely paused to let a word in edgewise, at least Billy didn't have the opportunity to gather his miserable thoughts.

"So, on to your questions about what the hell that was and what the hell this is. I think the best way to put it is that you, Billy Lopez, as of today, can consider yourself a high roller in the kind-of glamorous world of black market pornography!"

'Pornography?'

"Or, as I like to call it, doing the Lord's work! Ha! Exciting right? No need to answer, you've got a big 'hell yes!' written all over your face. You want to get acquainted with your co-workers?"

Billy's inability to gather his dour thoughts was replaced with a singular giddy focus. *'Pornography!'* The concept alone left him in a state of dumb awe. If what Clint said was true, he might as well have told Billy that he had stumbled into the world of dragon punching or cattle ranching. It couldn't be true. It was too good to be true! Billy had overheard reverent whispers from the other members of the track team about the sex photos of legend. He had always assumed there was no way something so incredible could actually exist. *'And with her! Oh man, I totally forgot! Please, please let this be true!'*

Billy's head was in the clouds, the attack from moments ago barely registered. He hardly realized that Clint was leading him down the main corridor of the cave. His astonished, buoyant thoughts of photographing naked ladies were cut short about halfway back to the Underwater Palace backdrop; he and Clint were stopped by a man with no legs and his eyeless counterpart. *'Whoa!'* They were enough to make Billy forget all about his new line of work, at least for the moment.

Billy wasn't great at guessing the ages of the physically deformed, but he deduced they both had to be about his age, more or less. They probably worked with Clint, or so Billy presumed from their close-to-matching, button down, western shirts. They were different colors, red for the guy with no legs and light blue for the guy with no eyes, but they all featured identical embroidered chest panels; a cowboy on horseback giving chase to a runaway donkey.

"Damn it, Clint! We've got to start screening these sickos! Next time, if we don't get the guy's name, I'm not turning on the camera!" the legless man chirped. He must have been the person behind the squeaky voice Billy heard during the melee. His babyface and thin, wispy brown hair matched his high-pitched pre-pubescent voice, but there was something world-weary about his demeanor that clued Billy in to his being a fair bit older than he appeared. The legless man stood on his hands, his shirt dangled down past where his beltline should have been, stopping just short of the ground.

"Yeah, that was awful! You took care of that bastard, right?" Croaked the eyeless man, accounting for the second unseen voice from the fight. It didn't look as though he once had eyes and had lost them; his smooth forehead kept going south until it met his mouth, interrupted only by his nose. He was tall, nearly tall enough to hit his head on the cave's ceiling. Billy couldn't tell if his head was covered in bruises, his bushy blond mop of a hairdo did a pretty good job of concealing any potential damage.

"More or less, sure." Clint replied. "He won't be back, let's leave it at that." Billy stood behind Clint, feeling particularly awkward and trying not to stare.

"Sure, whatever, you're the boss. You going to introduce us to the stinky new guy, or what?" The eyeless man asked, gesturing towards Billy with his chin.

"Aw, Jesus. Haven't been much of a host, have I? Billy, this here is Ry, my audio technician. Naturally God gifted at hearing, not so great at looking at stuff."

"Hey Billy. Not sure what things were like back in F, but we've got plenty of bath paste down here. Just so you know."

'He knows I'm from F? What else does he know? And bathpaste? Oh! Oh yeah...' Billy hadn't given much thought to the condition of his clothes recently, but Ry's remarks ratcheted up his level of self-consciousness. "Hi Ry, um... thanks. But uh... it's my clothes, actually. Usually I smell great. And, um, it's nice to meet you." Billy reflexively stuck out his hand for a shake, only to be left hanging. It didn't take long for him to figure out the flaw in his cordial formality. He withdrew it and gave a feeble wave, not having learned his lesson.

"See? Usually he smells great!" Clint chimed in. "He's going to fit in just fine! Ha! Not that there was ever any doubt. Now then, Billy, meet Norm, my director of photography. He might not have anything below his belly button, but he sure as hell can shoot some porno!"

"Hi Norm." Billy motioned to shake Norm's hand as well, but stopped midway as he took into account how Norm had to stand. A half-hearted slicking back of his hair was the best thing Billy could think of to try and save face.

"Yeah, hi." Came Norm's curt reply along with a curled lip and an emphatic eye-roll.

Clint continued. "And then, well, then there's nobody else! Aside from Mona that's it, and you've already seen what Mona's here to do."

'Mona...'

"Yeah and I bet he likes what he sees! Huh, Billy? Huh? Or maybe it's the cave? You always get boners in caves?" Norm blurted gleefully, dropping his snide pretense in order to poke fun. Billy had yet to register what the brief flash of Mona in his mind's eye had done to his stiffened member; now he couldn't ignore it.

Ry broke out laughing as Clint cut back into the conversation. "Don't let these jealous sons-of-bitches crack on you too bad, Billy! Hell, they'd both be rock hard all day long if they could be!" That managed to strip the smile from Norm's face, setting his expression back to petulant in an instant.

"Whoa, whoa, whoa!" Ry cut in. "Just because I'm not into Mona's 'ooh ooh ooooohs' doesn't mean I can't get it up! Just pop a smooth jazz tape into my cassette player and I'll prove it!"

Both Clint and Norm cracked into laughter as Billy let out a nervous chuckle. "Ah hell, seriously though, odors aside, it's nice to meet you Billy" Ry continued "It'll be great to have you doing our grunt work!"

Billy paused, partially to let the blood flow subside, partially to take in what Ry just said. "Grunt work? Like lifting stuff? Is that what I'm doing here?" *'How much lifting do you need to do to make sex pictures?'* Billy was less than thrilled by the prospect of manual labor, he really hoped 'grunt work' was some kind of cave code for sexing Mona.

"Yes sir, lots and lots and *lots* of lifting. But don't sweat it, we're going to start you off light. Granite slabs for the first few weeks. In the third branch of the cave on your left back there," Clint gestured over his shoulder. "We've got a good 25, maybe 2600 of 'em that we'll need you to haul into town. Sound good?"

"Uh..." That didn't sound good at all. Grunt work wasn't any kind of code for sex, it was just what it sounded like, work that would make you grunt as you did it. Billy was crestfallen, it was written all over his face.

"Ha! Gotcha with that one! Lightening the mood, remember?"

'Thank God.' Billy smirked.

"Hey, that's better! Nah, no lifting. Just joking with you. I've got a nice cushy job down here, but I'm getting old. Older anyhow. I just needed someone to help me out with some of the small day to day stuff that keeps the business running. That's where you come in. Dragging fatty out of here was *the* worst thing I'll ever have to ask of you, that much I promise. There may some physical stuff I'll need from you, but no lifting. At least not much. Running, though? Not going to lie. Yeah, you'll end up doing some running - you fast?"

"Hey Clint, Clint!" Norm interjected before Billy had a chance to brag about his exploits on the track. "I'm sure he's got rocket wheels under those nasty smelling pants of his. But, can't this wait? Mona's pretty rattled, I think you'd better go see her."

168

"You're right Norm, I think so too. Come on, Billy, let's get you and Mona properly introduced."

Billy's nerves were on edge as Clint led the way through the winding passageways of the cave. *What am I going to say to her? Some kind of compliment obviously. Her hair? Yeah. And her eyes. Nothing sexual. Keep it classy.* Clint laid out his one and only ground rule as they headed back to the main clearing. The rule would prove to be as calming as it was disappointing.

"Like I said, Billy, this job is pretty easy, pretty straightforward. With one exception. One rule. It's a pretty big deal, this rule, and you're probably not going to like it. But, it has to be followed to the letter, no questions asked."

"OK, sure." Billy had put up with what seemed like a million rules as cafeteria janitor. Only having to follow one rule didn't seem too bad.

"Good. Great... So, uh, I saw the way you were looking at Mona and hell, I can't blame you. She's quite something. But, looking is as far as things can go Billy. Even that might be too far. You're going to have to treat Mona like a sister. You get it? We can't have any funny business going on down in my cave. She needs to focus and focus hard. She won't be focused if she goes and falls in love with the help."

'Aw, Christ! C'mon! Well, you can still compliment her hair. Brothers probably compliment their sister's hair all the time.'

Clint went on. "Keeping things strictly professional hasn't been a problem for half-man, hasn't been a problem for no-eyes, hasn't been a problem for this old man either." Clint gestured to his tubes, then to his crotch. "The blue juice keeps me soft as a pillow. But a healthy young guy such as yourself..."

"Don't worry about me, I'm a gentleman." Billy tried hard to hide his frustration; he did a pretty good job of it. He wanted to be a team player in order to keep on Clint's good side. He sure didn't want to end up on the receiving end of a boulder to the head, no matter how hot Mona was.

"Glad to hear it." Clint gestured for Billy to stop as they turned a bend and reached a pink beaded curtain. Clint's tone was soft and gentle as he knocked on the tin garbage pail lid that served as a rudimentary doorbell.

PANG **PANG**

"Mona?"

"Yes?" Came the quiet response from inside.

"Billy's here with me, can we come in? I'd like you to meet him."

"Come in."

Billy followed Clint through the parted beads. He stopped, utterly transfixed, as the beads swung back into place behind him. No matter what Clint had said seconds earlier, now all Billy could think about was giving Mona the now explicitly forbidden 'funny business'. Goddamn she was sexy!

Wavy blonde hair, enormous blue eyes, full heart-shaped lips and a cute pert nose. Not to mention the smoking hot body that had no problem filling out her tiny, yellow flannel bathrobe. Her long, lean legs were on full display; the bathrobe just barely covered the firm, plump curves of her ass. And those tits... The way they were straining against the plunging neckline of Mona's tight robe forced Billy to daydream about them bursting free, settling with a heaving jiggle and a coy giggle.

Even as she stood rubbing the claw marks on her neck with a far-off, vacant look in her eyes, she made Gina Theoulis look like

Garbage Bag. *'So. Hot.'* Billy didn't mean to objectify this poor girl to such a degree but the pull she had over his most base emotions could not be denied.

"Hi Billy."

Billy's heart was pounding, there was no way he would be able to treat her like a sister. "H, hi Mona, nice to meet you." he stammered.

Clint rushed over to the gently quivering object of Billy's desire. "Mona, honey, you OK?"

"My neck hurts. Will that man be back?"

"No, no, never, that will *never* happen again. Billy here made sure he won't be coming back."

"Good. Thank you Billy."

Billy really wanted a way into this conversation. The problem was, he had very little idea what had happened between Mona and Mr. Lollipop and even if he had been better informed, talking about a beautiful woman's recent strangulation seemed like a bad icebreaker. "Oh, you're welcome... You have a nice dressing room." Billy lied. Aside from the mattress on the floor, the small four-drawer vanity dresser and the bucket of toilet powder in the corner, it looked just like the rest of the cave. Uniformly brown, smooth floor, craggy walls, lit up by a glowing plastic strip.

"Thank you, this is where I sleep."

'That's a weird thing to say. Is she trying to blow me off? Aw Christ, of course she is! I stink! Damn it! Now I've got to... Hey, wait! She sleeps here? In the cave? Does everyone sleep down here? Do I sleep down here?'

"Yes, very nice." Billy felt like kicking himself for not coming up with a suave reply that would help take some of the edge off of his ripe odor. Thankfully, Clint cut in.

"This kid has an eye for decorating style, I'll give him that! Ha ha ha! Speaking of sleep, Mona you must be tired, Billy, I'm thinking you must be tired too. C'mon, I'll show you to your room."

Billy was tired, exhausted really. It had been a long, bad day and he was happy to get out of there before things got any more awkward. "OK, goodnight Mona."

"Goodnight Billy." Mona turned her back to the men and busied herself pulling a hairbrush through her blonde locks.

Clint led Billy back into the main clearing and then down the furthest passageway on the right. It certainly seemed as though Billy would be sleeping in the cave. His suspicions were confirmed when the duo turned a corner and were faced with another set of beads, dark blue in this case. Clint pushed them to one side and gestured within.

'This is it? Hmm. Not bad. I suppose. For a cave.'

The underground pocket that had been earmarked for Billy was practically identical to Mona's, except he didn't seem to have a dresser. It was at least four times larger than the dorm room that served as his home at Castillo; plenty of floor space that would make a suitable resting spot for the crumpled heap he would be making out of his sole change of clothes.

"Here it is." Clint gestured across the room with a broad sweep of his arm. "A nice room of your very own! Ha ha! You're easy to please when it comes to decor, I like that! Ha! Say, listen. I like the way you handled yourself around Mona too. Thanks for not making too much of her, uh, condition."

Billy wanted to play it as cool as possible when it came to discussing Mona. The last thing he wanted to do was let word of his horny desires spill. "Yeah, no problem. Didn't want to make a big deal out of the choking thing. Shouldn't be any of my business."

Clint paused for a moment, perplexed. "No, not the choking. Although, I like the way you kept a cool head about that, too. Plus, Billy, so long as you're working with me, that kind of thing *is* your business. And, from the looks of it, you'll do just fine in this line of work! Letting the desert finish off that lousy bastard? Brilliant! I sure didn't want to have to get rid of a body, did you? Let him crawl away and rot, I say. Works for me, so long as he's not rotting on my doorstep! Ha!"

The nauseous guilt began to churn in Billy's gut. *'I let a man die. I'm no better than a murderer. Maybe I'm worse. I could've stopped it. I should've stopped it. I...'*

Clint pressed on, sending Billy's train of thought off the rails. "What I mean by condition was... Hell, how can I put this delicately? Mona's a brain retard, Billy."

'What?'

"What?"

"A brain retard. About as smart as a four year old, I'd say. Without any of that cute 'joy of learning' type stuff that four year olds have. She's hit her intellectual plateau. Pretty as a picture but not quite as smart." Clint paused to let this sink in. The dismayed expression on Billy's face told him it was time to go. "Get some sleep; got a big day of nothing planned for us tomorrow."

With that, Clint left. Mona's weird reactions made sense now, or at least a bit more sense. Billy stripped to his underwear and climbed into bed, feeling rotten for more reasons than he cared to count.

The exciting potential of making forbidden pictures with the sexiest woman he had ever seen had quickly dried up. *'Does she even know what's going on down here? How could she? I don't know what's going on down here! Why the hell am I down here? I don't care if this is where Ms. Hung told Garbage Bag to drop me off or not. This isn't right. It's not right for me and it sure isn't right for Mona.'* Billy wanted out. He didn't want to spend any more time in the violent pornography cave than absolutely necessary. His mind was made up, he'd be moving on as soon as he could. He wasn't sure where he would go, or how he would get there, but he was sure of one thing. When he left, he'd be taking Mona with him.

CHAPTER 21 - SABBATH

20.3 MILES SOUTHWEST OF TIERRA PODRIDA,
M PREFECTURE, THE UNION

SATURDAY, JUNE 26, 2010

Billy dressed with a grimace. He had slept well, far better than he had been able to on Bluebell, but waking to the prospect of spending another day wearing the crusted on remains of God-knows-who on his school uniform instantly soured his outlook.

His gloomy thoughts turned to the cave of depraved sexual violence he would be spending... some time in. No point in planning a timetable for a daring escape without getting a feel for the routine first, Billy figured. His resolve to flee with Mona helped Billy feel a shred of optimism about his situation. At least he had a goal, even if he didn't have much else.

With a zip-up of the fly of his Castillo issue trousers, markedly stiffened by the juices of humanity, Billy brusquely pushed aside his veil of beaded privacy, braced for whatever new cruel trick the world had planned for him that day. He didn't make it far towards the cave's central chamber before an ambush wiped the grimace from Billy's face.

"Open your presents!" Mona was ecstatic. The overt melancholy effects left by yesterday's attack had washed away. She was flanked by the rest of the cave crew. Smiles all around, with the exception of Norm's exaggerated sneer. Ry was holding a crudely wrapped package in each hand.

'Presents? Oh my God! Really?'

To Billy, this was a staggering gesture. These would be the first presents anyone had ever given him, aside from the used textbooks Ms. Hung gave him before each school year. He wasn't entirely sure what sort of things people normally gave as presents. Billy had a feeling that no matter what was hidden beneath the plain brown wrapping paper, nothing they could give him was going to beat the view of Mona's boobs dancing beneath her tight bathrobe. She was bouncing around with a level of glee that would have made a first grader blush.

"You should see the look on your face! Welcome aboard Billy!" said Clint.

'Good. Good. Keep looking at my face. Nothing to see below the belt.'

"Uh, wow, I mean thanks everybody, I never really..."

"Here." Norm squeaked abruptly as he yanked a package from Ry and tossed it Billy's way. "This was Mona's idea." Billy wasn't sure if he had done something to get on Norm's bad side, or if Norm was always in a foul mood. One thing Billy did know for sure was that Norm's effortless ability to balance on one arm was really impressive.

Billy deliberately unwrapped the oblong, floppy parcel. It was a full change of Western wear. Rugged denim trousers, a pair of high-cut leatherino boots and a pale pink shirt, complete with an embroidered runaway donkey chest panel. Billy was wrong. Fresh, clean clothes blew Mona's boobs out of the water.

"I don't know what you've got on now, but this'll be an improvement in the smell department!" Ry added with a laugh.

"These are great! I'll be right back." Billy ran back behind his beads, emerging moments later feeling like a new man.

"So handsome!" Mona said with a giggle and a heaving bounce. Billy was awfully glad he left his shirt untucked.

"I'll say!" Clint chimed in. "Billy, you might be the best dressed man in the Prefecture. But, you've got some pretty strong competition. Ha ha!" He gestured around the room. Everyone save Mona wore the same outfit, differentiated only by the pastel hues of their shirts. "Glad you like it, it's the only style they sell here in M. Does look good on you though. Here, this one's from me."

Billy was quicker to tear into this package, slower to respond to its contents. It was a used textbook, but Billy couldn't place the subject. The mustachioed man in the striped shirt on the cover was funny looking, posed sort of like he was slow dancing with himself. That was about all Billy was able to glean from the old, worn tome. Billy wasn't a big fan of reading but he appreciated the thought behind the present. Clint couldn't have known the book would trigger foggy, unpleasant memories of twelve first days of school.

Billy took his time sounding out the book's title. He butchered it. "Gentleman Girl... Gentleman Girled on Puggyliss. M. ...well, uh thanks!"

"Jesus Christ! Is he serious? Ry's a better reader than this guy!" Norm blurted incredulously, to no one in particular.

Clint cheerfully ignored Norm. "That's Gentleman Gerald on Pugilism. Wise words from one gentleman to another." He was calling back to the discussion he and Billy held the night earlier. The connection flew over Billy's head. "It's my old manual. A fella in your position has to learn how to handle himself out there."

'How is dancing going to help me handle myself?'

"Uh, yeah, thanks. Thanks everybody. But, uh, I don't get really get it. Why are you giving me these?" Billy paused to gather his thoughts. He caught himself losing sight of the bigger picture. "No, that doesn't matter. I mean it's really nice and all, but it doesn't matter. Well, maybe it might matter but... Who are you people and what the hell are you doing making pornography in a cave?"

Clint looked shocked. "Billy, this cave has every amenity available!. 72 degrees year round. Rich in minerals. Zero chance of a bird attack. I tell you, there's nowhere I'd rather be!"

"That's not really what I meant. I meant..."

"Ha! I'm teasing you Billy, do they do that in F? Now then, listen. You've got a good head on your shoulders, very inquisitive. So, why don't you quit asking so many questions already? Ha ha! Kidding, I'm kidding! C'mon, let's get something to eat. I'm not one for explaining on an empty stomach."

Ry peeled the top off of a firecup. Blue flames crackled to life just below the metal lip. Norm skewered the last of the gutted, brown and yellow striped lizards onto a blackened coat hanger. The rest of the lizards, close to twenty in all, each about nine inches long from nose to tail, had been skewered and piled on the flat stone slab that served as both prep area and table. Billy's eyes were wide as he knelt in the gap between Clint and Mona.

"Do we get to eat these?" He almost hated to ask. He'd been awfully lucky with food lately and didn't want to jinx himself.

"No. The new guy has to watch. Cave rules." Norm piped up with exactly the kind of answer Billy had grown to expect from him.

"Shut up, Norm." Ry croaked as he tested the fire's intensity with the palm of his hand. "Yeah, Billy. We'll be eating these. OK. Feels good and hot to me, let's roast 'em!"

Everyone but Billy took turns selecting a lizard and holding it over the flaming cylinder, waiting for the skin to blacken and peel before turning them. Billy went last, having ample chance to pick up on the simple cooking technique.

Clint broke the relative silence as they ate. "Mmm. Nice catch boys. You like them, Billy?"

"Mm. Yeah!" He turned to Ry. "You caught these?" He quickly turned to face Norm before he looked too stupid.

"That's right. Not everyone around here gets to sleep past noon. The rest of us have things to do." Norm grumbled with his mouth full.

Billy wasn't sure what he did to deserve constant scorn from Norm, but he sure was getting tired of it. "You don't have to be a jerk." Billy had never stood up for himself before. Then again, he had never been accosted by an annoying squeaky half-man.

Ry snorted. "Billy, he doesn't *have* to be a jerk. But he will be. Better get used to it."

"He's our resident ray of sunshine." Clint scraped the meat from the tail by pulling it through his teeth. "And we love you for it, Norm."

"We love you, Norm." Mona added without looking up from what was left of her lizard.

"Yeah, yeah." Norm busied himself with the fire cup, mindlessly poking at the flames with a bare hanger.

"Billy, there's a good reason I'm down in this cave. And it's not just because we're near a nest of these guys." Clint gestured with an uncooked lizard as he shifted the conversation away from Norm's petulance. "I'd be a dead man if I wasn't living the underground life, and I can't say I take kindly to the idea of being a dead man. I'm an outlaw, Billy. Norm and Ry, Mona, they're outlaws too. Same goes for you. You're an outlaw now, Billy, makes you feel pretty bad ass, am I right?"

Billy looked confused. "Yes?"

"Well, it should. Tell me. When you were back in F, did you ever see anything like what we were shooting yesterday?"

"No!" Billy's tone was defensive; offended that Clint would think him a sexual deviant, fearful that Clint might clue in on his curious desires.

"Calm down, calm down. I already knew the answer. Porno is illegal in the Prefectures – especially illegal here in M. It's not just illegal, though. It's in demand, high demand."

Billy couldn't quite believe what he was hearing. "Really? People want to see... that?"

"The choking? Nah, but you missed the good stuff yesterday." Norm chimed in. "Came in at just the wrong time. The stuff you missed, that's what people want to see."

"And they want it bad." Ry added.

"That's right. Things took an ugly turn yesterday. First time that's ever happened, and we've been doing this for years. But, I bet this tape moves just as fast as the rest, choking or no."

"Oh." Billy had no clue what Clint meant by 'tape' or why anyone would want to kill Clint over it. "So, what does pornography have to do with living in a cave?"

"Everything!" Billy's befuddled expression let Clint know he'd have to delve a bit deeper into his explanation. "OK. So, Mona, she's gorgeous, right?" He gestured to the beauty in the bathrobe. Still super hot, even as she gnawed burnt skin off a coat hanger, not paying any mind to Clint. "No need to answer. Don't want to embarrass you. Thing is, she's not just gorgeous; she's the only gorgeous woman left in all of The Union. No one comes close to looking half as good as Mona. Well, unless you ask Garbage Bag. You meet that mechanic of his on the way over?"

"Yeah. Gretl. She was really nice."

"Nice is nice, sure, yeah." Clint turned his lizard. "Would you give up eating for a month to stick your dick in her?"

Billy couldn't help but burst out laughing. "No! Oh, God no!"

"Ha! Exactly! And a month's worth of food is the least anyone's ever paid to 'star' with Mona in a tape. The men of M, they're a desperate, horny bunch, each and every one of 'em. They wouldn't think twice of slitting all of our throats and stealing Mona away if they found out where we were."

'Does he know? He couldn't. How could he? Plus, I won't slit any throats.'

"*That's* why we stay hidden down here. That, and because what we do *is* against the law. Or, at least what passes for law in these parts."

"Clint, you're putting Billy back to sleep." Ry interjected. He was wrong, Billy was eager to learn as much as he could about Clint's illicit operation. The sooner he had things figured out, the sooner he'd be able to hit the road. "Get to the good part, tell him about my idea."

"I was about to, Ry. I was about to. Billy, does the safety stuff make sense? It's important."

"Sure. Hide down here so we don't die, right?"

"Yep. You got it. OK, so Ry's idea. This is important too. See, for the first few years, we'd just set Mona up with the highest bidder, tape it all and sell the tapes once we were done."

'First few years? How long have they been doing this? How old is Mona? 20?'

"And that was stupid." Norm cut in.

"Sure, now it seems stupid, now. But we were living pretty well off of that stupid system."

"Are you going to get to my idea?"

"OK, OK. So, Ry, genius that he is, comes up with his lottery idea. Now we're not just getting paid by the highest bidder, we're getting paid by anyone who wants a piece of Mona. And *everyone* wants a piece of Mona."

Billy nodded, taking it all in. He didn't really like what he heard, it sounded like Clint was exploiting everyone he could. Especially Mona. She didn't seem to be phased by anything Clint was saying. Not in the least. She just kept chewing her last lizard, staring at the cave wall.

Clint went on. "You can only trade so many tapes, but there's no limit to how many times you can trade the chance to star in a tape. That's why we sell lottery tickets. And selling lottery tickets is where you come in. You're my new Runner, Billy, or rather I should say you're my Runner – it's not like I had an old one I'm replacing."

'Runner?' Billy liked the sound of that, even if he wasn't clear on what running had to do with Clint's sex lottery. "I love to run. But run where?"

"Run away mostly! Ha! There's more to it than that though. You'll see. I'll show you the ropes tomorrow. Sound good?"

"Sure!" Billy's enthusiasm was only half-acting. He figured that if information kept coming his way at this pace, he'd have a handle on the cave's routine within a week. Two weeks tops. His internal escape countdown began to tick deep within his subconscious.

"I love that can do attitude! Love it! OK, we done eating? I am." Clint rose from his knees and gave his back a little stretch. "Norm, why don't you and Mona clean up back here. Ry, let's show Billy how to pack up after a shoot."

"I can't wait." Ry croaked. He would've rolled his eyes if he could've.

"This way?"

"No, Billy, the other way. That's it. Roll it towards me. Keep it tight." Clint held one end of the Underwater Palace backdrop high in the air, Billy bent down to the floor to roll the rest of it towards Clint. Clint went on as Billy shuffled towards him. "So now that we've sold our tickets to the horny and desperate, it's time to pick a winner. I draw a ticket from a hat, doesn't have to be a hat actually..."

"Focus, Clint!" Ry called out with a chuckle as he unscrewed the fuzzy microphone from the boompole.

"Right, thanks Ry. Let's just say we have our winner. Best I can tell we don't have any psychics in these parts, so you'll have to head back into town and let the lucky son of a bitch know about his good fortune. You'll have to bring him back to the studio too."

"Do I have to blindfold them or something?"

"Good question. We used to do it that way, never went over well. Got really tired of smacking guys who were trying to take a peak. I'll get back to that. Where were we... tickets sold, winner picked, winner brought in, porno! Hope this doesn't disappoint, but once we're filming all you've got to do is stay out of the way."

Billy was disappointed. He tried not to let it show as he passed the loose, sloppily rolled backdrop into Clint's hands.

"Thanks. So our winner has had his fun, we have our footage, now it's time to cover our tracks. Some guys accept this part, most will try and fight back, but one way or the other I've got to shoot 'em full of special cocktail. Knocks 'em out cold, makes 'em forget all there is to forget. Once he's slumped over with a needle in his butt, it's your job to drag him back to town. I would've done all that yesterday, but, well, you saw what happened."

'Special cocktail? Dragging through the desert? Hell, it'll all be worth it for Mona.'

"OK. I can drag a guy. But, wouldn't it be easier to drive him back?"

"Drive! Of course!" Norm called out as he waddled around the bend with Mona close behind. "You're a genius! A regular Goddamn Ry-level genius!"

"Norm, shut up." Ry tossed back as he latched the microphone case shut. "He just got here, he doesn't know how things work. Plus, nobody's on my level."

"Ry's right. At least half right. Shut up, Norm. And pack up your camera. He's just teasing you, Billy. Here, hold this end." Billy did as he was told, grabbing onto the end of the rolled backdrop he was offered. Clint folded his end over to meet Billy's and set the doubled over canvas roll down behind a stalagmite. "I'd love to drive, but hell, this is M! No one drives in M – no cars! The EFT snatched 'em all at gunpoint years back."

"Oh."

"Good excuse for us to get some exercise though, right? Plus, the quieter we can get in and out of town the better."

The more he heard, the less Billy liked the sound of any of this. Always being in hiding. Using the luck of the draw to whore out his future wife. Drugging 'winners' and dragging their bodies. At least it wouldn't be long before he was through with it all. Or so he hoped. His hope flickered, briefly and he was hit by a flash of panic. *What if I can't escape? Even if I can get out of the cave, I can't get back into the U.S.A!* Cave life wasn't for him, but what options did he have? He couldn't go anywhere without a car. Maybe he could work in the factory? How bad could that be?

"Say, uh, why do you do... this... down in a cave when you could just go and work in that big factory?" Billy asked quietly.

Norm guffawed. "Oh man! Now you've done it!"

'Done what?'

"Why?" Clint was suddenly irate, his face flushed bright red. "Why? Why don't I work in *that big factory*? I refuse to be chained Billy, do you understand? I am a free man!"

"Yeah. No. I... I understand. Sorry, stupid question."

Clint took a deep breath. Then another. "Hey, it's OK. Don't be sorry. I'm sorry for losing my cool." The frenzied determination in Clint's voice had given way to a warm compassionate tone. Billy didn't really know what to make of their brief factory exchange. It was clear that Clint wouldn't approve of Billy asking about working in the factory himself. What wasn't clear is why the notion of factory work would get Clint so riled up.

"Why's a normal guy, normal sounding anyway, out in M if he doesn't have to be?" Ry asked, cutting the mild tension left hanging in the air by Clint's outburst.

'Should I? Ah, what the hell.'

Billy went on to tell the tale of how he came to find himself in the porno cave. Life in the group home. Life at Castillo. The race. The makeup. Garbage Bag. The corpses. Gretl. Dr. Timothy. Pretty much everything, aside from the Satanic Sacrifice lie. Things had been going downhill fast since he decided to let that story spill.

"Makeup? Bet you made for one sexy lady back in your fancy ass school."

"Shut up, Norm." This time it was Billy's turn. It didn't take long for him to pick up on the best way to deal with the director of photography.

"Seriously, shut up, Norm. Did you even listen to what Billy had to say?" Ry added.

"Shut up, Norm." Mona added with a grin.

"What about all of you? How did you meet up with Clint?" Billy asked.

"Met him when we were little." Ry was very matter of fact. "He killed our parents and brought us down here."

'There's no way I heard that right.'

"Ry!" Clint snapped.

"What? It's true isn't it?" Norm squeaked with an air of bratty nonchalance.

"Well, sure, but... he just got here! I mean..." Clint stammered out a non denial.

Billy was alarmed, but intrigued as well. This wasn't like the situation with Garbage Bag, or at least it didn't quite feel that way. Billy hadn't known Clint long, but he had certainly never felt threatened by him. *'A murderer? Really?'* Maybe it was just the gift of new clothes that skewed Billy's perception of the old pornographer towards the positive. But, from what Ry and Norm said and what Clint didn't say, it sure seemed that Clint was a murderer. From what he was about to do to the Lollipop of a Man the day before... *'Wait. I'm responsible for the fat guy. Damn it! Damn it! Whatever Clint did, he's no worse than I am! ...so what did he do?'*

"Clint, what are they talking about?" Billy asked.

"Well, see Billy, ah, hell, they're talking about the uh, the bad old days. Can't say I wanted you to find out about any of this. Sheesh... Tell you what, I'll tell you the Clint Masters story in full, OK? Maybe with some context my um, murderous, uh, leanings won't seem so bad to you."

"Yeah, OK." *'He is a murderer. But, he's not happy about it.'* Clint's admission of guilt was laced with regret. Billy assumed that whatever happened it was probably a case of self defense.

Clint let loose a heavy sigh. "OK then. Come with me. This isn't the kind of story I want to tell with an audience. Plus, these guys know how it ends. Norm, I thought I told you to pack up your camera."

Billy followed Clint through another branch of the cave. They had to stoop a little as they walked; the ceiling grew progressively lower as they pressed on. "It's a manly story. Action packed. Full of guys punching each other. Well, maybe not *full* but... Ever hear the name Jonathan Wright?"

"No, I don't think so."

"He was a loser, used to be our Chancellor before the war. Dead now, thank God. The EFT took him out a little while after the bombs fell. Put me in one hell of a spot before he died. If it wasn't for that jackass, well... No point in worrying about that. He did what he did and I am where I am. I'm getting ahead of myself though. Did I tell you I used to be a boxer?"

The gears in Billy's head spun quickly enough to put together a little white lie. "No, but I figured from the book you gave me." *'A boxer! OK, that makes sense. He probably killed someone in a fight. That's a bit better.'* They reached a set of dangling beads, black ones.

"Smart kid. C'mon, I'll show you something." Clint pushed the beaded strings aside and stepped over the tangled bead mass on the ground. He had to scrunch his head down into his shoulders to make it underneath the low clearance. "Watch you don't trip." There was just room enough for Billy to straighten fully upright as they passed through the beaded gateway. They were in Clint's room, or so Billy guessed. Sporting a mattress in one corner and a toilet powder bucket in the other, the room was nearly identical to Billy's. There was a purple and white poster taped to the rock wall. Masters vs. Hughson. Clint stopped to stare at the poster in silence. Billy did the same.

"Changed my life, that fight." Clint said eventually.

"How come?"

"Lost my family, had to be hooked up to all of this." Clint gave the tubes feeding into his nose a gentle tug.

"Oh, sorry."

"Thanks. See, I used to be a pretty good fighter. Actually, I used to be *really* good at taking a punch; I was only OK at dishing them out. My big claim to fame was that I never bled. I still don't – not as long as I'm all wired up with the blue juice."

'That's what the tubes are for? Not bleeding?'

"I was a big deal, I drew big crowds. That's where Wright came in. He was a huge black guy, only one in the Prefecture. Not totally sure how he made his way into M, still don't know how he became Chancellor. I heard a bunch of stories – that he was from Taiwan, some kind of kung fu whiz, personal bodyguard to somebody or other. Don't know how true any of that is, but I do know he was a God-nut. You religious?"

Billy had grown curious about religion since leaving F, Satan especially. He figured this wasn't the time to get into that though. "Nope."

"OK good, don't want to offend. You want to sit?" Clint gestured to the bare mattress. Billy perched on the edge, holding his knees in his crossed arms. Clint did the same. "Wright wasn't just a holy roller, turns out he was into boxing too. He used to show up at all of my fights. Uninvited, I might add. Eventually he came around to me, said he wanted to represent me – said I was something special. I was flattered, y'know? Really excited. There I was, 20 or so, and the most powerful man in the Prefecture wanted to be my agent. Lucky me, right? That's what I thought, but then things got strange. We got to talking and he didn't mean special like 'special boxing talent' he meant special like 'you are God, you will save us all.'"

"What?" *'Who would be stupid enough to think this guy was God?'*

"Yeah, that's what he said. More or less. Might as well keep coming clean with you Billy. I'm a sick man, or at least I used to be. Sick in the head, schizophrenic. Lucky for me, the blue juice takes care of that too."

"I don't know what that means."

"Schizophrenic?"

"Yeah."

"Means I used to hear a voice in my head, heard it all the time. Used to tell me what to do. I used to try and ignore it, had to fight back against it sometimes."

"Oh." *'Great. He's a lunatic.'*

"I'm a man of science. I knew there was an explanation for what was wrong in my head. Just couldn't figure what it was. Years after everything with Wright went down, I finally got a look at a

189

medicine book from overseas. That book clued me in to having been a schizophrenic. Explained my blood condition too, hemophilia – the disease of kings! Ha! But now I'm getting too far ahead of myself. Back to Wright. He tells me the voice in my head is God, and I tell him to shove it. Sure, I'd fight in the matches he set up, but there was no way in hell I'd join up with him on his crazy crusade to save the world. You following all this?"

"I think so. You were a crazy fighter and a black Chancellor who was also a fight promoter told you that you were God. But you aren't. And now you're not crazy anymore. Is that it?"

"Pretty much. The not crazy anymore part doesn't really come in until later though, I was still plenty crazy back when I told Wright to shove it. Now, Trixie, my sorta-wife at the time, she hated watching me fight, never wanted to see her man take a punch. Made sure our daughter Anna never saw any of it either. She was always begging me to retire, settle down and live a normal life. I was about to give in, too. I made up my mind to retire after the Hughson fight. And, in a way I guess I did. The fight got ugly, really ugly. Hughson made me bleed, only time in my life that's ever happened. It wouldn't stop either – the hemophilia I was telling you about."

"The which?"

"Hemophilia. Blood disease. It means once I start bleeding, I don't stop. Normally, my tough skin made it so it didn't matter. Hell, I didn't even know I had the disease until that fight. But, Hughson split me open and I started gushing like crazy. I'll never forget that feeling, felt like my life-force was dripping out of me. It put me into some kind of rage. I ended up killing him, Hughson."

'I knew it!'

"I still feel bad about that. He was just another stupid kid like me, and I beat him to death for a few bucks. I'd feel worse if Wright wasn't his agent."

"So... Norm, Ry and Mona are Hughson's kids? I didn't think they were related. If Mona was my sister..." Billy wasn't sure how to finish that sentence.

"What? No! Ha! No! Still thinking about the murder part, huh? Yeah, don't count Hughson in any of that. I'll get to that part soon, though."

'He's a murderer. An actual honest-to-God murderer. Or he's a liar.'

"So, Hughson's dead and I'm damn close to it. They had to take me out on a stretcher, but I never made it to the hospital. Wasn't even wheeled into an ambulance, the paramedic lady – wait, you know her! It was Gretl who carted me out of there."

"Gretl? Huh." *'Where the hell is this going?'*

"Yep. Anyhow, she skips the ambulance entirely, had a hearse waiting for me. Scared? Ha! You bet I was scared! Hell, I wasn't dead yet! Turns out it was all part of an act, or something. Trying to make things extra dramatic for me, I guess. A gentleman who went by the name of Satan was lounging in the back, had this blue juice drip ready and waiting." Clint gave an emphatic snort to send a rush of blue juice into his nose.

'Satan?' "Um, Satan?"

"It's just a name, that's all. Something to keep him straight from the rest of the weirdoes. No shortage of weirdoes out this way, even back then. Anyhow, this guy put on one hell of a show. Real theatrical. Left a big impression on me, even though I never really got a good look at him. You know those lights that make white things glow purple?"

"Uh yeah, I think." Billy had no clue what Clint was talking about. But, he needed to hear as much about Satan as Clint was willing to tell. Even if it was 'just a name' it was a name that had forever haunted Billy's dreams. The last thing he wanted was for his new boss to get sidetracked talking about lights.

"He had those lights set up in the back of the hearse, lots of 'em. I could see his track suit glow purple and I could see his headband glow purple, sure couldn't see his face though. Just a jet black smudge. Now, I couldn't see him, but I sure did listen to him. He knew what he was talking about, must've had some kind of insider tip or something. He tells me Wright got to Trixie, he got her to dope me with some kind of bleeding powder. Bitch. No. No, I shouldn't say that. She's Anna's mom." Clint paused. "I never saw them again after that night, Trixie or Anna. Can't say I wanted much to do with Trixie after she tried to kill me. But, Anna... I just hope she got out of the Prefecture, one way or the other. This is no place for a sweet kid like her."

Billy let it all sink in as Clint got quiet again and maybe grew close to tears. It was hard to tell through his permanent squint. *'How many Satans could there be?'*

Clint perked back up quickly enough. "Don't mean to drag things down too much, I still have to get to the bad part of the story! Don't worry, it gets real uplifting first. This Satan guy, he saved my life. Hooked me up with this weird rig here, stopped the bleeding no problem. Made my skin tougher than ever. He says he got the secret for making my skin tough from some guy in Italy, seemed to be really proud about that. Don't know why. Didn't matter to me where the juice came from, just so long as it worked. And it worked. Worked like crazy! Best thing about it, the juice even stopped that voice in my head. Haven't heard word one from that mouthy bastard for years! And, get this, on top of all that, even after everything he did for me, Satan didn't charge me a cent."

'Think Billy! How does this all tie together? Satan's sort of a doctor. He wears a tracksuit. He's been to Italy. Or he knows someone in Italy. He can fix crazy head voices and bleeding. Gretl knows him... Jesus Christ! None of this has anything to do with me!'

"And you're sure his name was Satan, this guy who fixed you up?"

Clint looked confused. "Well, I didn't see his birth certificate if that's what you mean, but, yeah that was his name. I mean, it's not the kind of name I was going to forget."

"OK. Right." Billy could tell Clint's well of Satanic knowledge had dried up and decided against pressing any further. He hadn't been able to mine him for any information of substance. Knowing that a man named Satan was a philanthropic hearse doctor was... well, in Billy's mind it was no better than being left completely in the dark.

Clint stood up from his perch on the mattress and began to pace back and forth as he changed the topic of conversation. "You rode in with parts, didn't you?"

"Parts? You mean, like, body parts? Yeah. Garbage Bag had a bus full." Billy wasn't pleased to relive the memory.

"Smelling the way you did yesterday, I figured that had to be the case. Yeah, Garbage Bag has been in the parts business for a long time, longer than I've been down here at least. Hell, I wouldn't have been able to get started down here if it weren't for that guy. Didn't even have a chance to get used to these nose tubes before I got his number through Gretl. And then, well..."

"Clint, what are you talking about? What do Garbage Bag and body parts have to do with anything?"

"This is the bad part of the story Billy. Try to keep an open mind, OK?" Clint took a deep breath and gave the ceiling a long hard stare. "Those body parts came from somewhere. From somebody. Somebodies. I don't know where the batch you were riding with came from. Don't want to know. What I do know, is that if you had been riding with Garbage Bag and a pile of parts in the 1980s... 1990s..." Clint lowered his voice to a near whisper. "I would've been the man responsible for those piles."

'Oh God!' Billy was appalled. Not only by Clint's admission, but by the sheer scale of his crimes. One bus full of chopped corpses was vile enough. Who knows how many bus trips Garbage Bag made over two decades. *'How many people did Clint kill?'*

"That's disgusting!"

Clint crouched down next to Billy. Billy flinched back away from him.

"I know. It sounds bad. Really bad. But, you have to understand, things were different back then. Worse than they are now. Far worse. Those were the Rooster Liquor days."

'What the hell?'

"Rooster Liquor?"

"Yeah kid. Worst thing that ever happened to M Prefecture, bombs included."

"I don't get it." Billy's curiosity overpowered his growing distrust.

"It was a drug. Addictive. Rotted people's minds, tore apart their decency. We didn't have much after the bombs fell. We didn't have anything after Rooster Liquor. It turned the city into a depraved hole. No one cared about anything aside from getting their hands on another bottle. I never drank the stuff."

"Too busy killing people?" Billy made no attempt to hide his disdain.

"Hey!" Clint straightened from his crouch. "Open mind? Please? I never drank the stuff because it was a city drug. I had to leave the city after the fight. Compelled to, like my brain wouldn't let me go back. Satan told me about this cave, said it would make for a good place to live. Seemed like a good idea. I spent some time laying low in a motel, then moved in here as soon as they could run a phone line out this way."

'I thought he was down here to hide his pornography business? How is living in a cave a good idea?'

"Now, this place wasn't always decked out like this. It was a lot more, I don't know, cave-like when I first made my way down here. Thing is, I didn't care much for living in the dark and I was starting to go hungry too. So I called Gretl up. She told me to be in touch if I ever needed anything. And I needed lots of things. She never showed, but Garbage Bag did. Scared the hell out of me, big green guy and all. He tells me Gretl sent him. Tells me his story, about the deal he and Dr. Timothy made. New skin for tons, like, literal tons of body parts. Told me he could get me set up down here if I helped him out. So I did."

'That's the debt Garbage Bag had to repay? Goddamnit, are there any decent human beings out here?'

"Before Trixie tried to do me in, I never would have... acted the way I did. Never. Something changed inside of me after that fight, though. I guess maybe since I didn't have to be a good dad anymore, I... Ah, hell I don't know. Doesn't matter why I did what I did. I just did it. I used to go into town at night. Late night. I was gentle. I'd find somebody passed out on the street, put a pillow over their face until the deed was done then I'd drag 'em to the bank.

Buzz Dr. Timothy, have him put the body on Garbage Bag's tab then wait for Garbage Bag to bring me stuff for the cave. Hey, I see the look you're giving me and I deserve it. In my defense, it wasn't like I would pick off anybody healthy, just the low lying fruit – the ones who were a bottle or two away from death anyhow."

"You're a real saint." By this point, Billy had forgiven himself for what happened to the Lollipop of a Man the day earlier. He hadn't sentenced him to death by desert heat; he had spared him from death by boulder. Clint was a murderer and Billy had stopped him from claiming another victim.

"It's not as bad as it seems. Like Ry said, the kids wouldn't be here with me if it wasn't for what, uh, what happened to their parents. It might not seem like it now, but I'm not a monster. I sped up the inevitable, sure. And yeah, I did it for personal gain. But, I got the kids out of some bad spots too. Started up a new family, I wanted to give them a better life."

'Better than what? This is no family. This is sick.'

"Ry was first, back in '90. I couldn't very well leave a three year old who couldn't see alone on the street. Then came Norm. '95? '96? One of those two. He was a little bit older when I picked him up, smaller though. A few more years went by before I brought Mona home. Probably 2004 or so. I'm damn lucky I found her when I did. She's a real rare one, a girl in M. She probably would've been able to take care of herself if she wasn't, y'know..."

"Yeah..." Clint's story left Billy feeling numb. He hoped that the more he agreed with Clint, the sooner it would be over.

"Once I found Mona, I knew my days of working with Garbage Bag were over. Didn't feel... right anymore. Something about having a daughter again, I don't know... So, I started up a new business. I even managed to put these kids to work. See? Not so bad, right? Altruistic even!"

'She's not your daughter. Fathers don't whore out their daughters. I'm getting Mona out of here.'

Billy stood from his spot on Clint's mattress, eager to make an exit. "Oh, yeah. I see your point now. I probably would have done the same thing. Listen, I'm really tired. I think I'm going to get some sleep." He wasn't certain what the time was but it felt as though Clint had talked for a week. It couldn't have been laughably early as Clint didn't offer Billy any challenge as he made his way out through the black beaded curtain.

'There must be something wrong with Clint. He almost seems like a good guy, but... He did say he was crazy... maybe the blue juice didn't fix him at all. Satan's blue juice. Satan. God, I wish I was back in the group home.'

Billy wasn't tired. He pored over *Gentleman Gerald on Pugilism*, eager to fill his head with anything other than thoughts of what Clint had done. The book was illustrated in great detail; the writing was scarce and simply phrased. It was as if it had been written specifically for Billy. He read it, re-read it and re-read it once more. This marked the first time Billy had even considered reading a book more than once.

His interest piqued, Billy checked inside the front cover to see if there was anything more to learn about Gentleman Gerald. There wasn't. Just a publishing date. 'Printed by Proud American Punching Press. K Prefecture, U.S.A. 1942.' Billy knew something was wrong with the line of typeset text, but he couldn't quite figure out what. Then it hit him.

'K Prefecture, U.S.A.'

Any lingering hopes that Billy was trapped in some kind of elaborate ruse were erased. The simple reference to a place and a time that no longer existed convinced him that everything he had learned in F had indeed been a lie. Billy wished that he could say the same about everything he had learned in M.

CHAPTER 22 - COXWELL

TAIPEI, ETERNALLY FREE TAIWAN

SATURDAY, JUNE 26, 2010

As far as Zhang could tell, his supernatural immortality came with only one trade off; complete and utter impotence. The longer he went without any form of sexual activity, the less he missed it. Any second thoughts he may have had about making his pact withered and died decades ago. The fleeting pleasures gleaned from furtive sexual exploits in his youth were nothing compared to the long lasting euphoric rush he felt every time he flexed his diplomatic muscle on the world stage. The downside to his flaccidity was that he was forced to fake the lifestyle befitting a man of his great importance. While chemically induced asexuality wasn't a concern to Zhang, keeping up appearances certainly was.

Twice a week, a parade of Eternally Free Taiwan's most beautiful concubines would file into Zhang's private chambers. The girls worked in shifts. Some would quietly discuss gardening and the latest trends in mens fashion with the President for Life. The rest would enthusiastically act as if they were in the throes of passion;

moaning orgasmically, making certain to drown out Zhang's small
talk. Then, they would file out, sometimes one by one, sometimes
in small groups. No matter who they left with, they always left
looking the same; appropriately bow-legged, half dressed, hair
mussed and makeup smeared. Occasionally, rumors that Zhang
impregnated a concubine would 'leak' to the Eternally Free
Taiwanese tabloid press to help bolster Zhang's ruse. He had been
maintaining this well choreographed routine for over a century.

Variations from this fraudulent display of virility were rare and
only occurred under great duress. A phone call during that evening's
faux orgy forced Zhang to stray from his routine. The concubines
did not file out, nor did they leave in pairs. They were shooed out
en masse, fully clothed and looking suspiciously prim. Keeping up
appearances had to take a back seat to compulsory loyalty; Satan
was on the line with a favor to ask.

Satan didn't wish to leave the American colonies, but it was
clear the time had come to move on. He was going to miss his
depraved little playground; he had accomplished so much there.
Orchestrating a civil war under Zhang's nose proved to be great fun.
Initially the war was only meant to serve as a distraction, a skirmish
steeped in just enough violence to prevent the Ashanti Orthodox
from easily locating the Messiah as he came of age. The war served
its purpose, and then some. Had Satan known his war would usher
in an era of warped misery, he would have held one years earlier,
Messiah or no. And the Messiah? Satan hadn't enjoyed a project like
Clint Masters in ages. Mentally reprogramming the man who
would be Christ under the guise of saving his life was a nice little
coup, but the act paled in comparison to what followed. Satan
marveled as Gretl called with periodic reports culled from her

network of mouthy lowlifes. His heavenly pious enemy took to murder? Then to murder and kidnapping? And then to sexually exploiting a mentally deficient minor solely for financial gain? Exquisite.

For years he had kept close enough to monitor the moral slide of Clint Masters and the fall of M along with him, but far enough away to avoid arousing suspicion. Now, his position had been compromised. The laughable threat from the skies was neutralized, but Satan knew that staying put could prove risky. There was no chance the second wave of attack could be as pitiful as the first. He could no longer keep close tabs on Masters, that was unfortunate. However, he could wrest political control over more than half the globe from Zhang. That would have to do.

"I look forward to it." Was all Zhang was able to say before their conversation was cut short by the click of the receiver on Satan's end. There was little else Zhang could have, or should have said. Satan's message was direct and firm. He would be moving into the penthouse suite of the Erect Dragon. He would arrive within the week. His stay would be indefinite. Zhang began to suspect that he was on the verge of paying the full price for his powerful lot in life.

Earlier that day, there had been only one pillar of light radiating over the old Coxwell Motel. Life 29 took a page from the coward's playbook and chose to retreat. It was a decision as wise as it was craven; the battle was over before it had begun.

Abundance 12 had kicked his way through three dry-rotten motel doors in a search for Satan's spawn without result. The prize lay in wait behind the fourth door. It was not who the Four Friars had been expecting. Should they have been prepared for an ambush? Always. They were not prepared. The Four Friars preached caution and constant vigilance in their hunt for Satan. Their ideals held little weight. The Knights in Satan's Service had claimed the lives of 49 previous Friars. The caution and vigilance preached did nothing to help those men. That afternoon marked the first face to face encounter between the Ghanaian Holy Men and Satan himself. They were sloppy, rash. They paid dearly for it.

Abundance 12 never made it into the fourth motel room. Not entirely. Not alive. His leg breached the flimsy barrier only to be snatched from within. His screams echoed throughout the vast rocky landscape as he attempted to hop away, eyes wide, down to three limbs. Blood spurted in jets from his hip, soaking the ground. Ethereal flames licked the ceiling of room 104, spilling out through the door frame. Abundance couldn't hop far before being grabbed by the flames and dragged back inside.

Daunted, but intrinsically brave, Peace 9 and Prosperity 4 recklessly followed Abundance 12's lead. One after the other, they met the same bloody fate; sucked within room 104 as if by magic, screaming out in agony as their limbs were torn from their torsos.

If one or more of the Four Friars was to fall in battle, the survivors were to return to Accra to lick their wounds and aid in the selection of replacement members. The official protocol of the Four Friars made this clear. Unofficially, the protocol was openly mocked, derided as gutless. Within the ranks, it was expected that in battle with Satan and the Knights in Satan's Service you were to return to Ghana victorious or you were not to return. Life 29's peers would have expected him to join his 28 forbearers amongst the ranks of the fallen. Life 29 never set foot within room 104. Following protocol in a cowardly, rational act of self preservation, he made a hasty retreat skyward as Peace and Prosperity met their grisly fates.

He never made it back to Accra. Really, he never came close.

As one of the Four Friars, rather, as the newly minted leader of the Four Friars, Life 29 had a sworn duty to destroy Satan and his Knights. That was not all that was expected of him, however. As a member of the Ashanti Orthodox, he also had an ideological duty to help those in need. The man Life 29 saw as he ascended eastwards was definitely in need. At least he appeared to be a man. The heat signature readouts displayed on the interior of Life's golden sphere matched those of a man with a bad fever. The enhanced visual display told a slightly different story.

Safely separated from the Coxwell Motel by miles of desert, Life 29 aborted the atmospheric launch stage of his retreat, aiming to set down next to the man crawling towards Tierra Podrida. The naked, pockmarked man's grotesque disfigurement grew increasingly obvious as Life made his way to the ground; he was bloated through the mid section and scrawny everywhere else. His unique body shape wasn't what forced him to awkwardly crawl through the desert, seemingly at death's door. From the looks of it, horrible bruising and still oozing lacerations, he had sustained quite the beating.

Night was beginning to fall; the pillar of light shone brilliantly over the man struggling to propel himself forward. The beaten man shielded his eyes as best he could and shirked backwards, trying to escape the mysterious glow. The Holy Man landed before he had the chance.

"You poor soul." Life 29 said softly, his golden orb fading from view. His tone soothed the bloodied man; he offered no resistance as Life produced his first aid kit and began to anoint his wounds. The fear in the man's eyes disappeared as Life injected him with a blend of amphetamines and painkillers.

"Who... who... thank.. you..." gurgled the Lollipop of a Man, looking up at his savior with great reverence, eyes as wide as the bruising would allow.

"You should be alright, now." Life spoke with conviction. The man's injuries were dire, but not life threatening. "Who has done such horrible things to you my child?"

"Clint. They called him Clint. And there was a half man. And a man with no eyes." The name Clint meant nothing to Life 29, neither did the descriptions of his accomplices. The Lollipop of a Man continued his labored list of assailants. "And some kid dressed in a bloody grey suit." This piqued Life 29's interest. Images of students in their grey suits gawking at him from Castillo classroom windows flashed through his mind. It was a long shot, but... He produced Billy's yearbook photo.

"Is this the young man you speak of?"

The Lollipop of a Man squinted in the dimming light. "I think so. Yeah. That's him."

"Where can I find him now?"

"Some cave, out there..." he made a weak sweeping gesture, indicating somewhere out west.

"Thank you. I will see to it that this deed will not go unpunished." Life 29's conditioning enabled him to disguise his emotion, the timber of his voice betrayed no hint of his excitement. Destroying the child was his chance to return a hero. He knew firsthand he was no match for Satan, but judging by the yearbook photo, this Billy Lopez was no one to be feared. He would not rest until the child was dead. That is, once he was certain the oddly shaped man would be safe. "Can I escort you into town?"

The Lollipop of a Man wanted to take this mysterious Holy Man up on his offer, but knowing his employer's view of the church, he decided it wouldn't be a good idea. Plus, he no longer felt as though his death in the desert was inevitable; with the drugs coursing through his system he could shuffle his way back.

"No. No thanks. I can make it. Thanks again." He stood with grim determination and began taking slow strides towards Tierra Podrida. Life 29 couldn't determine if his odd gait was attributable to the injuries he had sustained or to his physical deformities. He knew one thing for certain, it would be best if this strange man was given something to wear.

"Can I offer you my robe? Surely you could use something to protect you from the elements, something to shield you from committing the sin of nudity?"

The Lollipop of a Man bellowed "No!" without turning back. He knew he was in deep enough trouble with his boss already. Strolling back into Saint Basil's wearing an Ashanti Orthodox robe would make things far worse.

"Very well, if that is was you wish. Be well, my child." With that, Life 29 hovered over the desert once more. Heading west, optimistically blind to the difficulty of the search that lay ahead.

CHAPTER 23 - MEET THE PERVERT

20.3 MILES SOUTHWEST OF TIERRA PODRIDA,
M PREFECTURE, THE UNION

SUNDAY, JUNE 27, 2010

PANG **PANG** **PANG** **PANG**

Billy bolted upright in bed. In the windowless, clockless 'room' he had no concept of the time, but he knew it felt early. The metallic banging stopped; he could hear Clint through the beaded curtain.

"Billy! C'mon Billy! Time to get dressed and get stretched! We've got dreams to sell! Sexy, sexy dreams!"

Ugh. Billy felt stiff and groggy, but he had a job to do. Or so it seemed. He knew he'd be doing some running and Clint made it seem like he'd be selling lottery tickets too, but he was still unclear on the exact details.

Judging by what happened to The Lollipop of a Man and the stories Clint told him the night before, things were going to get unsavory. Billy knew that much. He also knew that until he figured out the ebb and flow of Clint's debaucherous operation, he'd never know the right time to make a break for it. Not only that, but without a better understanding of the lay of the land, he wouldn't know the first thing about where to go. Or where Mona would be safe. He sure didn't want to, but Billy knew he'd have to play along. For now.

"OK Clint, be right out."

Norm was waiting for them at the base of the ladder. "Here, it's cut and ready to go." He said as he tossed a videocassette tape to Clint in an impressive act of one armed balance.

'Oh, that kind of tape! That's what Clint meant!' Billy was shocked to see a cassette. He had vague memories of watching tapes on a VCR back in F. But he was a toddler then. *'Christ, this place is like some God awful time machine. Why don't they have Laserdiscs?'*

"Clint, you sure about using all of this tape? It's pretty sick at the end, don't you think?" Norm's voice had a faint pleading air to it, as if he was trying to soft sell Clint into passing on what he had filmed. Clint wasn't buying.

"Sick sells my good man! Or... So I assume. Only one way to find out! Make sure Mona gets some rest today, OK?"

"Yeah, yeah."

"Thanks Norm, don't know what I'd do without you."

"You'd have to hold the camera. It's pretty easy."

Clint climbed the ladder first and crawled out into the darkness with Billy following closely behind. The clock that was Billy's tired, aching body was right – it was early. The first sliver of sun illuminated the eastern sky ahead of them.

"So, first day on the job." Clint said with his hands on his hips, stretching his back, chest pointed up at the dark blue sky. "You excited?"

"A little, a little confused too. I'm still not entirely sure what I'm supposed to be doing here." Billy was hoping to fish Clint for a quick jolt of information, anything to help him get a leg up on his escape plan. When he started working in Castillo's cafeteria, Imelda gave him a list of exactly what he had to do and exactly when he was to do it. If he could get his hands on a list like Imelda's... "Think maybe you could make me a list of things you want me to do? Or maybe some kind of work schedule?"

"I'm not big on lists or schedules, Billy. I'm also all out of paper. Listen. Don't worry about any of that stuff for today. All you need to know right now is that we're headed to Tierra Podrida. After that, well, just follow my lead."

Jesus... Just give me one straight answer.'

They set out towards town in a slow jog, with Clint setting the pace. To Billy it was agonizingly slow. By the time they were close to town, they had been jogging for over three hours. It was now morning, not just technically morning. They were atop the same crest overlooking town that Garbage Bag had sped down days earlier. The breadth of Tierra Podrida spread out before them on the horizon; men the size of pinpoints were slowly making their way from their squat grey houses to the smooth white factory. It wouldn't be long before Clint and Billy reached the crumbling core.

Clint signaled for Billy to stop. He gestured down below to the dots of humanity swarming across the swath of dusty brown land. "This place is pretty depressing right? No need to answer, of course it is! But it's still profitable and that's why we're here. Hell, that's why those EFT bastards are still here, too. Unlike the rest of the world, they haven't given up on this place, not as long as everyone keeps slaving away at that factory."

Clint's talk about being a free man still rung in Billy's ears. He knew better than to suggest positives about making an honest living in the factory if he wanted to avoid another self righteous earful.

"Yeah, this place doesn't look so hot." Billy wasn't lying. Time had not been kind to Tierra Podrida. And Tierra Podrida was ugly when it was founded.

They made their way into the residential section the slow laborious way, taking a narrow winding trail down from the escarpment. Billy was awfully glad Clint didn't choose to take Garbage Bag's route into town. Clint led the way past dozens of seemingly identical cinderblock and tin shacks, each left to slowly deteriorate in the sun. He stopped Billy short in front of one of the hovels. #215 Progress Ave.

"Remember this spot, Billy. Most important building in town as far as you're concerned."

"This place?"

"You bet. This beautiful palace is home to The Pervert. He does all my dubbing for me – you'll be bringing him the master tapes." Clint said, holding up the videocassette. Billy didn't know what the hell 'dubbing' was and he didn't stop to put together what Clint could've been meant by 'master tape'. He had a bigger question on his mind.

"The Pervert?"

"You'll be the best of friends! He's a super individual that Pervert! You'll love him! C'mon, he's always home."

'Uh...'

KNOCK KNOCK

"Is that the Master? Is the new Master ready?" Came the wheezy reply from within.

"Yep, it's ready, like always. Can we come in?"

"Yeah. We?"

The door swung open, the inhabitant of #215 apparently not interested in waiting to hear the answer to his own question. The Pervert, as he was known to Clint, was a sweaty, greasy little man with horribly atrophied, gnarled stump limbs. His eyes were tiny, so small you couldn't tell at a glance whether or not they consisted of anything other than pupils. 30? 40? Billy couldn't guess his age.

"Oooh! Oooh! Don't keep me waiting! Bring it in, bring it in!" The Pervert made a surprisingly quick waddle-dash to his reclined swivel chair and scrambled up into it. He absentmindedly rubbed his jockey-shorted crotch bulge through his slimy, wide open, mint-green polyester robe. Billy made no effort to disguise his full body shudder.

The small square room looked like it made up almost all of the house. There was a door opposite the entrance that had to led somewhere, but judging by the house's modest exterior it couldn't lead far. The room itself was as stark as it was stained. The air smelled salty. The cracked, chipping concrete floor was littered with wadded up sustenance gel pouches and a variety of suspicious cylindrical items and hollowed out sundry. A washbasin bolted to the wall served as the only household convenience. The rest of the space was devoted to pornography. The wall to the left of the entrance was stacked floor to ceiling with TVs and VCRs, each TV showing Mona in a compromising position with a different man.

'Holy...' The half naked, deformed man. The squalor. The forest of televised cocks thrusting in and out of Mona. It was almost too much for Billy to take in.

"Who's this?" The Pervert asked without as much as a glance in Billy's direction.

"This is Bil..." Clint cut himself off "This is Mr. Lopez. An associate of mine."

"What do I care? Just give me the Master. I'll call you when the dubs are ready."

"You're the boss." Clint handed him the tape. The Pervert snatched it and spun to face the glowing wall of sex.

"Oooh! I can't wait! Ooooooh!" The Pervert wriggled out of his nestlike chair and lurched towards the VCRs. Clint clucked his tongue and made a gesture to Billy, his head and thumb cocked towards the exit. Billy wasted no time in picking up on Clint's cue. They made it outside before The Pervert was able to hit play.

Billy let loose a giant exhale as he and Clint hustled down Progress. Clint slapped his back with a laugh. "So, how do you like your new best friend?"

Billy broke out laughing with a chortle. "What do I care? Just give me the Master!" his Pervert impression was pretty good. "Does he have a real name?"

"Maybe, but not one I know. The Pervert is how he introduced himself, believe it or not. He lives up to it too. I can't stand him, but he works quick and practically free. That little twerp's got a real thing for Mona. Not that he's the only one. Ha! He'll do anything for a tape, though – and that includes making us tons of copies. Hungry?"

"Yeah actually, really hungry" Billy was amazed he had any appetite at all. Not only was he surprised by his rumbling stomach, he was caught off guard to find himself in a good mood. Billy felt as though he'd accomplished a fair bit that morning. Now he knew Clint liked to get an early start. He knew just how to get into town. And, he knew without any doubt that when it came time to run with Mona, they sure as hell wouldn't be paying The Pervert a visit.

"Me too. Let's get some lunch."

"Hey stud. Wanna party?" The voice came from the gutter that ringed the town square. She was sprawled out on the curb, legs splayed, her short skirt draping just low enough to maintain her last shred of dignity. Billy knew she was old, even if her face didn't quite tell that story. Her skin was pulled taut over her sharp cheekbones. Her bright red lips didn't quite move with her mouth as they should, jiggling long after she stopped speaking. Her eye makeup looked as though it had been drawn on in permanent marker and then left to fade in the sun. The work on her face was nothing compared to what was done to her body. She wore multiple sets of mismatched bikini tops, barely covering the rows of breasts that had been grafted onto her torso. "I wanna party!" She began aggressively miming fellatio with a bone dry bottle. There was a woodcut print of a Rooster on the label.

Any appetite Billy once had dried up.

"Uh, oh God! Um..."

"Ha ha! Leave him alone Pretty Becky! He's on the clock!"

Clint took Billy by the arm and quickly led him away from the painted sow-woman. Billy didn't dare speak until they were across the street from the town square.

"Thanks! What was... Who... I mean..."

"Try not to be too hard on poor ol' Pretty Becky. She's a relic, a product of the Rooster Liquor era. She's only trying to make a living like everyone else. Just so happens her method of making a living is nasty enough to turn a man's dick inside out. And that's a good thing, believe it or not. With gutter beauties with her as our competition, it's no wonder I don't have a hard time moving these!" Clint said, reaching into his pants pocket and fanning out a stack of tickets with a flourish. "And it's not just the tickets that move fast, my tapes fly off the shelves! They're rarely on shelves, actually, and not literally flying of course..." Billy didn't tune Clint out intentionally, but his attention had shifted to the big butt in the tiny navy blue shorts swaying back and forth in front of him.

"Billy. Billy! C'mere!"

Clint grabbed Billy squarely by the shoulders and slammed him against a steel door, spilling into a dingy little restaurant. It didn't look like the man behind the counter was expecting anyone; all of the chairs were upturned on the tables.

"Jesus Christ! You are *so* lucky we were right outside Rollo's. Hey there, Rollo." Clint nodded to the old man, who slowly nodded back. His face was an odd patchwork, mostly freckled and leathery with strips of younger, pinker flesh scattered around his mouth and eyes. By the time Rollo had completed the upwards half of his nod, Clint had turned his frantic attention back to Billy. "Never, ever let yourself get hypnotized by an ass out on the streets! She was a Beat Cop, Billy, and that is *exactly* how the Beat Cops lure you in!"

"Beat Cops?"

"Yeah, pull up a chair." Billy did as he was told, overturning a chair for himself, then another for Clint. "Beat Cops – lady pimp death squad. Hot body right?"

"Yeah, I'll say." *'Lady pimp death squad?'*

"Hi Clint. Can I get you and your friend something?" Rollo asked as he shuffled towards their table.

"Sure, two soups. Thanks." Clint waited until Rollo shuffled back into the kitchen before continuing. "Course they're hot. That's what you're supposed to think, moth to the flame – see the mustache?"

"Uh... Mustache?" Billy wondered if M had any slang he had yet to pick up on.

"That's right; consider yourself warned – big thick ol' mustaches. One minute it's all 'Ooh, yeah!' and the next, it's nothing but 'Ugh, no!' Attraction and repulsion are powerful forces, so keep a cool head."

'Like, a real mustache?' "OK sure, but..."

"Here you go, guys." Rollo returned from the kitchen and set two bowls of murky brown in front of his guests. He was missing all of his right hand, apart from his index finger, thumb and a thin wedge of flesh that joined them to his wrist.

"Thanks." Clint paused until Rollo was out of earshot. Even then, he spoke in a half whisper. "Billy, I agreed to take you in for a reason; and running from the Beat Cops is a big part of that reason. You don't want to mess with them, ever. If there's trouble in town you need to bolt back to the cave, no questions asked, OK? Nasty as she may be, Pretty Becky and the rest of the working girls here in M still do kinda well for themselves. And the Beat Cops? They make damn sure they get a slice of whatever pie those girls are bringing home. Thing is, the better the tapes do, the smaller that pie is going to be. You follow?"

"More or less."

"Good enough. Listen, all you really need to know is when in doubt, run. Fast."

"Sure. OK." Billy took a sip of his soup. It was vile. He leaned into Clint, mouth covered. "What *is* this?"

"Like it? It's boiled desert. Some of the best boiled desert I've had, too." Clint's reply was completely free of sarcasm.

'I hate M Prefecture.' Billy had his fill of lunch, but he was eager to reap as much information as Clint was willing to provide. He needed out.

"So, where do they come from, the Beat Cops? Who's in charge?"

"The factory's in charge. But, not in charge of the Beat Cops." Clint said with a slight slurp, polishing off another spoonful of brown liquid.

Billy cut to the chase. "That doesn't make any sense!"

"Damn straight, welcome to M." Clint replied without batting an eye, completely missing Billy's intent, but catching his exasperated tone. "If you're so big on matters of authority, tell me. Where did the cops in F come from? Who's in charge there?"

Billy knew that question wasn't a fair one, not fair to him at least. Billy would have loved to put the old pornographer square in his place with a detailed account of law and order in F. Thing is, he had no idea how the police force back home was run.

"Yeah, yeah, alright, fair enough. I don't know. What's with their name then?"

"They'll beat your ass, Billy. What do you think?"

"Oh."

Clint set his spoon down in his empty bowl and looked at Billy's, still full of boiled desert. "You ready to go?"

"I guess."

"Alright, let's move some tickets." Clint produced the stack of tickets from his pocket and peeled two off as payment for lunch. "Feeling lucky Rollo?"

"Lucky enough!" Rollo made his way back to the table to bus their plates. He tucked the tickets into the pouch of his apron. "Thanks Clint. Knowing that I have a chance to nail that broad is just about all that keeps me going."

"Ha! You're not the only one, Rollo! You're not the only one. See you around. Maybe soon, if things go your way."

"Hope so. Dear God, I hope so."

Billy shielded his eyes from the noon-time sun as they stepped out onto the street. Clint's squint accomplished the same effect.

"He's a good guy that Rollo. Course, I'd say that about any man who hasn't sold his soul to the factory. Speaking of, want to check out the belly of the beast?"

Billy did, badly. He needed to know what his options were. He needed to know what could be worse than a life of making dirty movies in a cave or selling dirty soup near freaky hookers.

"I can't wait."

CHAPTER 24 - RETURN OF THE FRUITLESS ASSASSIN

TIERRA PODRIDA, M PREFECTURE, THE UNION

SUNDAY, JUNE 27, 2010

Brian Gordonson was a thief by trade and a henchman by chance. He had set off to work in the Phase 2 Manufacturing Center just after the turn of the 21st century. Like the most men in post-war M, he began working in his early teens; childhoods spent without purpose, guidance or readily available food tended to be short-lived. He was not a smart man. None of the men born to Rooster Liquor addicts were particularly bright. Physical deformity and early death had been bred into M through tainted sustenance gel; Prefecture-wide stupidity was part of Rooster Liquor's lasting legacy.

With his youthful vigor and an intellect best suited to menial tasks, he should have made for an ideal employee at the Phase 2. Unfortunately for Gordonson, his oversized torso and spindly limbs were not conducive to spinning the turbines in the factory. Decidedly ill-fitting in a machine designed to harness the energy of the average physique, he couldn't complete the rotations he needed to sustain himself. No matter how hard he labored in the conversion dynamo, he never came close to meeting his daily wattage quota. Gordonson didn't last a week in the Phase 2.

He turned to burglary to feed himself. It was a simple job. The quality of the town's locks left a lot to be desired and he had firsthand knowledge of when the rest of the men would be at work. The downside was that by the time Gordonson turned to a life of crime, no one in Tierra Podrida had anything worth stealing. Sure, he could snag a few sustenance gel pouches here and there, it did keep him fed, but as the weeks spent burglarizing turned into months, Gordonson felt the urge for a bigger score.

To the best of the Black Pope's knowledge, pornographic video cassettes appeared out of nowhere in 2004. By 2005, the cassettes were everywhere.

Combination TV/VCRs were one of the last things the workers of M were able to purchase from the old factory. They proved to be incredibly popular, nearly everyone ended up buying one back in the late 70s. The big grey boxes weren't only popular, they were heavy; far too heavy to casually trade for bottles of Rooster Liquor. Nearly 30 years after they were taken off the market, you could still find a TV/VCR in almost every shack in Tierra Podrida. The VCRs sat unused for years; they weren't much good unless you had a tape to watch. Once the porno cassettes hit the market, VCRs were whirring all over town.

This made the Black Pope furious. *He* was to control vice! Not... not... His inability to place blame on anyone only angered him further. Not only had he lost his sex trade monopoly, his profits from pandering were down across the board. Men who once laid with his bevy of working girls were becoming content to stay home and take matters into their own hands, so to speak. This would not do. He could not lose control of M's underworld. Without Dr. Timothy's aid, The Black Pope feared that which could not be was close to coming to pass.

He and Dr. Timothy had grown increasingly distant over the years; speaking less frequently, rarely seeing one another in person. This was all Dr. Timothy's doing, he seemed to make a point of avoiding the Black Pope as best he could. The Black Pope had never been able to figure out why his right hand man was abandoning him. There was no falling out between the two, just a slow steady drift apart. Dr. Timothy had been unable to round up a fourth subject for Beat Cop conversion. Could that be why he grew cold? Fear of failing to please the man he once considered his partner? If that was the case, it was certainly out of character. The Black Pope didn't know Dr. Timothy to fear anything.

By the time the porno tapes were established as a full-fledged societal mainstay in Tierra Podrida, Dr. Timothy had become almost completely incommunicado, fortified behind the bank vault door. He and the Black Pope had not met face to face in months. Dr. Timothy refused to venture outside of his vault. Even worse, he refused to produce any more Rooster Liquor. The Black Pope's pleas had no effect. Dr. Timothy said his heart just wasn't in it any longer and that there was nothing more to the matter. The last batch was brewed in October 2007, drunk dry halfway through that November.

Tierra Podrida was sobering up and the Black Pope's fears that he was losing his grip were becoming reality. His empire of vice was shrinking without a reliable man about town to do his bidding. The Beat Cops served their violent purpose on the streets and their sexual purpose within Saint Basil's. But, he needed a proper representative amongst the people. He needed a new Dr. Timothy.

It was Brian Gordonson's desire to steal bigger, better things that eventually led him to Saint Basil's Cathedral and Nightclub. It took him quite a while to get there, his addled brain kept Gordonson mired in a fog of petty crime for years. He was terrible at following instructions, even his own. He would forget his meager goal of being a better thief for months on end; falling back into his simple pattern of break-and-enters for sustenance gel. Tierra Podrida was still suffering from Rooster Liquor withdrawal when he finally hit upon the notion of looking outside the town's core for better stealables. It was January 2008, Gordonson was 23 years old. He had spent nearly half his life re-remembering to improve himself through better thievery.

When Gordonson chanced upon the converted warehouse, he found far more than he had ever dreamed of stealing. Mounds and mounds of pre-war items were haphazardly stacked in the shadow of the spiral dome. Gordonson couldn't recognize most of the piled goods, he was fascinated by them nonetheless. Some of the seemingly ancient junk was so intricate, so complex... He forgot all about theft. Gordonson wanted to play, to test out this mysterious bounty. Engrossed with his new toys, he failed to notice the enormous, porcelain masked black man and his trio of mustachioed amazons as they approached from behind. Circumstance and good timing were all that kept Brian Gordonson alive that afternoon.

He was especially fortunate a particular typewriter caught his eye. There were literally thousands of discarded items he could have been tinkering with; during the heyday of Rooster Liquor people pawned anything they could carry to get their hands on a bottle or two. The Black Pope amassed so much stuff that he took to letting it pile outside his Cathedral, heaped monuments to both his greed and his sloth.

Gordonson sat on the ground, legs sprawled, prodding the typewriter with a curling iron. The carriage return was stuck, the keys locked in place. The Black Pope silently ordered the Beat Cops into position, they were to attack on his command. They stood at the ready, eager to crush the man's skull as punishment for stumbling upon their master's fortress.

KA-TING

The spring was released, flinging the carriage to the left. Startled, Gordonson leapt to his feet, dashing the typewriter to the ground in panic. The Black Pope roared with laughter and motioned for the Beat Cops to halt their attack. Unphased by the noise, the Beat Cops remained poised, ready to pounce on the man should the Black Pope change his mind.

"You there!" The Black Pope rasped. Gordonson spun to face him, but not before snatching the typewriter off the ground and hugging it close.

"I fixed it!" He snarled. "It's mine!"

Amused by the Lollipop of a Man's clumsy antics and charmed by his capacity to lie so brazenly, the Black Pope felt a twinge of opportunistic compassion.

"Yes. Indeed it is." The Black Pope gestured to the piles. "All of this can be yours as well. If you do as I say."

"OK." With Brian Gordonson's dim-witted consent, their pact was forged.

Gordonson was set to task. He was to go undercover and stop M Prefecture's burgeoning pornography racket. It was a tall order. Gordonson was best suited to duties like dropping typewriters. But, this scourge was his to stomp out; he was truly the only man for the job. He was paid handsomely for it, at least in comparison to the rest of the populace. The piles of pre-war goods shrunk slowly as Gordonson picked his favorite items and transported the rewards back to his cinderblock shack one by one. He had finally found purpose in life, even if that purpose was doing the bidding of a man who had most likely lost his mind.

After years on the periphery, it wasn't difficult for Gordonson to meld back into the 'society' of Tierra Podrida. All it took was showing up at the factory on time and keeping the conversion dynamo spinning for hours on end. It didn't matter that he was incapable of keeping up with the other factory workers. All that mattered was that he was back among his peers. At least that's what Gordonson thought. His method of 'show up and hope a clue falls in your lap' made him a terrible detective, at first. After weeks of generating power, he had no leads and a boss with thinning patience. Then came the day that the Old Man with the Tubes paid a visit to the Phase 2 Manufacturing Center and everything started to become clear.

It took months and months of playing the Old Man's lottery before Gordonson was able to win. It wasn't until he hit upon the idea of tampering with the punch cards that he even had a chance. A particularly stupid man in a prefecture full of them, Gordonson had unwittingly discovered a method of outsmarting the Eternally Free Taiwanese. By altering the punch cards that contained the wattage readings, he could reap far more reward than the other workers, by doing a fraction of the actual labor. He swapped those rewards for scores of lottery tickets. He was bucking the system, brazenly. It's a wonder he didn't win the lottery sooner.

Had he decided to share the trick he invented to fool the Phase 2's payment system, he would've been revered. 'The Man who brought M back to life' they might have called him. Unaware of what could have been, Gordonson remained loyal to the man who paid him in surplus stand mixers and toasters. He kept the secret to himself, even up to the day the Old Man with the Tubes came to lead him out into the desert, winning lottery ticket in hand.

Brian Gordonson's crawl most of the way back to Saint Basil's was a slow one. Champagne, the second of Black Pope's three Beat Cops, had been sent out to scout for him. He had been gone for far too long. She found him just outside the city limits. The last leg of Gordonson's trip was completed unconscious and slung over Champagne's shoulder. It finally culminated with Gordonson's limp naked body being dumped onto Saint Basil's dance floor.

At the far end of the dance floor, the Black Pope sat in a leather recliner studded with jewelry pilfered from the women of M. He had been waiting. Snadra, the third Beat Cop, was sprawled across his lap. One giant hand kneaded her fleshy butt as the other hand twirled her bushy mustache. He shooed Snadra away from his makeshift throne as Gordonson hit the floor.

"Excellent." He rasped. "Thank you Champagne. Please join Candi in town. Your patrol shift begins shortly."

"At once." Champagne replied, her voice as beautiful as it was soulless. She turned on her heels and made her way back towards town.

"Gordonson." The Black Pope steadied himself on his ebony staff and stood to hover over his nude henchman, his voice tinged with equal parts anticipation and malice. "Wake up Gordonson. The girl is dead, but her captors put up a brave fight during your

223

escape. Nevertheless, you have returned a hero and there will be no further impediments to prostitution in Tierra Podrida. I am pleased and you are to be commended. Am I correct?"

Gordonson had regained consciousness once his body hit the floor, but was too ashamed by his failure to show any signs of life. The Black Pope's bizarrely assumptive speech left him with few options. He could either own up to his shortcomings or continue to play dead. After playing dead for a solid twenty minutes, desperately thinking up lies that he hoped would help lessen the sting of his failure, Gordonson feigned awakening in order to confess.

"I tried, but..." Gordonson trailed off, remembering the fun he had with his intended victim before his attack was cut short. He opted to omit that part of the story. "There were... there were, too many of them. I'm sorry, Black Pope. I was overpowered before I could attack."

The Black Pope helped Gordonson to his feet with a grimace. The malice in his voice had overtaken the anticipation. "I prefer my version of the story. How many of them were there?"

"Let's see. Four? No five, I think. Including the girl."

"Girl aside. These were four strong, healthy men? In M Prefecture?"

"Uh, yeah. Yes! Big strong guys. Four of 'em."

"And they did... this... to you, before you had the chance to attack the girl, but after you removed your clothes?"

"Yeah."

"Gordonson. I do not expect much from you. You know that. I do not even expect the truth. But, on this occasion, perhaps you could try to exceed my low expectations. Tell me what really happened."

"I'm telling you the truth, I swear to uh... yeah, I swear! They swarmed me as soon as I took off my clothes!"

"They stopped you from fornicating with the girl." The Black Pope paused to take a deep breath. He gave his head a little shake before he continued. "The prize for winning the lottery was fornicating with the girl. You won the lottery. And they stopped you from fornicating with the girl?"

"Yeah! They said I was too ugly." Gordonson was treading water, but he didn't know it. Quite the opposite, he thought had the wool pulled snugly over the Black Pope's eyes.

"You are an ugly man, Gordonson. We are ALL ugly men in M Prefecture, it is who we are. I have seen many of these tapes, if not all of them. Each and every one of the tapes 'stars' a man no better looking than yourself."

"Well, sure... I don't know. They were all 'He's too ugly, get him!' and then they attacked."

The Black Pope began to circle Gordonson on the dance floor. "Yes. I can see that you were attacked." He poked and prodded at Gordonson's wounds with his staff. "You were struck here. And here. This looks painful. Did this one hurt?" The Black Pope was leisurely with his light torture.

"Yes." Gordonson hissed through clenched teeth as the Black Pope ground his staff into an abrasion.

"Good. Now then... They brought you to an undisclosed location. To film you fornicating with the fourth most beautiful woman in the Prefecture. Only, instead of following through with that plan, they beat you AND let you live to tell the tale?"

"Right! I mean, they were going to off me, seriously." Gordonson picked up that this was going to be his last chance to weasel out of the situation. He had to talk as fast as he could.

Maybe that would work. "One of the guys, the oldest one, he was going to pound my head in. But then, the biggest guy of the four he was like 'Clint! Clint! No! Let the desert kill him! He don't deserve the rock!' So they let me crawl away. I would've died too but then a black man from the sky saved me. It was some kind of miracle, I swear! Do you know him?"

The Black Pope was stunned. Lightheaded, he shuffled back to his bejeweled recliner and collapsed into the cushions. It could not be a coincidence. The man who ruined his life was back... to continue ruining his life. He had to be absolutely sure his dullard of a henchman hadn't misspoke. "What did you say?"

"I asked if you knew the black guy." Gordonson tossed back, a finger lodged halfway into his ear. "On account of you and your skin and all."

The Black Pope had no patience for Gordonson's moronic jabbering; a head injury likely exacerbated his henchman's already profound ability to spout utter nonsense. "Allow me to rephrase, so there can be no confusion. The 'biggest guy of the four' what did 'he' say?"

"Uh..." Gordonson had to try really hard to recall what he had just said. His delivery was not nearly as emphatic this time around. "Clint. Clint. Um. Don't hit him with that rock? So, did you know that black guy? Did you send him for me?"

"That matters not. Not now." The Black Pope rose to his feet. He struck the shaft of his staff against his palm; the loud smack snapped Gordonson to attention. "Tomorrow morning, you will return to the scene of your failure. You will bring my wives with you, all three of them." He wished he could sic his harem on Clint Masters without delay, but thought it best to wait until they were once again at full force... His harem! The Black Pope silently chastised himself for not thinking of this earlier! "Killing the girl is no longer you're goal. You are to bring her to Dr. Timothy, alive."

Gordonson nervously shifted his attention back and forth between his boss and the orange smear on his finger. "But, I'm not sure if I can find them again! It's in a cave, somewhere out in the desert, but you know how everything looks the same out there."

The Black Pope walked slowly towards Gordonson and slapped the waxy finger away from his face. "You will find them again and you will return the girl to Dr. Timothy."

"It was hard to get in there, I don't know if we'd all fit and..."

"I will provide you with explosives, use them as need be. There will be no further questions, no more excuses. Understood?"

"Yeah. Sorry. OK. I'll be here before the sun rises." Gordonson backed away from the Black Pope and limped out of the Cathedral, naked and aching. He was secretly delighted, convinced he had managed to pull a fast one over on his boss.

The Black Pope didn't notice Gordonson's smirk; he was lost in thought, barely able to believe his luck. Long awaited revenge on Clint Masters. His prostitutes working without video competition. A potential reconciliation with Dr. Timothy and, if that went well, a new bride. It could all be his, provided Gordonson didn't allow his idiotic failure in the desert to become habit. The Black Pope's optimism was tempered with regret; he should have held out for a higher caliber of underling.

CHAPTER 25 - PHASE 2

TIERRA PODRIDA, M PREFECTURE, THE UNION

SUNDAY, JUNE 27, 2010

Billy and Clint stood at the massive entrance to Tierra Podrida's
Phase 2 Manufacturing Center. They were dwarfed by the wide,
low slung 'door' designed to allow entry to thousands at a time.
Billy craned his neck to try and see the top of the factory, it couldn't
be done. There were no straight lines in the Phase 2's form, but the
curvature of the building was subtle, only clearly discernible from a
distance. The lip of the roof was up there, somewhere, kept just out
of view by the exterior wall's slight inward slope. The scale of the
structure was massive, its footprint larger than the official city limits
of Tierra Podrida.

It was shiny like nothing Billy had seen before, looking as if it
was constructed out of a plastic-metal hybrid. That was Billy's best
guess at least, he had no idea if such a substance existed. He
couldn't venture a guess as to how the huge complex was assembled.
As far as he could see there were no joins, nothing welded or
riveted. Like it was created in a giant mold. "Shouldn't we be

careful?" Billy asked, once he grew tired of gawking. "Disguises or something?"

"Don't worry about that Billy, the factory isn't picky. It'll let anybody inside who's dumb enough to want in. You'll see."

True to Clint's word, the pair had no problem making their way into the factory. The superwide door could not be closed, entry into the complex was as simple as crossing a yellow line embedded in the smooth white floor. They walked down a wide corridor for what seemed like miles. Inside, like out, was sloped ever so slightly, bright white, incredibly shiny and constructed using techniques Billy couldn't fathom. He remembered being wowed by the futuristic look of the Castillo Academy when he first walked its halls. Castillo had nothing on this place.

They hadn't come across any workers as they made their way further into the building. Not only that, there wasn't so much as a security camera in sight. Billy thought he heard someone off in the distance. As they pressed on, his suspicions were confirmed, the voice grew from a low rumbling to rhythmic muffles to honest-to-God words. The words were getting louder, but that didn't mean they were becoming any clearer.

"...in my position, or positions like mine. Strive. Aim to be your best. Make your best better than that of your neighbor. Both the fool and the wise man say toil is its own reward. The fool is selfish. The wise man divine. Stretch. Stretch farther than you believe possible. Peak productivity can be achieved. If it can be achieved, it must be. Family. Nourish your family. Feed them your fears. Feed them your tired body. Bathpaste..."

Billy tried to wrap his head around what the loud guy just around the bend was saying, but he was having a hard time keeping up. He knew all the words, but the message the man was trying to convey sure came across in a weird way. Things got weirder as Clint's voice joined the unseen. He spoke in perfect unison with the man around the corner.

"...your body must be vibrant. Sharp. Use the whetstone of effort to hone your soul. Strive. Wattage counts. Cowardice in the face of lactic acid counts for nothing. Thirty years in your position. Rise to the top. I did. Always. Calluses bleed. Blood is not the cure..." It was at this point Clint broke out in peals of laughter, drowning out whatever else the invisible loudmouth was talking about.

'If he's gone crazy I'm running.' "Clint? You OK?"

"You like my Shift Supervisor? Pretty good right?" Clint pointed to the corridor wall on their left. The slow curving swath of white gave way to a glowing man's face, 10 feet tall. *'Mike?'* The man did bear a slight resemblance to Mike Chan, Billy's ex track teammate. That is, if Mike were middle aged, wearing a suit and broadcast onto a factory hallway.

"Ha! That Taiwanese son of a bitch has been saying the same Goddamn thing for years!" Clint mouthed full, quasi-intelligible sentences along with the 'Shift Supervisor' to prove his point. "See, it never changes!"

"Weird. Why's he Taiwanese?" Billy realized how stupid that question must've sounded. "I, I mean, if he's from Eternally Free Taiwan what's he doing in the factory for white people?"

"He's not *actually* here, but I bet you already knew that. He's just in charge. I think. Or maybe he was. Probably dead by now. Like I said, they've been playing that on a big, long loop for years."

"They? The EFT? They run this place, right?"

"Smart kid! Yeah, they run this place. Running it right into the ground. You'll see. We'll be there soon."

The pair disappeared around the bend as the Shift Supervisor droned on. "...process. We do so that we do not want. Ever forward. Strive. Peak Productivity can be achieved..."

Clint and Billy trudged onwards. The long corridor grew wider and wider, eventually opening into a gargantuan circular room. The room buzzed with the sound of non-stop rotation, hundreds of thousands of conversion dynamos were aligned along an invisible grid.

The dynamos bore some resemblance to the stationary bikes Billy remembered from the Castillo Academy fitness room, operators sat astride a low slung machine and pumped bicycle pedals with their legs. The conversion dynamos didn't stop at harnessing the energy of the operators' legs, they came equipped with additional pedals to be operated by hand and a helmet-like pedal of sorts that seemed to be operated by swiveling one's neck.

Most dynamos were unmanned, operated instead by small, jet black, piston and gear based devices perfectly designed to keep the machines humming. The rest of the dynamos were operated by M's last vestiges of humanity.

The working men of M were scattered in small clumps throughout the spacious chamber. They were surrounded by the black, piston pumping contraptions that easily outpaced the production of their living counterparts. The men didn't have much reason to stick close to one another, it wasn't as if they could converse while they worked. Each human operated conversion dynamo was encased in a clear membrane, heavily fogged from the rider furiously chugging away inside.

The high percentage of mechanized labor allowed Billy to freely wander the aisles between dynamos, inspecting the bizarre display of energy generation. A rolling counter embedded in the base of each dynamo would click up by a single digit as the operator awkwardly contorted his body to complete a full rotation cycle. The human-operated dynamos had counters that numbered in the millions, piston powered dynamos all surpassed the billion mark, most by a fair margin.

Clint motioned for Billy to join him near a pod of three human operators. "Welcome to the factory!" He said with a wry smile. Clint's abject refusal to work in the Phase 2 made a lot more sense to Billy now. If this is all there was to factory life, Billy was starting to think it wasn't for him either.

"Is this everything? Like, are there other jobs here?"

"Only the job you and I are about to pull off. You ready?"

"Maybe, what do we do?"

"Just watch. Watch and learn."

Clint walked to the nearest human operator and peeled open his membrane, releasing a small steam cloud. The eyes of the naked man inside lit up. He began to shout out in joy. "Tubes! Tubes!" Clint peeled open another membrane, then another. Two more voices rang out. "Tubes!"

Soon the cavernous room was a din of muffled, but clearly excited shouts of "Tubes!" The shouting died down as the operators wriggled forth from their sheer plastic skins, each emitting a wet, sticky, sucking noise as they freed themselves.

The sweaty, naked men began paying rapt attention to the rolling counters affixed to their dynamos. Working against their obvious physical exhaustion, they frantically pushed buttons marked 'PAYOUT'. Low, impatient mutters were uttered as the men waited. The muttering gave way to yelps of elation as the dynamos spat thick paper punch cards out of their payout slots. Before long, the throng had surrounded Clint and Billy, cards in hand, eyes glinting.

Initially, Billy tried to pay attention to how Clint was swapping his tickets for the punch cards, but his concentration was drawn elsewhere. Every one of the dynamo operators was a freakshow of some variety, and Billy made no effort not to stare. The men fell into two categories. There were those who were merely deformed. Lots of burnt looking skin, half drooped faces, abnormal humps and missing limbs in that group. Then there were those who decided to 'upgrade' via plastic surgery. They were the ones who really made it hard for Billy to concentrate. Each member of the second group was a patchwork of parts, not all of which fit perfectly.

Plastic surgery wasn't reserved for revolting hookers, or so it seemed. Nearly half of the men in the throng had extensive work done, and those were only the obvious cases. The pile of body parts in the back of Bluebell started to make a lot more sense. Had he been granted more time to assess the situation, Billy likely would have been pleased to see that some of these unfortunate people were able to deal with their physical hardships. There was no time to assess. His gut reaction was one of sheer disgust. He vowed, then and there, that he would never go under the knife, even if his back sprouted five humps and his nose fell off. Billy knew firsthand what it was like to live in skin that wasn't your own, it wasn't a lifestyle he wished to revisit.

By the time Billy grew accustomed to the unsettling sea of desperate white guys, Clint had both hands full of punch cards and a beaming grin that only made him squintier. "Thanks boys! You know the routine, I'll be in touch with the winner, and then one of *you* will be in touch with the lovely Mona!" He announced to the dispersing crowd before turning to Billy. "I've been making that same corny speech for years! Come on, let's go get paid!"

Clint scampered away from the sweaty masses as they dethronged, heading back to their machines. He was headed for another large doorway that branched off of the conversion dynamo chamber. Billy followed closely, still trying to piece together what just happened.

"What do they mean, tubes?"

"That's me, in the factory at least." Clint gave a little snort, shooting vibrant blue into his nose for emphasis. "The guys in here, most of their memories are totally shot. Too much time breathing in their own stink, I figure. Ha! My name doesn't ring a bell, but they can't forget the guy with the blue tubes. Bet they'll give you some kind of nickname before long."

"Oh." *'I wonder what they'll call... ah, hell, I don't care.'*

Clint stopped in front of a giant vending machine just outside the main chamber, Billy followed suit. Column after column of consumer goods labeled with a sunburst flag logo were held aloft by metal spirals. Clint began feeding the stack of punch cards into a slot at chest height one after another, watching the digital readout marked 'kW' tick upwards. The counter stopped and Clint began to punch a combination of buttons. The spirals spun and an assortment of sundry goods dropped to the tray below. Firecups, toilet powder, a few pouches of bathpaste, disposable hair knives, 3 12-packs of socks, nothing that seemed all that exciting to Billy. Clint opted not to purchase any Sustenance Gel, but Billy failed to notice.

'That's it?'

"*That's* what you work for? The same stuff as the factory workers?"

"You bet!" Clint said, as he produced a net bag from his pants pocket and began to cram the spoils inside. "I like my food hot, my face hairless, my feet comfy and my body smelling fresh!"

Billy didn't get it, he couldn't get it. Factory work looked awful, sure, but at least it wasn't morally reprehensible.

"But, you could get all of that by riding one of those bike-things! Then you wouldn't have to live in a cave! Or whore out Mona! Or kill people for God's sake!"

"Billy." Clint's tone turned somber. "You've got a good head on your shoulders and your heart's in the right place. I respect both of those things. But, there is no way you will catch me on one of those soul-suckers. I am a free man. A free man! Now c'mon, we're done for the day!" Clint stormed back through the conversion dynamo chamber, net bag slung over his shoulder. Billy followed at a distance.

Clint might live 'free', but as far as Billy was concerned, he sure didn't live right. To hear him tell it, Clint hadn't made a good decision about how to live his life since he fought some guy 30 years back. God knows what he chose to leave out of his unsavory history lesson. Clint's talk of Satan from the day before began to worm into Billy's mind, swirling around with the Satanic Sacrifice Lie, transforming into a hazy feeling of helpless uncertainty and unfocused guilt.

He followed behind in a daze as Clint made his way back through the operators. To a man, they had re-sheathed themselves in their sheer membranes and had resumed their furious pedaling. A muffled thud from behind almost brought Billy to attention. The wailing siren that followed the thud snapped Billy the rest of the way there.

One of the operators had keeled over. Billy turned in time to see the man's last breaths inflate, deflate and then inflate his plastic casing one final time. He looked young, or at least most of his face did. Billy would've pegged him at 25, 30 on the high end, if not for the top of his head. It was bald, speckled with liver spots. Deep furrows creased the upper half of his forehead; the lower half was unnaturally smooth.

A small, orange point of light began to glow on the ground next to the downed man's dynamo. The dot traced a faint orange circle of light on the floor, about two feet in diameter. Once the circle was complete, the white floor contained within popped upwards with a **FWUMP**, as if it had been held back by some great pressure. What had been an unremarkable patch of shiny, white ground seconds earlier was now a shiny, white, five foot tall pillar. The pillar opened from within with a hiss. Curved partitions swung aside revealing two of the black, piston driving automatons. Nearly man shaped, featureless, slender and wholly mechanical, they set to work, moving in time with the siren.

A thin blue flame flared out from the 'head' of one of the black contraptions. It bent down to grab the limp man by the shoulders and then burnt his membrane free from the conversion dynamo. The second mechanized worker took the man's spot on the dynamo; the siren stopped the moment pedaling resumed. Flame retracted, the first automaton dragged the operator into the pillar, contorting his lifeless body to fit within the cylindrical confines. With another **FWUMP** the pillar disappeared into the ground, the orange light retraced its path. By the time the light faded from view, the floor was perfectly smooth once again, completely unmarred.

Working, dying, being swallowed whole by the Phase 2, the whole process took less than a minute. Billy had never seen anything like it. But, Billy had seen a lot of new things that week, the technological wizardry behind the grim automation barely registered. His concern was with the young looking old man, he knelt to rub the spot where the pillar once stood, hoping it would pop up once more.

Clint clucked his tongue over Billy's shoulder and let out a low sigh. "Damn it. Billy, remind me to cross Ken off the lottery list, would you? Poor bastard."

"Isn't there anything we can do? I mean..."

Clint cut Billy off abruptly. "No Billy. He's dead and gone. Probably lived longer than he should've, anyhow. Let's get out of here."

"But... Yeah. OK." Billy knew the floor wasn't going to open again. Not without another dead body.

"Life is cheap here in M. Dirt cheap. Hell, life itself is cheaper than any other energy source out there. That's what this place is all about. Using people to power the factory; using you 'til you're all used up, just like old Ken. Don't think Ken was special. He wasn't. Everyone goes the same way here, you work 'til you die, you get replaced by a machine. No fond farewell, no gold watch, just a one way trip into the floor. Won't be too long now until those black leg things take all of these jobs, if you can even call them jobs." Clint sermonized as they made their way back to the entrance. "This place is rotten, and I mean that. Not just this factory, this whole Prefecture. Just living here does some ugly things to people. I mean, if Ry wasn't born here, he'd probably have a normal face. A little on the ugly side maybe, but normal otherwise. Norm would be walking, Mona would be smart. Smarter, anyhow." Clint was practically screaming at this point, as loud as he was sanctimonious. His speech effectively drowned out the nonsensical drone of the Shift Supervisor as they walked the long corridor. "In a way, those kids are lucky to even be alive, most people here are 100 percent sterile. Have been for years. Population's been shrinking fast since the war. Give M another twenty years, maybe thirty, and I betcha there won't be a soul left. Yep. Won't be long before the whole Prefecture withers and dies. Good riddance, if you ask me."

"Huh." was about all Billy could manage in reply. What he had seen in the factory coupled with Clint's bleak view of life in M didn't excuse the way Clint lived, but it did help to put it in perspective. *If lives are so cheap, is it so wrong to take a few? Use some others however you want? Is Clint any worse than the factory? Yeah. He is. Much worse. The factory doesn't kill people, it just... There's no sex stuff in the factory. But, that's what the people want. They want it bad. At least life in the cave doesn't rot your memory. I think. Hell, I don't know.'*

Clint picked up on Billy's melancholy expression. "Sorry. Don't mean to be too much of a downer. This place gets to me sometimes." He spoke softer now that the Shift Supervisor was out of earshot. "But, you can't change the dirt you were planted in. You just have to try and grow as big and as strong as you can, right?" Clint didn't wait for a response and Billy didn't have one to offer. "C'mon, there's something I want to show you on the way back." They stepped over the yellow line and back out into the desert.

"No! Don't! Aaugh!" Rollo's hollered pleas reverberated through Tierra Podrida's town square. "I paid her! I did! That bitch is lying!" Blood was streaming down Rollo's face. Two identical women, both dressed in child size police uniforms and seemingly sculpted by a horny twelve year old, took turns pushing him to the ground as he tried to make his way to his feet. Pretty Becky lay nearby, topless, sixteen nipples bared to the world. She cackled, coughed, retched, spat and then cackled some more. With Rollo's head apparently bloodied to an appropriate degree, the Beat Cops turned their attention to his limbs. They held them taught, one at a time, and hammered vicious blows against the joints, forcing them back the wrong way. The attacks paused only once a satisfactory crunch could be heard, then they would move on to the next one.

"Wait! He did pay me, I forgot!" Pretty Becky blurted, followed by a dirty chuckle. Rollo was down to his final usable limb by the time he was granted his 'reprieve' from the half naked hooker. The timing didn't seem to matter to the Beat Cops. His left arm was broken to complete the set.

"Area secure." one of the Beat Cops intoned before she and her partner dashed off into the night, heels clacking on cracked cement. Pretty Becky spat on Rollo's battered body before she passed out face down in the gutter.

Billy and Clint poked their heads out from behind their concrete bench cover. Clint pointed skywards, up towards the flagpole that still held the caged skeletal remains of the man said to be Jonathan Wright.

"So, uh, as I was going to say, that's Wright up there." Clint said, with a slight quiver to his voice. "Probably should've picked a better time to show you, I guess."

"You weren't kidding about those mustaches." Billy replied, obviously shaken. "We should help him, right?"

"Yeah, yeah we should."

The pornographer and his apprentice ran over to the crippled restaurateur. Rollo was wheezing hard. Clint knelt down beside him. "Keep still, we'll get you fixed up right."

"I can't... I can't..." Rollo couldn't complete a sentence without lapsing into a series of labored breaths.

"Can't walk? I figured. We'll carry you."

"Can't... pay..."

"This one's on me, Rollo. Don't sweat it. Help me prop him up, Billy." Billy did as he was told, supporting Rollo's weight on his shoulders, briefly raising him off the ground to allow Clint to shoulder his half.

The three set off for Tierra Podrida Savings and Loan, ambling awkwardly, weighed down not only by Rollo's body but by Clint's haul from the factory as well. The old bank wasn't far from the town square, but their shuffled trek there was a slow one. Once inside, Billy gingerly propped Rollo against the wooden teller's desk as Clint sounded the intercom buzzer. Rollo's eyes had drifted back into his head, his wheezes had grown ragged.

"Dr. Timothy? I've got a man here who could use your help. Bashed head. Four broken bones, I think. He doesn't sound too good."

"And in return?" the dry Australian voice buzzed through the speaker.

Clint dumped the contents of his net bag onto the dirty maroon carpet for a quick inventory count. "Fourteen pouches of bathpaste. Firecups, two ten packs. Can of toilet powder, family size. Five disposable hair knives and uh, twelve, twenty-four, thirty-six pairs of tube socks. White, with blue stripes."

"No sustenance gel?"

"No. I don't touch the stuff."

"Pity. Still, a generous offer. Quite generous. Leave the man and leave my reward. I will tend to him immediately."

"Thanks, doc. I'd say I owe you one, but I already paid out the ass for this."

"How poetic." The intercom hiss went dead.

Clint let up off the button. He gave the pile of stuff that was to be his a look over and shook his head. "Some day, huh, Billy?"

"I'll say. Can Dr. Timothy help him? I mean, is he a real doctor, or does he just do plastic surgery?"

"Real enough. I mean, he's the only doctor we've got. He'll do a good job though. For that many Goddamn socks, he'd better! Ha! What do you say we head back?"

"Yeah, let's." Clint's generous gift muddled Billy's conflicted feelings about his boss even further. Billy felt he should acknowledge Clint's good deed after harping on everything else he had done. "Awfully nice of you to do this, Clint."

"Guess so." Clint said with a shrug. "Be safe out there Rollo!" Clint called out as he and Billy made their way out into the growing dusk. "And for the love of God, keep it in your pants next time!"

Clint and Billy ran back towards the cave under the cover of night. They still weren't moving as quickly as Billy would've liked, but they were maintaining a brisker pace than they had in the morning.

The moonlight glinted off of Clint's broad, toothy smile. He had planned on waiting, he didn't want to make his big announcement until they were back home. He was too excited, he couldn't wait.

"Billy. Hold on. There's something I want to tell you."

'What now?' Billy jogged back to Clint. "What's up?"

"You did good these past few days."

'I did? How?' "Thanks."

"Real good. So good... See, I'm getting old and I'm really glad you came, I mean... You've seen what we do, and... Hell, never had to make this speech before! Harder than I thought! Suppose I'd better just come out and say it. I'm retiring Billy." Clint gave Billy an emphatic slap on the back. "And, I want *you* to take over for me!"

'Jesus Christ!'

CHAPTER 26 - BOSS

10.1 MILES SOUTHWEST OF TIERRA PODRIDA,
M PREFECTURE, THE UNION

SUNDAY, JUNE 27, 2010

"Retire? What do you mean retire?"

"It means I get to sit back and wait to die, Billy. And, I tell ya, it's going to be fantastic! When you get to be my age, you'll understand." Clint said with a wink. "Now come on, it's getting late." He took off through the desert, leaving Billy no choice but to chase after.

"You know that's not what I meant. I can't take over for you, I just got here!" Billy could've kicked himself. This was his chance to change things, to make things right on his terms. And now he was turning it down? "I mean, don't get me wrong, I want to, but I still have a lot to learn."

"I'm not going anywhere, not for a while. I'm just going to pass the torch and take it easy. I'll be around. You'll learn. Plus, Norm and Ry aren't going anywhere either and they've been doing this for years."

'Right. Those guys.' "You don't think they'll be upset? I mean, they probably won't like me giving orders and stuff after just a few days on the job... Wait. Did you tell them about this?"

"No sir. That's the kind of thing best left to the boss. And as of tonight, that's you. Ha! Norm is going to be so pissed off!"

'Boss. Yeah! I'm the boss.' "If Norm doesn't like it, he can go work in the factory!" Billy said with a chuckle.

"See? You're a natural!"

Billy set the receiver back on the cradle and turned to Clint as Clint made his way down the ladder. Billy didn't mean to outpace the old man on their way back to the cave, but his mind was racing and he unconsciously allowed his feet to follow suit.

"Hey Clint, The Pervert called. He says the dubs are ready. Now what?"

"Now it's on you to go pick 'em up, speedfreak. Jesus, Billy, you do know I'm old, right?"

"Yeah, sorry about that. Do I have to go now?"

"Now, in the morning, a year from now, whenever. You call the shots." Clint headed down the passageway towards his segment of the cave. "I'm a retired man now, Billy. And this retired man is headed to bed! Night."

"OK. G'night."

Billy had been in charge of the cave-based pornography operation for about two hours at this point. He had yet to actually do anything as boss, and Clint was the only soul who knew of his new position. Neither of those things mattered to Billy. For the first time in his life he had the power to make decisions. So far, Billy was really enjoying that power. He decided he'd head back into town tomorrow. In the meantime, he'd spend the night feeling pretty pleased, both with himself and with the big decision he made during his run back to the cave. *'Tomorrow morning! Another good call, Billy!'*

Billy's mind was made up long before he completed his trip back. Sooner or later, he was going to shut this operation down. He knew this wasn't the kind of thing that could happen overnight, even though he wished it was. He figured they'd have to make at least one more tape before going out of business. Billy didn't want to find out how the men in the Phase 2 would respond to a refund and an apology. He couldn't imagine a positive outcome to that scenario, and besides, Clint already spent all their earnings on Rollo.

Shooting one more tape would buy him some time with Norm and Ry as well. Billy hoped he could find a way to avoid ever having to fill them in on his promotion, but he had his suspicions that Clint was going to spill the beans in the morning. Being passed over in favor of Billy wasn't going to sit well with Clint's tenured employees. Finding out that they would be losing their jobs would only add fuel to that fire. Billy would wait until he came up with a new business plan before telling the crew they were closing down production. And Clint, well, Clint just handed Billy the reins. Billy figured he'd let him settle into his retirement before telling him anything that might make him change his mind.

Someday he would do right by Mona, hopefully someday soon. Even if it meant that Billy had to slave away in the factory to make ends meet, things couldn't keep on this way. He wouldn't have admitted it if asked, but Billy was banking on his 'doing right by Mona' leading to an awful lot of sticking his penis inside of her. In the meantime, he wasn't her savior, just her boss. He'd have to settle for wowing her with some mild boasting. He found her in the dining area, picking her teeth with a coat hanger. Billy was smitten.

"Hi Mona."

"Hello Billy."

"Looks like I missed dinner."

"Yes. We had lizards."

'New rule. Save leftover lizards for the boss.' "That sounds good. Wish I was here for it, but I had business in town. Important business. I'm going to head back in tomorrow." Billy lowered his voice to what he presumed was an appropriately seductive level. "I'll be heading in alone."

Mona shuddered. "That is very scary. I do not like it there. I like it here with Clint and Norm and Ry. I think you are very brave for going into town." Her voice lowered. "I also think you are very good looking." Billy couldn't tell if she was mocking him until she leaned in and gave him a quick peck on the cheek. She broke into a fit of giggles and ran out of the dining area. Billy blushed a deep scarlet watching her butt bounce rhythmically as she ran off. Things were looking up, especially in Billy's pants.

It was mid Monday morning when Billy set off for Tierra Podrida; he wasn't overly eager to go. Sure, this would be his first taste of adventure completely on his own, but another meeting with The Pervert was something he could happily delay. Without Clint to slow him down, Billy made great time. Even with his leisurely start, it wasn't even noon by the time Billy made his way to residential section of town. Things were going well. Billy just wished that his feet didn't ache so badly. His school dress shoes had been awful to run in, but these new cowboy boots were even worse. They were absolutely killing his feet. He completed his trip to #215 Progress Ave. in socks, boots in hand.

"Come in!" came from the yell from inside before Billy had a chance to knock on The Pervert's door. Billy pulled his boots back on, took a deep breath and barged in.

"This is a good tape, really good tape." The Pervert gushed. He was lounging in his swivel chair, slowly rubbing his jockey shorts, engrossed by his wall of pornography.

Billy didn't want a review. "Uh huh, where are the dubs?"

"Bathroom. You get them. Mmm. Mmmm."

'Oh God.' Billy wanted to get in and out of The Pervert's as quickly and smoothly as possible. If that meant setting foot in his bathroom, so be it. *'Oh God.'* He headed for the door opposite the entrance, avoiding the semen encrusted detritus that littered the floor as best he could. It wasn't easy. Bracing for the worst, Billy cracked the closed bathroom door, and then opened it quickly, holding his breath. He was almost disappointed in its sterile cleanliness. Cream colored tile, neatly hung towels, fuzzy purple toilet seat cover, four big cardboard boxes of pornographic video cassettes in the bathtub. *'At least that's weird.'* Billy paused as he thought this. *'I've been in M for too long.'* Billy had yet to spend four full days in the Prefecture.

Balancing the large boxes wasn't easy; it was going to have to be a slow run home. Billy may have been in charge, but that certainly didn't mean he knew what he was doing. Making a few round trips between the Phase 2 and The Pervert's house would've been the economical way to peddle the tapes. It was the method Clint had been using for years. The thought never crossed Billy's mind. All he wanted was to get out of The Pervert's house and to avoid coming back for as long as he could. He stood at The Pervert's front door, boxes awkwardly cradled in his arms.

"Think I could get some help with these?"

"No."

"Thanks..." *'Asshole.'* Billy set the boxes down and crooked the door open with his foot.

"Oooooh! Choke her! Choke her!" The Pervert's absentminded mumbles sure as hell didn't sit well with Billy, but this was no time for an argument. He figured ignoring him and making a hasty exit was the best plan of action.

"Oooh! Her pussy squares! Ooh. Ooooh!" *'Pussy squares?'* This was too much for Billy to ignore. He glanced back to the monitor wall. *'Oh.'* There they were. Two sort-of square shaped moles sat just above Mona's clit hood. The squares went in and out of view as Mona's legs kicked and thrashed, trying to escape the grip of the Lollipop of a Man. The clip played in a loop on every monitor; The Pervert was masturbating furiously.

Billy had seen enough. This was not the part of the cave filmed, brain retard, pornographic videotape he wished to be associated with. "Turn that off! Now!"

"Make me!" The Pervert replied, defiantly jerking off, angry-red pecker pointed squarely at Billy.

Billy strongly considered taking the Pervert up on his offer. For the first time in memory, rage was simmering inside Billy Lopez. But, a cooler head prevailed. He was in charge now. And that meant dealing with disgusting associates, like it or not. While he would have loved to lay into The Pervert, he didn't have the desire to get anywhere near his slimy little wiener. A half-yelled dressing down would have to do.

"You're a sick, sick bastard, know that? Idolizing Mona like this, moles on her vagina?" Billy was livid; words were flowing out of his mouth without the buffer of thought. "She's the kindest gentlest person in this toilet bowl of a Prefecture and you get off on watching her get strangled? You disgust me. I'm in charge now. That's right. Me. And, I'll see to it that this is the closest you'll *ever* get to Mona! In fact, I think I might start dubbing these tapes myself. Asshole."

The Pervert stopped stroking himself and began to whimper about fairness, tears flooding his beady little eyes. Billy was new at making impassioned speeches, but he felt pretty good about himself after his brief diatribe. The part about making the dubs himself was a lie of course, but it got the response he was looking for. Billy left without saying another word.

Now the hard part began. Billy had to carry an impossibly bulky load, still full of this new queasy, angry feeling. And, he had to do it quickly, invisibly. Uphill. In boots that made him wish his feet would fall off.

Billy was quite sure he wasn't followed back to the cave, just as Clint had requested. He may have been invisible, but he was far from quick. The return trip took hours. Each step had to be precise in order to keep the load of tapes from spilling. That precision took time, more than enough time to assess and re-assess his surroundings. His deliberate pace also gave Billy plenty of time to wonder about the new cave dynamic. Surely, Clint had filled Norm and Ry in on the new workplace hierarchy by now. Billy wasn't certain if he should expect outright hostility, indifference, or a combination of the two from the men who were now under his command.

'What the hell?' Whatever he was expecting from Norm and Ry, he wasn't expecting them to do this. The small rock outcropping that marked the entrance to the cave was gone, blackened stone rubble was scattered around the hole in the ground in its place.

'They blew it up? How'd they even...' Clint screamed out in agony down below. Precision and caution were tossed aside. The boxes of tapes hit the ground, Billy slid down the ladder.

Billy choked up, the lump in his throat made it hard to breathe. Ry and Norm weren't angry. They didn't do anything to the entrance of the cave. Ry and Norm were dead. Their lifeless bodies, bloodied and beaten, lay on the cold stone floor of the cave's main chamber. *'No! God damn it! No!'* Billy felt terrible, but there was no time to attend to them now. Three Beat Cops were bent over Clint, savagely laying into him with feet and fists.

Billy racked his brain for something he could yell to draw their attention. Something intimidating. Anything to make them stop their attack.

"Hey!" was the best he was able to come up with. Trite though it may have been, it worked. Next thing Billy knew, they had abandoned their assault on Clint and were towering over him. Blinding white smiles. Big blonde hair. Tiny navy blue cop uniforms. Exposed midriffs, impossibly tight stomachs. Muscular thighs. Tits aplenty. Eerily identical, apart from names stamped on shiny brass badges. Candi. Champagne. Snadra. Inch-thick mustaches. Menace. Loathing. When he had time to reflect on it later, Billy figured Snadra had to be a typo. But, this was no time to question stupid names, Billy was furious.

His years of conditioning to avoid conflict had begun to show cracks in The Pervert's house. Now, faced with three augmented warrior women brazen enough to break into his place of business and viciously attack the only group who had ever come close to accepting him, it was as if he had never been conditioned at all. The lump in his throat dropped to his stomach. It was time for retribution. Billy swung, right fist clenched. He connected with

Champagne's wafer thin nose. The crunch was sickening, blood began to pour. Time slowed to a crawl, sounds were drowned out by rushing white noise. Candi and Snadra attacked Billy from behind to no effect. Their punches and kicks connected, but it was as if the impact from the strikes were cushioned before he could feel a thing. If Billy had been able to see himself, he would have seen a rosy glow surrounding his body.

"Clint! Are you OK?" Billy yelled as he continued to bash Champagne's face towards the back of her head. Clint groaned and allowed himself to slump against the wall. He was bruised and swollen beyond belief, but not a drop of his blood had spilled. Clint's disgustingly hoarse voice cut through the din of static in Billy's head. "No! Billy! Get out! You've got to get out of here!" Billy had no intention of leaving. This was his mess now and he had to clean it up.

Even before Champagne's body had the chance to fall lifeless to the ground, Billy had Snadra in a headlock, her long limbs flailing frantically, heels clicking and scraping against stone. This technique wasn't mentioned anywhere in *Gentleman Gerald on Pugilism*, instinct had taken hold. Gripping Snadra's neck tight, Billy abruptly bent at the waist, heaving her over his shoulder. She hit the ground headfirst and she hit it hard. Blood spurted from the top of her head, mussing her hairdo, pooling with Champagne's. The rosy glow surrounding Billy had grown into licking crimson flames of energy.

Billy caught a glimpse of Candi trying to blindside him with a punch. He ducked down, dropping a knee on Snadra's neck to keep her from squirming away. The punch skimmed over top of Billy's head. With Snadra firmly pinned, Billy grabbed hold of Candi by her hair, she was slow to recover from her near miss. He smashed

Candi's face against the nearest stalagmite, breaking it clean from the floor.

He let go off what was left of Candi's head, mostly blood-matted hair, and hoisted Snadra back up off the floor. Lifting her up over his head, he flung her clear to the other side of the cave's entrance. Billy lunged, broken stalagmite in hand. With a final emphatic thrust, he impaled Snadra's abdomen with the calcified cone.

Time sped back to normal, the white noise rushing between Billy's ears gave way to the sounds of his own deep breaths. Doubled over from exertion, a sly smile broke out across his face. He had murdered three women. Three police women. He felt strangely at ease, blithely detached from the gravity of the situation. A groan from across the main chamber snapped Billy out of the euphoric haze imparted by his violent retaliation. *'Clint!'* Billy ran over to check on him, his flames now reduced to a mere flicker.

"Clint! Are you OK? Oh God, what happened here?"

Clint was face down on the floor of the cave and was slow to speak. "I think I'm OK. That fat son of a bitch didn't die. He came back and took Mona. We tried to stop him, but then they... I should've..." Clint coughed, too weak to finish.

'Mona! No!' Billy's mind had been elsewhere as he was forced into the middle of the violent melee. He had completely forgotten about Mona. As the revelation that she was gone sunk in, so did the gut-wrenching guilt. None of this would have happened if not for Billy. Norm and Ry were dead. Clint was probably almost dead. And Mona, well, Billy felt worst about Mona by a long shot. He was supposed to save her, supposed to get her out of here. Somehow. But, certainly not like this. He buried his head in his hands, agonizing over what he could have done differently, only to

pull his hands away again with a startled yelp. Ghostly flames still danced on Billy's fingertips.

The panic was clear in Billy's quivering voice. "Uh, Clint? Do all white people catch on fire when they fight?"

A strange smile broke on Clint's face as he mustered the strength to look up to Billy.

"No Billy, only the chosen few."

CHAPTER 27 - DOCTOR

TIERRA PODRIDA, M PREFECTURE, THE UNION

MONDAY, JUNE 28, 2010

"I am ever so sorry to report that there have been setbacks in her surgery." The lilting Australian tones of Doctor Timothy's voice buzzed through the Black Pope's telephone receiver.

"Go on." The Black Pope rasped, making no effort to disguise his displeasure. Failure to convert had yet to cross his mind and now that if had, he didn't care for the thought of it. Things had gone so well to this point. Gordonson miraculously managed to find his way back to the cave and he had succeeded in safely delivering the girl to Dr. Timothy. After coming so close, securing a fourth Beat Cop for his harem seemed inevitable. At least Clint Masters would finally meet his violent end at the hands of his three existing Beat Cops, or so the Black Pope was led to believe. The solace he took in misinformation was short-lived.

"There were... severe complications with the lobotomy. She has died." Doctor Timothy wasn't lying. Mona was dead, the result of an aggro-tranq gone wrong. However, while Doctor Timothy wasn't lying, she was deceitful. This was nothing new. Doctor

254

Timothy's very existence had always been steeped in lies and trickery, even before she was born.

15 years earlier, Dr. Timothy told the Black Pope that Snadra would not be an easy conversion. He said he'd have to take his time, he had to make sure everything went as smoothly as possible. The Black Pope readily agreed, candidates for conversion were not easy to come by and he did not want to waste this one. It had been nearly a decade since Champagne's transformation by the time Dr. Timothy managed to drag Snadra back to the bank vault.

She was to be the third, and likely last of the Beat Cops. She was not to be the last one by choice. If the Black Pope had his way, he would have dozens, maybe hundreds of Beat Cops at his command. That wish was one that could not be fulfilled. As the sustenance gel pouches wreaked their special brand of genetic havoc on the people of M, the female population had dropped off to nearly non-existent. To the best of Dr. Timothy's knowledge at the time, Snadra who was both young *and* alive, was the last girl in the Prefecture who would fit the needs of the Black Pope. She should have been an ideal candidate, but Snadra was pregnant.

Dr. Timothy had no idea of Snadra's condition at the time of her abduction, she was a month along, if that. Terminating a pregnancy would have been a simple procedure, but it was not one that Dr. Timothy was going to perform. Snadra's baby was going to be a girl. Quite possibly the last baby girl M Prefecture would ever see.

Dr. Timothy's devotion to the Black Pope had been born out the desire to perfect what he considered his art, pushing the human body far past its natural limits. The Black Pope's ideal of ushering a New Sodom unto the world merely acted as a means to that end. By the time the streets were fully awash with Rooster Liquor, Dr. Timothy had already operated on over half of the town. His skill had hit its zenith. He yearned for new challenges, but they were not to be found in grafting on replacement digits or refining the remains of men into alcohol. Fatherhood however, that was a new challenge, duplicitous fatherhood especially. He knew the Black Pope would not approve, but Dr. Timothy sought a bold new endeavor, not approval. He would raise the child as his own. Train her in the ways of medicine. Keep her from the Black Pope at all costs. He strove to raise a surgical genius, not a mindless sex brute.

Dr. Timothy had little difficulty keeping the nagging demands of the Black Pope at arm's length for the final eight months of Snadra's pregnancy. A host of excuses, rooted in imaginary ailments, were enough to placate his boss. The Black Pope had been at the height of his power in 1996; M was still as horny as it was thirsty. Tales of delayed surgical procedures had been easy to brush off while he joyfully controlled the vice that ran rampant.

The birth of Snadra's daughter had not been easy. The infant's abnormal physiology led to complications that nearly proved fatal for both mother and child. Both pulled through, thanks to Dr. Timothy's skillful hand. Snadra's subsequent conversion to a Beat Cop was a light, breezy affair in comparison.

Snadra's delivery to Saint Basil's thrilled the Black Pope, at last he was able to add a new piece to his wife collection. He couldn't have known at the time, but Snadra's arrival marked the beginning of the end of his professional relationship with Dr. Timothy. Catering to the twisted Holy Man's whims had to take a back seat; Dr. Timothy had a secret daughter to raise. He named her Doctor, partly to pass on his surgical legacy, mostly because he was a wiseass.

Her mother's typical M Prefecture diet left Doctor with a fiendish taste for tainted sustenance gel from birth. Dr. Timothy didn't have any pouches on hand when she was born. He knew of the damage M's foodstuff of choice inflicted on the human body and he didn't wish to poison himself. If he wasn't going to poison himself, he certainly wasn't going to poison his daughter. Or, so he thought. His resolve didn't last.

After days of Doctor caterwauling and vomiting, Dr. Timothy abandoned his attempts to feed her a nutrient paste of his own creation. He reluctantly allowed her to sample the sustenance gel. She took to it as if it was mother's milk. Dr. Timothy conceded his will to the needs of his daughter's addiction. She had to eat something and given the extent of the mutation she was born with, he figured the gel couldn't do any further harm.

The problem was Doctor's head. It was enormous, especially in contrast to her tiny, frail body. It took quick thinking, even quicker scalpel work and jury rigging a set of triple-wide forceps to keep her from suffocating within Snadra during birth. Initially, Dr. Timothy thought that correcting Doctor's glaring genetic defects via surgery would be simple, certainly nothing compared to what her mother went through. He didn't count on the paternal bond he would form with Doctor. By the time it was clear Doctor's weak little neck would never be able to support the weight of her whopping cranium, Dr. Timothy couldn't bring himself to operate on his baby girl. He cursed his soft heart and set about creating a support system, a metal framework designed to sit on her shoulders and hold her head in place. She learned to sit up in her brace, then to crawl and eventually to approximate something of a walk. Running in the brace would prove impossible, but Doctor would never really have room enough to run.

Security and secrecy took on more importance than ever before now that Dr. Timothy had a daughter in the workplace. The citizens of Tierra Podrida had a terrible track record when it came to proper treatment of the fairer sex. No one could know of Doctor's existence, for her own safety. This rule sheltered her from not only from danger, but from the outside world as well. She had never seen sunlight or the starry sky.

Given the nature of Dr. Timothy's patient-driven business, this presented an interesting wrinkle. The vault door kept most of the outside world at bay, but something needed to be done about those who sought surgery. The solution was chemical. He devised a powerful amnesia inducing agent to be administered post-surgery. His patients would learn of Doctor's existence prior to their operation, it was unavoidable. Once they awoke outside of the vault, any potential lingering memories of the deformed young girl would be written off as a dream.

This solution eventually proved profitable. Dr. Timothy didn't ask why Garbage Bag needed a memory wiping drug for his 'friend'. He had no business questioning what his big, green parts man would do with the stuff, or who he would do it to. Dr. Timothy would happily sell off some of his surplus, so long as the price was right.

Dr. Timothy strove to give Doctor an early start on her education. It didn't take quite as he planned. Aside from certain illustrations, his one year old daughter showed little interest in medical texts. Something was wrong. She was a bright child, exceedingly so. The battery of cognitive tests proved it. Despite her far above average intelligence, infant Doctor showed no interest in reading. This worried Dr. Timothy to no end. She was an eager pupil in other ways. She would eagerly watch each procedure her adoptive father performed and began to gurgle questions about the tools he was using and what functions certain body parts performed before she was able to stand on her own. But, reading was a non-starter. To his chagrin, Dr. Timothy conceded that he had set the bar too high, she likely needed to start on lighter reading material. He would have to see what he could scrounge up outside of the bank vault.

Books were scarce throughout The Union. Dr. Timothy was lucky he was able to amass as many as he did. The subject matter may not have been entirely appropriate for a toddler, but the complete 34 volume collection of the *LaRue's Longing* series of romance novels was still quite the score.

She took to these new books immediately. Tales of broad shoulders, ripped bodices, throbbing manhoods and timely face slapping eventually led her into the world of heart arrhythmia, inert marrow replication, tumor excision and interlaced muscle grafts. Dr. Timothy's plan to encourage love of the written word was a success, more or less. By the time she was four, Doctor could recite every word of his medical texts from memory. She could also do the same with every volume of *LaRue's Longing*.

Once her knowledge base was established, she began to assist in surgeries. Her assistance led to performing surgeries on her own, under her father's watchful eye. By 10, she took over the family business full time, without assistance or supervision. Dr. Timothy was ever so proud of what he taught his daughter. He was also rather jealous; he could tell that her innate skill dwarfed his own.

There was no telling what she could accomplish in time. Dr. Timothy knew he was unlikely to live to see her achievements. He was an old man by the time Doctor took his scalpel for good; he could feel his time was coming soon.

A drastic measure had to be taken to ensure that their ruse would last beyond Dr. Timothy. Days before his death, Doctor relocated her father's vocal cords, and his voice with them, from his throat into her own. The legacy transfer was complete. For those outside the vault, it would seem as though Dr. Timothy was immortal. His name, his skill, his voice, his love of the art of medicine, his unflinching apathy towards human life, all had been gifted unto his daughter.

When Dr. Timothy died in the fall of 2007, Doctor brewed him into the final batch of Rooster Liquor. It seemed a fitting tribute. She figured another batch would sully his memory, strip the 'special' from the bottles that contained her father. She also figured that cutting off the flow of Rooster Liquor would really rile up the Black Pope and that sounded like good fun. If there was one thing Dr. Timothy failed to pass on to Doctor, it was respect for his boss.

The Black Pope envisioned the fourth Beat Cop as being the finest in his fleet. Just like the others, only with that new wife smell. She was to be the statuesque, mustachioed whirlwind of feminine violence that proved he was still in firm control of M Prefecture. Reality was doing cruel things to the Black Pope's delusions. With his number of wives capped at three, he had to take out his frustration on someone.

"You have failed me Dr. Timothy. If it were not for that vault door, I would come down there and put an end to your incompetence myself!"

"How very rash. Perhaps in future, there will be other women to suit your needs." Doctor was fairly certain that there wouldn't be.

After years of being told she was the last of M's females, she was quite surprised to have Mona dropped at her doorstep. This mysterious girl was older, but not by much. The odds of a third girl their age slipping through the cracks were slim. Doctor was feeding the Black Pope lip service in hopes he'd hang up in frustration, he was always so dull. He didn't hang up.

"No, Dr. There will not be." The Black Pope knew the extent of M Prefecture's decline better than anyone else. This had been his last shot to grow his ranks. Had he known of what Billy Lopez had done to his wives hours earlier, he would have known it was his last shot to have any effective presence in the streets of Tierra Podrida.

Doctor had to think fast, listening to the Black Pope bitch and moan was such a boring chore. She needed something to shut him up. "Your conjecture differs from mine. I see. What shall be done with the body? If you wish we could sell her off, one part at a time. I imagine the Prefecture's most sought after body could fetch quite the price." She stole the idea from volume 21 of *LaRue's Longing*. In this case it wasn't a broken heart divided amongst five spurned lovers, but the concept wasn't far off.

The Black Pope pondered this over. The girl would not be returning to life... It would send a message to any potential upstart pornographers... "Yes. That will do."

With the unenthusiastic approval of her boss, Doctor Timothy set to work. The last daughter born to the once proud people of M Prefecture began to disassemble the second last, piece by piece.

CHAPTER 28 - FALSE BOTTOM

20.3 MILES SOUTHWEST OF TIERRA PODRIDA,
M PREFECTURE, THE UNION

TUESDAY, JUNE 29, 2010

THWUNCH **THWUNCH**

There was no longer any point to hiding. With nothing left to protect, Billy slammed the shovel against the sunbaked earth. Brazen, out in plain sight. The rocky crunches kicked out by the shovel resonated throughout the desert. Clint lay on his side nearby, feebly fashioning crosses out of the thickest pieces of scrub brush he could find.

Norm and Ry were wrapped in their bedclothes. Ry was left clutching his portable cassette player. Norm didn't really own anything worth burying him with.

It had been a long, awful night. Billy split his time between trying to nurse Clint back to health and yearning to chase after Mona. He had no clue where to start looking. He didn't know the first thing about Mona's captor and neither did Clint. Billy's worry kept him from getting any lasting sleep. He had been out since dawn, Clint joined him not long after.

THWUNCH **THWUNCH**

"I figured you'd be making pentagrams." Billy said with a bit more of a sneer in his voice than he had intended. They were the first words either of them had uttered all day.

"These only take two sticks." Was the weak reply, followed by the sound of uninterrupted shoveling.

The holes were dug and the sun was high in the sky by the time either of them spoke again. "I'm sorry Clint. We should have killed him when we had the chance. None of this would've happened if it weren't for me." Letting the painful events marinate in his mind hadn't done Billy any favors. He had never felt guiltier.

"Couldn't be helped Billy. I was the one who agreed to let him go, anyhow. Seemed like a good idea at the time. Hell, I bet you didn't have any idea what was going on that day." Billy knew Clint was right, it didn't make him feel any better about the situation.

"Yeah."

Billy was able to lift Norm into his grave. He considered dragging Ry into his, but figured it would best to ask for Clint's help; despite how swollen the old man's battered and bruised body had grown.

"Could you get his feet?"

"Of course."

The graves were shallow, shallow enough that the bodies could be lowered in, and not dropped. They both deserved better, but that could be said about most of the people in M Prefecture, living or dead.

"I am really going to miss these guys. Y'know Billy, losing a second family is just as hard as the first."

"Sorry Clint. I hope Mona's OK. And we'll find her if she is."

They both knew she wasn't OK, they just didn't know the degree to which things had gone sour. Billy's attempt at making Clint feel better left both men feeling terrible.

"Should we say something?" Billy had to break the silence, lump in his throat or no.

"I'm no good at these things Billy. But, yeah. I should. I want to. Um. I'll miss you boys. We had a good thing here for a while and none of it would have been possible without you. Sleep well."

Billy wasn't sure how good a thing they possibly could have had; he still viewed the life Clint's crew led as a decidedly horrible existence. But, Billy could tell how badly Clint felt about his loss. The old man was staring off into the distance, struggling to stay upright.

"I'm sorry Billy, I never should've accepted Garbage Bag's offer, never should've brought you here. Just figured I could get some proper help around here, finally hang it up. Help some poor kid get out of a jam at the same time. Sounded good, really good. Then it all got shot to hell. Still, I'm glad you came Billy. It's selfish of me, I know, but you've made me do some thinking. About how I live, how I used to live. New perspective, you know? Yeah... If you never showed up, well... Hell, Billy, I hope you're not sore, I hope you know you're too good for a place like this." Clint said, without breaking his stare off to the mesa in the distance, choked up with a waver in his voice.

"Don't feel bad for me, I like it here." Billy was lying, but at least he meant well.

"That's nice of you to say Billy. I'm going to get some rest."

"OK." Billy began to shovel the dirt back into the graves as Clint sniffled his way back to the blackened crater that now served as entrance into the cave.

'What now? What the hell am I doing here? He's right. I am too good for this.'

Billy's thoughts of hopeless self pity were briefly interrupted by a muffled telephone ring from below. Clint must've got it, the ringing stopped abruptly. Billy finished shoveling the thin layer of freshly turned dirt onto the blanketed husks of Norm and Ry and tamped the desert back into place with his cowboy boots as best he could. The makeshift crosses were shoved into the ground above the heads of his onetime co-workers. The act didn't hold enough finality for Billy's tastes, but prayer never crossed his mind. A sigh and a solemn trip back down the ladder were all Billy had to offer.

"Uh huh. Uh huh. OK. OK! I'll tell him." Lying prone on the floor, Clint weakly let the receiver drop onto the cradle. "That was your best friend, The Pervert. Says he has something to show you, 'push hares' or something. Hard to tell though, he sounds like some kind of robot."

"Oh good, I'd better head right over." said Billy with a sarcastic sneer. Billy's upturned lip slowly drooped back into position as he pieced things together. "Wait. Did you say push hares?"

"Pardon?" Clint wheezed.

"Push hares! You know, you must know. Mona's got um, those squares, you know?"

"Oh right! Sure. I don't follow." Clint lowered his head to the ground, too worn down to steady his focus on Billy.

Billy had little patience for Clint's confused ignorance. His mind was going a mile a minute and his mouth had a hard time keeping up. "Listen! He made a big deal about them, and the choking, and I called him some names, and... oh man, I really messed this up! He wants to rub this in my face, he must! I've got to go!"

Clint's strained reply came without the courtesy of lifting his face off the stone floor. "Slow down, Billy. Are you talking about The Pervert?"

"He has Mona! I know he does! The fat guy must've kidnapped her for him!" Billy scampered up the ladder.

"I don't know Billy. Don't think The Pervert is friendly enough with anybody to call in a favor. But, if you're right, we'll go bring her back together. Hold on." Clint made an effort to follow Billy up to the surface, only to awkwardly fall back to earth with a groan, betrayed by his beaten body. He managed to stop short from a complete faceplant by stiff-arming the ground, his hand came to rest in what was once Candi's head.

The cave was still a gruesome sight, streaked with spattered blood trails, sprinkled with chips of bone. The remains of the Beat Cops lay where they fell, cleaning up didn't seem all that important compared to giving Ry and Norm a decent burial. The stream that trickled through the main chamber ran clear until it flowed through the pulpy remains of Champagne's mangled skull. It ran pale pink after that. The blood that had fallen onto the light strips on the floor cast vivid red, blotchy shadows onto the ceiling and walls.

Billy clambered back down into the bloody mess to help Clint to his feet. "You alright?"

Clint rolled his shoulder in place to make sure things were in working order. "Alright enough, I think. Maybe you should head into town on your own for this, Billy."

Billy never had plans to the contrary. "Sure."

"Jesus Christ, Billy. You really did a number on these stupid broads." Clint said in a reverent near-whisper as he wiped Candi's blood from his hands onto his pants. "You always catch fire like that when you fight?"

"Dunno." Billy called down as he ascended the ladder. "That's the first fight I've ever been in. You get some rest, I'll be back with Mona."

When Life 29 left the beaten man in the desert days earlier, he had only a vague understanding of where to find the spawn of Satan; he was to be found in a cave, out west. At the time, he rationalized that his tracking expertise could take care of the rest. After 60 hours of futile searching, he had to concede he was in over his head. His Halo revealed thousands of natural formations that could be considered caves, but unfortunately revealed little else. He had been checking them one by one. His frustration grew with his tally of empty caverns. The notion that the beaten man could have lied about Billy Lopez' whereabouts was not a thought Life 29 would entertain. He was a man possessed. He had to save face, not only for himself, for his fallen comrades as well.

The Four Friars had failed in their battle with Satan. They failed badly. Life 29 refused to fail again. He had to destroy the child. But, he would have to find him first. And to find him, he would have to take to the sky once more. He had lost track of how many times he had to re-launch to look for clues. It felt like hundreds. His airborne body yearned for sleep, for food, for a hot bath to wash away the coating of dusty grime that had permeated his tan robe and pasted onto his body.

He was finally in luck. His body would have to wait. Unless he was misreading his infra-red scanners, the next cave he checked looked like it just might be the last.

Billy's shoulder slammed into the plywood door of #215 Progress Ave. The first blow buckled the wood, the second cracked it wide open along the buckle. Billy stormed through the ragged wood. He was greeted by silence, the cacophonous pornographic soundtrack was no more. The wall of televisions had been turned off and partially dismantled.

The swivel chair in the center of the room spun to face Billy. The Pervert did not look as Billy remembered. Surgical bandages wrapped around the bottom half of his face and a speaker, not unlike the one affixed to Dr. Timothy's bank vault, jutted out of his neck. The massive pupils that once filled his eye sockets from lid to lid were gone. In their place were tiny black pin pricks, languidly floating in a sea of bright white, seemingly unable to focus.

Crudely synthesized giggles emanated from the speaker. "Hello, Mr. Lopez!" The Pervert buzzed, followed by more mechanical tittering.

"I don't have time for this, Pervert. Where's Mona? The bathroom?"

"They say painkillers kill the pain but..." The Pervert lapsed into another set of giggles. "Oh, Mr. Lopez it is *so* good to see you again!"

Billy stormed over and grabbed The Pervert by the lapels of his slimy green robe, yanking him up halfway out of his seat.

"Where's Mona?"

"Who?" The Pervert followed this with more giggling and a weak little struggle. "Put me down. Put me down. I've got something to show you." The Pervert waved his scrawny arms in an attempt to brush Billy off of him. Billy lifted The Pervert up and all the way out of his seat, only to fling him back down, hard.

"Don't play games with me." Billy snarled. "Where is she?"

"I was just about to show you." The Pervert said, followed by more synthesized titters. He began to remove his bandages, slowly at first, gradually building speed and finally yanking the bloody gauze off with a poorly coordinated flourish.

Mona's vagina, pussy squares and all, sat underneath The Pervert's nose. Lying sideways, filling the spot where his mouth belonged. His tongue slithered between his new lips. "See something you like, Mr. Lopez?"

'NO!'

Mona wouldn't be saved. Billy had rushed over for nothing. No, it hadn't been for nothing. He had rushed over for vengeance.

Billy grabbed The Pervert by the speaker and swung hard with his free hand, his fist connecting with The Pervert's right eye. Blood poured out of the socket, flames burst forth from Billy's arms.

"Ont ill e! Ont ill e!" The Pervert screeched repeatedly over the noise of cracking bone as the assault continued. Billy loosened his grip on the voice box to hear what the little weasel was trying to say.

"Don't kill me! Don't kill me!" He wheezed through the box. "I thought you'd be happy to see her again!" Billy's grip tightened, the beating resumed.

"O! O! E uz ed en I ot it!"

'What was that?' "God*damn* it! This is your last chance, Pervert." Billy eased off the speaker once more.

"Don't kill me! I didn't *do* anything! She was dead when I bought it!"

"What?" Billy meant to continue punching through his interrogation but he was new at this kind of thing, not to mention shocked. *'That fat asshole sold her?'*

"I just bought it, that's all. I bought it from the auction."

"Auction? What auction?" Billy's line of questioning was countered with quiet snickering and a lot more lip-licking than he wanted to see. He smashed his flaming fist into The Pervert's badly broken eye socket. "Where?"

The Pervert giggled through the pain. "If I told you I wouldn't be keeping it a secret! Oooh! Ooooh! Such strong hands! Punch lower."

Enraged, Billy kept pounding away at The Pervert's smashed eye only to stop abruptly, mid punch. He turned from his bloody handiwork and left without another word. The vengeance he sought couldn't be found here, but he had figured out where he had to go to find it. Probably.

'Even if I'm wrong, what does it matter now?'

Life 29 alighted between the crudely constructed crosses that marked Norm and Ry's final resting spot. He had seen the heat signatures picked up while flying high over the desert before. Oblong rectangles, tinted a cool blue in contrast to the fiery red ground. Fresh graves. If this wasn't the cave, the child would not be found in a cave.

The crosses confirmed his initial suspicion, these were certainly burial sites. He wondered why the spawn of Satan would choose to mark a grave with a cross, or bother to grant his victims a proper burial at all. It had been days since Life learned of the Lopez boy's location. Perhaps he had moved on. Perhaps these graves were the work of another. They were freshly dug, the upturned soil still relatively cool to the touch. Doubt began to set in, but Life 29 was unwilling to concede defeat. Not without first venturing through the scorched hole that led into the bowels of the Earth.

Clint had long since shuffled and crawled his way to the comfort of his bare mattress by the time Life 29 made his trip down the ladder. He was unable to hear the Holy Man's shocked cries, the cave's labyrinthine quality made it difficult for sound to travel from one room to the next. Clint could have set the matter of Billy Lopez straight had Life 29 checked down the corridor that led to Clint's room. It didn't play out that way. Life 29 saw more than enough in the cave's main chamber to know he was on the right track.

The extent of the injuries the dead women suffered spoke of a man capable of inflicting incredible damage on a human body. Only the bloodbath at the Coxwell Motel could match the level of carnage. This was the work of Satan's son. But, Life could tell he would not find the child down in the cave. The blood spray was centralized in the main chamber and his sensors did not detect any telltale drips leading down any of the cave's passageways. The drips didn't continue up the ladder either, but a trail of fresh, cool, dirty footprints did.

The footprints continued in a north-eastwardly direction above ground, but their signature was incredibly faint, growing ever fainter as the hot sun baked the desert. Even with his expertise and advanced equipment, Life 29 would have a difficult time locating Billy Lopez based on that trail alone. Luckily, the trail of fresh dirt had a friend. A small piece of yellow fabric was snagged on a scrub brush not far from the cave's entrance. Flannel, badly frayed. It was not the only piece, far from it. Life 29 adjusted his sensors, his path became immediately clear.

The mysteries behind the fresh graves and the underground lighting grid would have to go unsolved. The trail of cool dirt and the frayed fibers marched in lockstep, both heading directly towards

Tierra Podrida. Life 29 set off to finalize his mission in M Prefecture. He had a high school senior to destroy.

CHAPTER 29 - WE NEED TO TALK

TIERRA PODRIDA, M PREFECTURE, THE UNION

TUESDAY, JUNE 29, 2010

BZZT **BZZT** **BZZZZ-ZZZ-ZZZZZT**

"Dr. Timothy! Open up! Dr. Timothy!" Billy impatiently pounded on the thick metal door, mostly for dramatic effect, even if that wasn't his intent. Regardless of the adrenaline racing through his veins, Billy wasn't strong enough to get any kind of sound out of the solid steel.

Eventually a snide reply buzzed through the intercom. "Her choice parts have been sold. How else can I be of service?"

Billy knew Dr. Timothy was involved with Mona's death long before he arrived at Tierra Podrida Savings and Loan, Mona's pussy didn't end up sitting beneath the Pervert's nose without a little help. The confirmation that Dr. Timothy was behind the parts auction didn't come as a surprise. That was to Billy's benefit. He would need to hang on to the little cool he had left in order to take advantage of the opportunity offered by the man behind the door.

"It's my um, arms. They're swollen up and they're uh, starting to change color. I think they're sick." Billy was worried about the quality of his lie, the intercom was silent. He'd have to make his visit worth Dr. Timothy's while. "I can only pay you in sustenance gel, but I've got lots of it. 40 pouches, is that OK?"

"That is more than OK. Please, come in."

Billy wasn't sure exactly what to brace for as the vault door slowly swung to the side. He didn't have much information to work with and *'Kill whoever killed Mona'* was about as far as his plan had evolved. One way or the other, things were going to get violent. Billy counted on that much. He didn't count on things getting horribly weird first.

A sickly girl stood beyond the open vault door. No more than 14, slightly built, aside from her enormous, bald, heavily veined head. She wore a lavender surgical gown, white tube socks with blue stripes and a reinforced metal latticework designed to keep the weight of her head from snapping her neck. She had the business end of a blunderbuss trained on Billy's face.

The bitter rage left over from his visit to The Pervert's kept Billy from reeling in fear. It didn't do much to help him with his confusion. "Uh... Dr. Timothy? Is he... here?"

"No." Her voice was definitely the one Billy heard through the intercom. Weirdly accented, decidedly male. "Please, call me Doctor. Step closer. And take off your shirt."

Billy did as he was told, fearful that refusal would leave him headless. That wasn't his only concern. He hoped that whoever this girl was wouldn't take gun-firing offense to his lie about his arms and the sustenance gel pouches. Billy couldn't turn back now, he unbuttoned his shirt and let it fall to the floor as he made his way inside the vault.

Doctor tried to approximate a seductive sashay in Billy's direction. Hindered by her abnormal physiology, the best she could do was a series of off-balance lurches. Despite her lack of poise, she never once lowered the bell end of the blunderbuss away from Billy's face. They met in the center of the vault. She nuzzled the cold metal spokes that held her head in place against Billy's neck and ran her free hand back and forth across his bare chest ever so slowly.

'Um...'

"Mmm. I didn't think I'd ever meet a man like you. A man so... perfect. Young, pristine. A LaRue to call my very own, after all these years." She purred as Billy stood stock still.

"There is nothing wrong with your arms and you have no gel. You do not need my services, you must need *me*. Oh, how I have dreamt of this day!"

'Help me.'

Billy wanted answers, but he *needed* to keep his head attached to his body. He let her continue as she wished; shifting his focus to the operating room, trying in vain to drown out the seductive Australian man's voice that was as unnerving as it was complimentary. The converted bank vault was immaculately clean. It stank of bleach. Folded cots stood next to what Billy presumed to be an operating table. A series of copper boiling pots were stacked against a far wall. Safety deposit boxes had been retrofitted with glass doors, nearly all of the boxes housed 'fresh' body parts. *Body parts. Damn it! What are you doing, Billy?'*

Billy was as frightened as he was determined. It took a few tries before he managed to spit out "Did you sell Mona?" through clenched teeth.

"I did, yes."

At least he was on the right track, even if he was on the receiving end of glacially paced, sexual assault committed by... hell, whatever or whoever she was.

"Did you kill Mona?" Billy could barely squeak out the word 'kill'. Luckily, the conical tube poised to blow his brains out acted as a decent amplifier.

"Oh my no." Her hand was now trailing up and down his stomach, grazing ever closer to his beltline. "I'm sorry, I never caught your name."

"Lopez, Billy Lopez" Billy choked on his words as he strained to deliver them through his clenched jaw. *'How do I get out of here?'*

"I am a surgeon by trade, not a murderer, Billy. Although there is a first time for everything. I would like to remind you that I *could* end your life with a single pull of this trigger, tragic and wasteful as that might be." Her hand had snaked down within the confines of his elastic waistband. Quietly terrified, Billy felt his penis shrink away in response. "Perhaps you would like to change your tone. Try one more befitting a gorgeous man holding a civilized conversation with the object of his, shall we say, lusty affections." Doctor batted her sparse eyelashes as she toyed around in Billy's trousers.

'I'm going to die here. She's going to kill me. Cut me up and sell me. Just like Mona. Keep my dick as a trophy.'

"Of course, my apologies" Billy tried to evoke a suave tone of voice and to coax a rise out of his member. She had been furtively fishing for a solid handful for a while and Billy didn't want to prove to be a disappointment at gunpoint. "I don't mean to offend... beautiful. I just need to find out what happened to Mona."

"Mmm. Why is that?"

The answer flared up in his brain and coincided with a rush of blood to his phallus. "I need revenge."

She squealed, or came as close to a squeal as her vocal cords would allow. "How romantic! But your Mona is gone now. And we are here, all alone. Just like LaRue and Josephine. Or Margaret. Or Stable Girl Sally. Or Vice-Princess Bernice!"

'What is she talking... No! Concentrate! I need to get out of here. Alive!'

She pressed the gun's muzzle tight up against Billy's chin and fondled his half-hard member. "Kiss me. Caress me. I have been a stand in for my father for too long. Make a woman of me, Billy!"

'Father? Doesn't matter. Not now. She's serious. Oh God. Oh God. Do what she says. Just get it over with.'

'OK.' Billy leaned away from the gun, and tentatively bent down to kiss his sexual captor.

A booming voice bellowed from the bank lobby through the wide open vault door. "Stop right there!"

Billy snapped upright, eager to make use of the diversion, thrilled to be interrupted by this noble stranger. *'Thank God! Someone came for me!'*

The mysterious savior, a black man swathed in tan robes with a golden ring hovering over his head, shoved Billy aside to get to the girl. He ripped the gun from her weak grasp. *'Yes! Oh God, yes!'* Billy's relief was short-lived. *'Wait, no! God no! Her! Shoot her!'* The bank vault's new guest picked up where Doctor left off. He had the gun trained on Billy's nose.

'What kind of rescue is this? I don't want to die! I don't want to die!'

"Spawn of Satan, you have eluded our reach for too long. The time has come to cleanse the Earth, to ensure that the future will be free from your dark deeds! Do you wish to repent your sins?" Life 29 hollered as Billy wriggled backwards, further into the confines of the bank vault.

'Spawn of Satan? How could he... that doesn't...' Billy looked towards Doctor in the hope that she could psychically shed some

light on who his current attacker was, or what he wanted. She looked to be as baffled as Billy felt.

"Me? You've got the wrong guy! It's not me!" Billy hated to raise the ire of... whoever this was, but he had to try and convince him that he wasn't Satan's son. Even if Billy didn't completely believe it himself.

Life 29's fellow Friars had been torn limb from limb. He had spent three sleepless days on Billy's trail. And, he was about to pass into lore as the Holy Man who destroyed the Son of Satan. This was no time for doubt, this was time for action. Life 29 had the child in his sights; pleas would not keep him from ending his life. "Do not play coy with me. The time for repentance has passed."

"Shoot him! Shoot him, please!" Doctor cried out in her manly voice. "He was attacking my chaste virtue!"

'Hey! That's not tr-'

KA-RRRROOOOOOOOOOOOOM

Life 29 had pulled the trigger. The blast was earsplitting, the acrid gunpowder cloud blinding. Billy shouldn't have been able to register either of these. His ears and eyes were supposed to have been blasted to paste by the thundering hand-cannon. Billy was just fine, physically. Emotionally, he'd been far better, but his head was still in one piece and he was very much alive.

The same could not be said for Life 29. He lay dead on the ground with a gaping, bloody hole where most of his torso should be. The blackened remains of the blunderbuss had fallen from one hand. The frayed yellow threads that made up the last of Mona's nightgown bread-crumb trail had fallen from the other. The golden ring fell from his head and rolled to a stop nearby.

The gun had misfired, the barrel exploded. Doctor Timothy knew it would end up this way. Her father never missed an opportunity to caution her about his faulty firearm and his lessons stuck. Delighted to have saved her fine-looking stranger, she hobbled over to Billy as quickly as she could.

"Spawn of Satan? Oh my! Handsome, vengeful and devilishly mysterious? I do believe I am in love with you, Billy Lopez."

Billy didn't really register what Doctor was saying as she knelt down to run her fingers through his hair. His heart was pounding, his ears were ringing. Concentrating on his vital signs helped chase away thoughts of what just happened, but it only worked to a point.

This had not come to a head as Billy had hoped. His trip to the bank raised more questions than it answered. Dr. Timothy was some freaky girl, somehow. That black guy was dead, whoever he was. And vengeance wasn't his, but apparently there were some sinful dark deeds he could lay claim to. They probably had something to do with his lineage, or so Billy figured. Mysterious black guys probably wouldn't say he was Satan's son and then try to kill him without reason.

Billy only knew one thing for certain. It was time to go. *'Where's my shirt?'* He swatted Doctor's hand off of his head and rose to grab his pale pink top.

Doctor Timothy was no threat without the blunderbuss in her hands, Life 29 had been felled by Tierra Podrida Savings and Loan's last line of defense. Gun or no, she still carried on as if she was in the position to off Billy. She grabbed him by his lapels and pulled him close before he had the chance to slip his second arm into the shirtsleeve.

"What are you doing?"

"Getting dressed. Leaving."

"You can't leave, Billy!." Doctor pleaded. "We need one another! Here I am, all alone, uniquely gorgeous and undeniably

279

brilliant. And here you are, all alone, magnificent to the eye and clearly stupid as a rock, if your diction is any indication. Our love was destined, Billy. You were meant to be the LaRue to my Bernice!"

"What love?" Billy shook her hands free of his lapels, slid his free arm into his shirt and buttoned it up to the collar. "And don't call me stupid." He was done. M Prefecture had beaten him. It was too weird, too horrible. And there was no escape. *'That gun shouldn't have blown up.'* Suicide only crossed Billy's mind briefly in his most petulant moment. No, he'd play the awful hand he was dealt. He'd explain things to Clint, wish him luck and start working at the factory tomorrow. He was a white man, and that was what a white man was meant to do. He headed for the vault door.

Doctor Timothy had other ideas. She toppled over with a **CLANG** as her supports hit the polished floor, desperately clawing at Billy's legs.

"Don't go! I need you Billy! And you need my help!"

"I don't need anyone. I certainly don't need you." Billy kicked himself free from Doctor Timothy's soft grip.

Sobbing, she scrambled to her feet and hollered as Billy strode through the lobby, and out onto the street. "The Black Pope! The man you are looking for is the Black Pope! Please, come back to me!"

Billy hated his curiosity for overpowering his better judgment. He took a deep breath and slowly surveyed the decaying city before turning back towards the bank with a deep sigh. "Who?"

"The man I work for. The man who runs things. The man my father once knew as Jonathan Wright." She said as she made her way out onto the street for the first time in her life. She wiped the tears from her eyes, her brows furrowed hard into a squint. "Is the sun always bright like this, Billy?"

'I thought you said you were brilliant, stupid. Of course the sun's bright.' Billy had no time to deliver insults, he'd have to save that one for later. He dashed past Doctor to grab the phone in the operating room. *'Come on! Come on!'* It took ages for Clint to pick up. Once the old man coughed up a "Hello?" Billy spared no time filling him in.

"Clint! I'm so sorry, Mona's dead. But Jonathan Wright's still alive. I know. I don't know! Of course I remember seeing his bones! But he did it, he killed Mona! Doctor Timothy told me. No, a she. Well, sure, but, I don't know! How would I know? It's complicated, OK? Also, some black guy tried to kill me. No, not Wright. I don't know! Some black guy! He's dead now. Yeah, I'm fine. I'll tell you later. Are you sure? In your condition? OK... Three hours? Sure, I'll meet you there in three hours. Oh, he calls himself 'Black Pope' now. I don't know why that matters, you're the one who knew him! OK. OK! Three hours. Yeah! Damn right, we'll make him pay!"

Billy slammed the receiver and turned to Doctor Timothy, who had retreated from her first glimpse of the sky to sidle up against him in the vault. "I really, really, *really* hate to do this, but Doctor, you've got to take me to Saint Basil's!"

CHAPTER 30 - FINAL FIGHT

TIERRA PODRIDA, M PREFECTURE, THE UNION

TUESDAY, JUNE 29, 2010

Gordonson didn't care much for lugging televisions through the streets of Tierra Podrida. His stick-thin arms certainly weren't well suited to withstand the weight of a cathode ray tube. Then again, Gordonson's body wasn't well suited for much. It was a regrettable genetic one-off that nature would have to correct through death.

The plastic casing on the bottom of the TV cut into his fingers. He had almost grown used to the feeling. This was the seventh television set Gordonson was transporting to Saint Basil's. Mona's vagina came at the price of 'everything you own' and The Pervert had been overjoyed to pay. Gordonson had been tasked with settling the bill by rounding up all of The Pervert's worldly belongings. Only six of The Pervert's TV sets ever made it to the Black Pope's lair; but the seventh came awfully close.

Tierra Podrida Savings & Loan sat along the path between #215 Progress Ave. and the town's lone Onion Dome. Gordonson lumbered down the street in front of the bank, bent over at the waist, television set weighing heavy on his fingertips, knuckles nearly scraping the ground.

Doctor had been stalling for time just within the bank's main entrance. She breathed a silent sigh of relief as she caught sight of Gordonson off in the distance. She had eagerly accepted Billy's offer of acting as an escort to Saint Basil's, but had neglected to mention a few key details. She had never set foot outside of the bank and had no clue where to find the Black Pope's hideout. Now she could use the Black Pope's hired brute to lead the way. Very, very slowly.

They would have to follow at a distance, in secret. Doctor coyly motioned for Billy to head back inside. Billy missed the signal completely, having just caught sight of the man who had ruined everything for everyone. *'Now, I'll have my revenge.'* Billy was wrong. Revenge would have to wait.

He was getting closer, too close. Gordonson's none-too-subtle grunts and groans drowned out Doctor's hissed "Get back in!" Her third attempt to grab Billy's attention would have to be impossible to ignore. She quickly crouched down and sprung into action, delivering a jarring headbutt to Billy's sternum. He tumbled back into the bank, his fall cushioned by the dirty carpet. Doctor lurched in after him.

"What the hell are you doing?" Billy fumed as he rose to his feet. "Do you have any idea who that is?"

"I know exactly who that is, Billy. The question is, do you?"

"Well, no not really, but..."

"But Mona, yes, I know. Vengeance will be yours, and soon, but for now, keep quiet and listen..."

Conspiring in speedy whispers, Doctor Timothy filled Billy in on the work Gordonson did for the Black Pope. He would have preferred to learn this lesson from someone who hadn't manhandled him at gunpoint, but Billy was in no position to be picky.

He began piecing things together. *That Gordonson guy works for this Black Pope guy and Gordonson wanted Mona dead. So, the Black Pope probably wanted Mona dead. For some reason. And Doctor Timothy works for the Black Pope...*

"Why did the Black Pope want Mona dead?"

"Dead? That was the last thing he wanted. He wanted her for his fourth wife."

'Four wives?' "What? You said the Black Pope killed her!"

"No. I said he is the man you are looking for. She died on the operating table."

It took a while for her words to sink in. When they did, Billy was livid. Whispers had given way to full blown shouting. "*You killed her!?*"

"No Billy, I'm afraid her ill-health killed her." Doctor had to choose her words carefully, sugarcoat her involvement as best she could. She didn't wish to further upset her delicate Billy, his reaction wasn't likely to be civil if he found out that she recommended Mona be sold in parts. "The Black Pope unwisely ordered her surgery and I did all I could to keep her alive. I assure you, I did her no harm."

Billy's shouts gave way to meek mumbles. "Right. Yeah. Sorry. Listen, if I follow this Gordonson guy, he'll lead me to the Black Pope, right?"

"You mean if *we* follow him, he'll lead *us* to the Black Pope."

'Fine. Whatever.' "Fine. Whatever."

"Then yes, I'm quite certain he will."

Together, they followed Gordonson through the streets of Tierra Podrida, over the rubbled building fortification that sat atop the highway and then south along a long, desolate stretch of road. Finally they arrived… somewhere. If this wasn't Saint Basil's, Billy couldn't reckon what else it could be.

A forest of carelessly piled consumer goods spread out in front of them. Gordonson made his way through the stacks of discarded small appliances, heading towards the blue and white spiraled onion dome that loomed not far in the distance. Billy and Doctor followed close behind.

Billy turned to Doctor and mouthed "Now?" Doctor nodded her consent, nearly tipping over in the process.

Gordonson couldn't have known what hit him. In a flash, Billy had tackled him from behind, knocking his top heavy body onto the ground. Billy hoisted the fallen television set high up into the air and flung it back down, driving Gordonson's head deep into the desert.

Ethereal flames engulfed his body as the blood poured out from underneath the smashed plastic and glass. Billy wasn't expecting his body to put on a personal pyrotechnic show, he wasn't particularly adept at picking up patterns.

'Again?'

"Hey Doctor, have you ever seen anything like this?" he asked, a twinge of panic in his voice.

She was stunned. Partially due to the extreme violence she was just witness to, mostly because of the ghostly flames shooting out of her fantasy beau.

"No…"

"Yeah, I didn't think so."

Clint Masters was slowly trudging through the desert towards Saint Basil's. Each step was painful. He had been making his way there for the last six hours, one foot plodding after the other. His stiff, swollen body felt like it was on the verge of completely giving up, maybe even shutting down for good, but, he was close now. Close enough to see Billy and... someone... crouched near the Cathedral and Nightclub's heavy double doors, relatively out of sight, their cover aided by nightfall. His final steps hurt the least, he had made it. It wouldn't be much longer now.

"Sorry I'm late Billy." Clint wheezed. "Who's this?"

"Yeah. This... is Doctor Timothy." Billy's reply was devoid of enthusiasm, bordering on a moan.

Clint eyed the strange girl from head to toe. "No it's not."

"I assure you, sir, I am indeed Doctor Timothy. And from hereon I will be forever by Billy's side!"

Clint glanced over to Billy and Billy's defeated grimace.

"Not today, sweetheart."

Clint summoned all the strength he could to hoist Doctor off of her feet. He wedged her face up into a big pile of second-hand merchandise.

"What are you doing? Pick me up!" Doctor kicked and struggled to no avail. Weighed down by the rods that supported her head, she was completely unable to escape the stack of pre-war goods.

"Sorry to leave you like this, but it won't be safe for you in there." Clint said, nodding in the direction of the converted warehouse building. "And Billy, I've been thinking, it probably won't be safe for you either. So if you want, I mean, you don't have-"

Billy didn't give Clint the chance to let him off the hook. He had to speak up over the racket of Doctor trying to right herself. "No Clint. You're right. It won't be safe, but, this is my mess to clean up. I'm in charge now, remember?"

"I do remember." Clint was beaming with pride. "And I see I picked the right man for the job. Thanks, Billy. Let's go kill a dead man."

"Yeah, let's."

They made their way past Gordonson's remains as they plodded towards Saint Basil's entrance. Clint had missed the final moments of the Lollipop of a Man's life and the subsequent display of Billy's body-fire, but the corpse and the television set that rested upon it spoke volumes. "Did that help any with the guilt, Billy?"

"No. Not really. I wish it did."

"That's not the answer I was hoping for. Say, is she *really* Dr. Timothy?"

"I think she is. She was the only one in the vault."

"Huh. Go figure. She's got the voice for it, I suppose. You said some black guy tried to kill you?"

"Yep. Ended up killing himself though."

"Ha! Weird. You'll have to tell me all about if we get out of this."

"Love to. And it's 'when' we get out of this."

The Black Pope had prepared a celebratory meal for the Beat Cops the night previous. He wanted it to be special. After all, the opportunity to send your three identical wives to murder the man who ruined your life by winning a boxing match over 30 years ago didn't come along often. The long awaited death of Clint Masters was not to be the only cause for celebration that evening. He would be adding a fourth to his harem, at long last.

It was to be a night to remember. Saint Basil's light-up dance floor was turned on for the first time in years and he had dipped into his private reserve of delicacies from overseas.

His three Beat Cops didn't return home in time for dinner. Dr. Timothy called with news that there would never be a fourth. A despondent Black Pope tucked into his tin of macaroni and pork alone, sitting in his jewel studded leather throne, watching the lights on the floor change color in turn. White, yellow, pink, blue. White, yellow, pink, blue. They'd be home soon. Evening gave way to night. Night to day. The Black Pope ate a second tin of macaroni and pork for breakfast. He set about polishing the bronze statues and lighting the freestanding incense burners, hoping superficial tasks would put his mind at ease. White, yellow, pink, blue. He ate another tin for lunch. White, yellow, pink, blue. He knew they were never coming home.

The Black Pope had finished his fourth tin in two days by the time Billy Lopez kicked open the doors to Saint Basil's Cathedral and Nightclub. He rose from his chair to meet his intruders, steadying himself on his staff. He still cut an impressive figure, even at his advanced age.

"Clint Masters." He rasped through his tall porcelain facemask. "What a shame."

Even after all the years and the deconstruction job performed on his face, there was no mistaking his voice. This man was Jonathan Wright.

"It *is* you! How are you still alive?" Clint was near pleading he was so confused.

"The skin of a transient bus driver was all it took to complete my little ruse. It is not as if I have been ruling over an intelligent people. I see you bought a young homosexual consort to do your dirty work for you."

'Hey!'

"Handsome lad, inviting buttocks." The Black Pope continued as he stepped closer to his unwanted visitors. "Not how I would spend my earnings from a pornographic empire, but to each his own. He makes you look absolutely terrible in comparison, Clint."

"He's in charge." Clint sneered. "And he's all man."

"Just the way you like it, I'm sure. I say, I do wish my hired goon had the good sense to tell me that you were the man with the tubes. I would have paid a personal visit to that cave of yours had I known I could find your rotting carcass there."

"I hope you and God are still on good terms, Wright." Clint began to stagger towards the hulking masked man. "You've taken two families from me. It is a damn shame I'm only going to get to kill you once!"

"Kill me? My, my, how dramatic! Two *families* is it? And I *took* them? If you were to have asked Trixie I have a feeling that she would have told you a very different story. One about a man who left his loving wife and young daughter. That is, she would have told you a story *if* you managed to catch her when she wasn't servicing a man with her mouth. Not an easy task, as I recall."

Clint staggered harder, faster. Billy followed behind at a distance, not entirely sure what role he was to play in the showdown.

"As for your second *family*, a caveful of crippled pornographers and some girl you were whoring out? Well, that does paint a delightful family portrait."

"She was a brain retard, Wright! What choice did I have?"

"What choice indeed. I would have done the very same in your position. Hard to believe? Not surprising. You always were weak of faith. On the other hand, I have seen the light, renounced my past. I am a man reborn and my faith has never been stronger! God and I are on better terms than ever before. And to think, I owe it all to you. Had you not rejected your divine role, I would have remained blind; forever subservient to a false doctrine. You should feel no regrets for abandoning your holy destiny. You have done this Prefecture a great service through your weak inaction, and for that, I applaud you."

The Black Pope gripped the top of his staff tight and pulled back with a twist, revealing a glistening sword concealed within. "Then, you went and cut the profits of my holy pandering to the bone. For that, I will kill you."

The sword thrust should've pierced Clint's heart, but Clint's skin had lost none of its resiliency. The second thrust should've perforated a lung, at least. Clint's body wrapper deflected it as well.

"Your pale hide is even tougher than I remembered, Masters. No matter, a bloodless death will be easier to clean up after. Your innards must be crying for freedom. Such a pity you cannot let them out."

The Black Pope continued his rapid thrusts and slashes, driving Clint back past Billy, all but ignoring the young man he presumed to be Clint's sexual Boy Friday. The old pornographer's skin may have been free from perforation, but his swollen, discolored body didn't look like it could withstand any further abuse. Knocked to the ground, he labored to scramble away from the one sided assault. Forced against a wall, he finally collapsed into a quivering heap, barely strong enough to give voice to the pain each subsequent attack inflicted.

Billy had seen enough. Clint wouldn't able to settle his grudge. He would have to step in, but first he needed the Black Pope's attention. "I killed your wives, Wright! I'm the one you want!"

The Black Pope spun to face the pornographer's apprentice, his sword at the ready. "Your end will be messy."

Billy had never ducked under a swinging blade while running at full speed before. He wasn't sure if he was naturally gifted at that kind of thing, or if his success should be chalked up to beginner's luck. One thing was for certain, he had a clear shot. He lunged, fist aimed squarely at the Black Pope's porcelain faceplate. His punch connected, shattering the mask, revealing the Black Pope's never-healed face underneath.

Billy waited too long before swinging again. He wasn't distracted by the Black Pope's skinless, featureless visage, he had seen more than enough of M Prefecture to accept grotesque deformity. He stalled because he expected to catch fire. He should have kept punching, ethereal flames or no.

"Nice punch, sex boy." The Black Pope scoffed. "Tell me, are you familiar with the phrase 'an eye for an eye'?"

"This is no time for talk, Wright." Billy wasn't eager to admit that he had no clue what the Black Pope meant.

"If what you say is true, you have taken more than my wives, you have taken the very hands with which I gripped the throat of this Prefecture. Too bad you have but two hands to atone for my three wives. I shall collect them both as repayment for Candi and Champagne. I will have to make do with your head for Snadra."

With one swift, graceful, figure-eight motion, the Black Pope effortlessly cleaved both of Billy's arms from his body. Two distinct thuds could be heard as they hit the ground and two thoughts sprung to mind as Billy stumbled backwards. *'My arms!'* and *'Snadra wasn't a typo?'* Adrenaline may have kept Billy from toppling over completely, but it didn't keep him from backing into an incense burner and knocking it to the ground. Its smoldering contents spilled, pockmarking the colored plastic tiles on the floor and igniting one of the defaced religious tapestries. The flames jumped from that tapestry to the next and then the next in turn. In a matter of seconds, the main hall of Saint Basil's had caught ablaze. The temperature within the stuffy, windowless space was growing intolerable.

Billy's thoughts of survival manifested in one word. A word he had learned in the first aid segment of health class years earlier, then had all but forgotten. *'Cauterize!'* His bloody left shoulder stump met the hot bronze statue of King Solomon with a **KSSSSSSSSS** and a wail. The right stump underwent the same. Billy slumped to the ground. Too weak. The bleeding might have let up, somewhat. Billy couldn't tell. His focus was on the faceless man pointing a sword at his neck.

"Setting a man's home on fire is hardly a fitting apology, sex boy."

"His name is Billy! Billy Lopez!" Clint hollered. "Damn nice work lighting this dump up, Billy!" Clint's exposed skin was now bruised vibrant purples and greens, but he had made it back to his feet. He struggled to step in between the armless Billy and the slowly advancing Black Pope. Clint unbuttoned his shirt and wrapped his fingers around the reinforced IV bag that served as the hub for his nasal tubes.

"What are you doing, Masters? Get out of the way!"

"Never too late to tell Satan to kiss your ass!" Clint pulled hard on the IV bag, ripping it free from the sutures that had held it place for decades. The tubes that snaked out of his nose ripped free from the bag and ran dry, the bright blue liquid gushed out of the plastic pouch and onto the floor. Clint's body went limp and fell to the ground.

'Clint! No! What the hell was that? He cut off my arms! Clint!'

Fire had eaten most of the way up the tapestries. Thick, black smoke had billowed to the ceiling and began to sink to the floor. The lifeless body of Clint Masters was all that stood between the Black Pope and the now incomplete Billy Lopez. Merely stepping over Clint wasn't an option, not after what he did to Jonathan Wright years earlier. Suppressing a fit of coughs, the Black Pope reared back and booted Clint's body, hoping to get it out of his way in one last act of disrespect. It didn't work. He wouldn't have the opportunity to try a second time.

The kick jerked Clint's body back to life with a series of violent spasms and loud, joint-cracking pops. Laying face down on the dance floor, his limbs contorted into impossible angles. The twitching grew faster, the popping louder. He planted his feet on the ground and snapped up to his full height with one emphatic supernatural spasm. He didn't say a word as he pinched his nose, but he grimaced just a little as he wrenched it hard to one side.

"Masters, what have you-"

The tubes left to dangle from Clint's nose began to spew torrents of blood, drenching the dance floor. Ethereal white flames erupted from his body, bright enough to cast shadows on the orange flames climbing the walls. The Black Pope never finished his sentence. Clint drove a flaming fist deep into his gut, crushing his spine. He dropped to the ground, legs immobilized, forced to support the weight of his torso on his massive arms. He would've been better off playing dead, Clint wasn't done.

Each punch left a flaming white trail in its wake. The furious flurry broke bones, shredded flesh. The Black Pope died long before Clint let up. His head and torso were completely destroyed, just as Rex Hughson's had been years earlier. The Black Pope's arms fell to the ground, Clint dropped to his knees, drenched in his own gushing blood.

Billy had been drifting in and out of consciousness, but he was dead certain that he was awake through all of Clint's flaming rampage. "You catch fire too!?"

"Only when I bleed Billy and I've spent most of my life trying not to..." Clint and Billy were speaking in strained whispers, hunched low under the blanket of smoke. "Listen, I was wrong Billy. I can feel that now. I know it. I haven't been a free man. I've been a slave. Satan's Goddamn slave. I was weak. Foolish. I've done horrible things. When the time comes, be strong. Be wise. You're a good kid, a special kid. The time will come. Whenever you want it to." With that, Clint collapsed.

Billy tried his best to drag him outside, doubled over at the waist, clenching onto Clint's bloody orange shirt with his teeth. Clint was too heavy, Billy was too close to death. Clint groaned his last.

"Clint! CLINT!"

The heat had become too much to bear. It was stifling, nearly impossible to breathe. Tears in his eyes, Billy ran.

THE END